THE
RATS OF
REFRACTION

AN INFINITES NOVEL

ELLEN CURTIS
MATTHEW LEDREW

THE RATS OF REFRACTION

AN INFINITES NOVEL

ELLEN CURTIS
MATTHEW LEDREW

Published in Canada by Engen Books, St. John's, NL.

Library and Archives Canada Cataloguing in Publication data available on their site.

Distributed by:
Engen Books
www.engenbooks.com
submissions@engenbooks.com

First mass market paperback printing: April 2021

Cover Image: Ellen Curtis

For our friend,
Ali House
and, for
Zillah Tiller.

PROLOGUE

Aisli's hair whipped around her face as she leaned out the window of her helicopter and stared down at the sand dunes below. She pressed herself out as far as she could, hanging onto the sides of the fuselage until she could not even see it in her peripheral vision. The blades of the copter made a steady *whomp whomp whomp* that droned out everything else, so loud that she became deaf to it — became deaf to everything — and all that was left was her, lifted up by the hot air of the never-ended sand.

As she watched, structures came into view. She watched it as though it were on a screen, burning pillars of smoke coming into view like black stalagmites reaching for the atmosphere. The smoke rose so uniformly that it was hard to picture a fire even fuelling it. It looked still, like it had always been there.

There was a hiss in her ear suddenly, the static of white noise breaking through the constant drone of the helicopter. A voice crackled over her earpiece and said: "We're due down in three minutes."

Aisli pulled herself back into the belly of the whirlybird and turned. She found Crenshaw looking back at her, chiseled features and unshaven jaw, with an expression that told her he'd tried to get her attention several times before using their comm system. She looked past him to the two others sitting to the side of the cabin, waiting with automatic weapons strapped to their chests pointed towards the ceiling.

She pressed her finger to her ear. "Recap me on the situation." She looked back out the side as she waited for him to speak, the pillars of smoke getting closer and closer.

Crenshaw looked back at the other two —Forrest and Davies – to make sure their comms were working as well. They both nodded that they had heard her and tapped their ears.

"We got a tip in that there was an Engen test site that had been abandoned. It had been a military town once. Meant to be a stopgap. We sent in drones to see if there was anything that could be salvaged, but the town's dead. Or so we thought. They'd been testing a biological agent and it was still active; the mission went sideways, fast."

"Sounds like a job for the Cleanser," Aisli said. She was now able to see the fires at the heart of each stack of smoke, and her eyes danced from it. "Why wasn't it sent in to deal with the problem?"

"The Cleanser *is* the problem."

She turned sharply to look at him. She met his eye for a long moment but said nothing, then turned back to the town below.

The main area was small – small enough that in a more densely populated area it might have been called just three city blocks. It was surrounded by a high wall that curved inward at its peaks, giving the appearance of a dome with no roof. It made it look like an arena, though she knew on some level that it was just so the solar panels could capture as much light as possible throughout the day. There was a section further down the track that was connected to it by a road made only by use, and at the end of it were several large oil drums and a helicopter pad. They were not aiming for that, though. They were aiming for the wall of the town just beyond the mouth of the blaze.

They were close enough now that the smoke was no longer a stagnant column. It was retreating from the force of the copter blades, the draft pushing them back and making them take new paths into the atmosphere.

"You taking your strap?" Crenshaw asked.

When she turned back to him, he was holding a pistol out to her, butt first. She looked at it as though taking it into consideration for a long moment, looked back at the fast-approaching walls of the town, then took the gun and cocked it.

They landed on the outskirts of town and the four of them marched away from the chopper as it took off again, entering a pattern circling around the town until they needed pickup. Flak jackets flapped in the breeze of the blades until it disappeared into a plume of smoke, and the four of them made their way through to the decayed walls of the town.

"Forrest. Davies. You two veer left," she said, motioning to an alley that ran alongside the interior of the wall. "Crenshaw, stay with me."

Her gun was drawn as she stepped beyond that first

row of homes that lined the outer rim and into the main hub.

The streets were not straight but existed in concentric circles, each one getting smaller and smaller until it reached an open park at the very centre of the town. It was pretty, and the sort of thing you could only accomplish when the entire township was going to be pre-planned. Stapleton could never grow or expand or become more than what it was. It had the same number of units now as it had when it first opened its doors, all potential stagnated by the looming walls of concrete and rebar that always cast some shadow.

The circular formation was cute, but it meant that they could never see very far down the street. They curved away from their fields of vision like funhouse mirrors, with Forrest and Davies disappearing around a slight bend not long after they started off.

The homes looked like model homes, each one a safe, controlled colour scheme that was meant, above all else, to *calm*. They were pastel pinks and sky blues and faded lime greens, the colour of the candy in your grandmother's dish that had no taste and the texture of chalk. They were colours that no one would have picked and were too symmetrical. Every pink house had a green house in front of it and a blue behind, a green to its left and a blue to its right.

It was supposed to be welcoming but it was eerie.

As the two of them got closer and closer to the centre, more and more of it was distorted and out of place. Mailboxes – the sort you'd see on *Leave it to Beaver* with the little red flag on the side – were ripped up by their concrete bases and laid a few feet from the craters they left. Some were splintered and splayed at their ends, as if they'd been met with a great force.

They reached the third street in and the park at the centre of the town was in full view now. There was a playground and a small fountain, which was turned off.

The pink house next to them had a stain of dried blood up its side. It came from the lower left corner and arched up before it started to come back down, as if someone had lost their throat while clinging to the corner of the home and the spurt had trailed the slope of the structure. There was no body at its base though, and the blood was so old it was a deep black even in the harsh light of the desert sun.

Crenshaw stepped towards it, lowering his weapon a little. A plume of smoke came between he and the stain for an instant, stinging his eyes and obscuring his view of it. It arched up and back down like the swirls and loops of a Jackson Pollock with the contrast turned too low and the brightness too high.

There were bones scattered along the front step of the home, a human skull only just visible peeking out from beyond the steps.

"What the hell happened here?" he cursed, stepping toward the tableau with his mouth agape.

"Don't touch the blood," Aisli snapped, her eyes locked forward on to monkey bars. "Remember the report."

He stopped and nodded. He hadn't been about to touch the blood but did not argue the point.

The town burned around them, and they reached the playground at its centre, the sand of it smooth beneath their boots.

There were bodies in the still water which had turned them the putrid black of rot.

Crenshaw squat down and looked at the bodies, at how the light from the fire and the sunlight that got through the plumes made them move and dance. It played over their muscles with smooth, wispy fingers, massaging them to life and making them seem alive again.

Aisli did not stop to look at the bodies. She stood erect, both of her hands on the butt of her gun, turning to look at each of the surrounding houses and then spinning quickly to look at one of the ones behind her, as if it had started to sneak up on her. They all had the same basic design, and each of them had front facing windows and doors that became faces staring back at her. Door-mouths open like the waiting lips of a pitcher plant.

"This isn't right," she said. It was someone both firm and commanding and meant-to-be-heard and to herself. Her red hair whipped around in front of her eyes and she tried her best to ignore it. She squinted, examining every nook and cranny and shadow between each house. She raised a hand to her ear. "Davies, you made contact?"

Crenshaw turned back over his shoulder to her. "Maybe it's at the hospital ruins," he ventured. "How's its resistance to fire?"

Aisli turned to him and her eyes went wide. She started to raise her gun even as he turned back around; one of the 'bodies' that had been laying face-up in the fountain shambling to its feet. It let out a loud, guttural series of clicks at it arose, slipped, and splashed up the black rot-water, then rose again. Its mouth hung agape as if the muscle that would have held it closed had withered away, and it reached out and grabbed Crenshaw, catching him by the scruff of his flak jacket.

"Jesus!" he screamed, standing and backing up all at the same time. The action made him trip and stumble, smacking his back against the concrete base of the fixture. He pulled his gun around, but it had gotten too close and the muzzle went past it. He fired anyway, sending a hail of automatic bullets out into the pink siding of the house across the way.

The muzzle got so hot it seared the creature's damp flesh, making it sizzle like water droplets on a stovetop.

"Get down!" Aisli ordered. She raised her weapon and fired twice, both shots connecting with the creature's torso. It let go of Crenshaw and turned toward her, face red and hot with rage, as Crenshaw kicked back away from it.

"Get those shoes off!" she yelled, seeing the creature's blood on them.

He reached down to grab the army boots off, thought better of it, then started to kick at them. It was hard: they were laced tight and made to stay on in fierce conditions.

She backed up and fired again, striking the creature shambling towards her in the shoulder. It sprayed blood from the wound and she cursed herself, then backed up enough that the clicking, snarling thing was far enough away, took a deep breath, aimed, and landed a shot directly between its eyes. It went down on the steps leading up to the fountain, and she breathed a heavy sigh of relief.

"Good shot," Crenshaw said, still edging off his second boot.

"After three horrible ones, yeah," she replied. She clicked, took out her clip, inspected it, then replaced it with a new one. She stepped over to the body. It had been wearing a nurses' scrubs, and she wondered briefly who it had been. The sewn-on name over the right breast was obscured by a bullet hole.

"Was that it?" Crenshaw said, stepping over to her in his stocking feet, mindful now of where he stepped. "Was that the Cleanser?"

The house at the far end of their vision erupted, its front door bursting clear as something too large for it pressed through. It was large and black and hulking, a mass of swirling black muscle and sinew and teeth and glowing, monstrous red eyes.

It was easily seven feet tall and as broad across as Crenshaw was up and down. It saw them at the source of the noise it had come to investigate, leaned back its massive head, then bellowed: "Za-Kron!"

"*That's* the Cleanser," Aisli snapped, checking her gun and stepping forward again. She pressed her hand to her comm. "Converge on the town centre. We've found it."

The Cleanser lopped down on all fours and started toward them, lumbering but with great speed, like a gorilla. Light from the fire glistened off its wet surface, constantly changing and swirling like an oil slick over the top of water. Its muscles were large – inhumanly large – each one bulging and swirling as it passed through the smoke coming towards them.

Crenshaw brought his gun up to fire, paused only momentarily to aim, then erupted a hail of bullets from the barrel of his gun. The muzzle flashed and black sections of soft tissue and bile splayed off the creature, spattering against the street but leaving no hole where they left behind. The gaps filled in almost instantly, the black swirling like suction and filling them in.

"It's still got charge!" Crenshaw yelled. He ejected the cartridge from the bottom of his weapon and loaded in a second one, with a red stripe along the side of it. When he fired again, the projectile landed with an explosive charge, taking off more of the creature's mass. It kept coming, the sucking swirl of its healing not even slowing it down.

Aisli lobbed to the side, circling around to its starboard side and waiting for it to get close enough that she could fire with some accuracy. When it was less than one hundred feet away, she fired all six of her shots in quick succession, each of them piercing the creature's neckless head and upper torso.

It turned towards her.

The fire blazed in its red eyes, adding a hint of orange to them, warped by their curve. They were shaped like cat's eyes, curving at either end, down where its nose would be and up, extending into the sides of its head. They glistened like the scales of a fish she saw now, each one moving and expanding individually, a mob working together rather than one solid hole.

Out of the corner of her eye, she saw Forrest and Davies enter the fray from what was now the creature's bow, but did not turn to look at them.

It turned to them without moving its head, the flesh and eyes shifting to the bow side of the skull before shifting back. Skull was the wrong word, she realized. There was no skull underneath, no central hub that all of this swirled and whirled around. This was what it was: a black mass of anger and violence and hate all wedged into a humanoid shape like a Jell-O mold.

More mouths formed on it, lending credence to her theory. There were long, yellow-stained teeth on the creature's arms and coming out of its centre, each of them moving and snapping in her direction. It drew back its great head again and yelled at her: "Za-Kron!"

It galloped toward her again, and she loaded a new clip and started to unload it.

Crenshaw, Forrest, and Davies all raised their guns and started firing explosive rounds. Each of them individually did not slow the creature's progress, but together they pushed it to the side and made it stagger.

It turned, bellowed that same nonsense word again, then started towards the three of them.

"No!" Aisli yelled in frustration. "Keep it on me!"

They continued to fire, black blood streaming off of it as it closed the distance between them.

It reached them, grabbing Davies in its great right hand and hurling him a good five feet, sending him skidding along the pavement and his weapon sliding away from him. The creature turned on Crenshaw then, who was keeping his fire trained on it. It turned and grabbed him, and suddenly not only did it have a neck, but its neck was long and malleable, extending forward with no movement from its torso, making its mouth into a projectile. It clamped on to the firm muscle between Crenshaw's clavicle and shoulder and took off a large chunk.

He screamed, and the creature threw its head back

and bellowed that horrible word again, the only word it knew.

"No!" Aisli screamed, the fire around them reflecting in her eyes and turning them a stark red.

She pulled the trigger three more times in rapid succession. On the third, the gun jammed, and she cursed, stepping up closer to the creature as she did.

Suddenly, the fires consuming the town of Stapleton all around them got closer. They bent in from all sides, some going with the draft of the wind and some impossibly against it.

Forrest backed up but kept his discharge trained on the creature, Aisli stepping out of his peripheral vision and into focus. He saw and understood that her eyes were no longer merely reflecting the flames around her but housed them: he'd seen it before.

The creature turned, wide-eyed, and dropped Crenshaw.

Crenshaw fell into a clump and started to clutch at his wound through gritted teeth. He reached into one of his deep pockets and pulled out a large gauze adhesive strip. He ripped off the plastic backing with his teeth and slapped it on. It was immediately thick with blood.

The creature turned and stepped toward Aisli, the scales over its eyes shimmering and clacking like sequins. It stared at her for a long moment as if suddenly seeing her. Crenshaw picked up his weapon and resumed fire into the creature's back and Forrest continued his volley as well, but now the creature barely noticed. Its flesh flew off and then reformed itself, but it was as if the moment it truly noticed Aisli, all of that was beneath it.

It yelled, "Zak-ron!" putting the emphasis on a different syllable than it had before, teeth coming off its body at the ends of long tentacles of ooze and becoming sharp implements; and it started forward at her.

The air around Aisli warped and waved, the way the air above pavement does in the hot noon sun of summer. Her eyes became alight with dancing oranges and reds and her hair blew back away from her face and back behind her head, as though a sudden blazing draft had just shot up from her middle. It exposed the pale flesh of her cheeks and the sharp, subtle incline of her ears.

The fires of Stapleton rushed toward her, swirling and twirling like flame tornadoes, catching smoke in their wake and bringing it into itself. It swirled around her and lifted her hair and even the thick, heavy edges of her clothes flapped in its wake. It was in her eyes now, it was all of them, and Crenshaw stopped firing, transfixed by it. Forrest followed suit. The former had seen this before, and still could not articulate what of that orange was reflected and what of it came from within her.

"Za-kron!" it bellowed, reaching back a mighty claw to slash at her.

She brought her arms forward and the fire stopped swirling, blasting forward in an eruption of heat and destructive force. It pushed into the creature and through it, forcing it back several feet before forcing its way through and blasting a hole the size of a small child in its leftmost side.

It screamed, for the first time making a sound different from those two syllables it uttered constantly, then staggered back and stumbled to the ground alongside the fountain.

"Jesus!" Forrest yelled excitedly.

"Stay back!" she commanded, her voice haggard and hoarse, like the echo of a fire's roar inside a furnace. He did and she stepped forward, flame swirling around her and into her and out again in an infinite loop, losing its glow and then travelling through her and coming out again, reborn.

As she watched, black ooze slid from it, trying to re-form its missing matter. It fell like water from a dropping faucet, unable to gain cohesion, dropping instead of so-lidifying into new material. Eventually it stopped trying to grow back the lost material and just sealed itself shut.

Aisli loomed over it, her teeth barred and black in the glow coming from the back of her throat.

In front of her she watched Crenshaw balk and push back, and knew she had reached that point she always did – there was a trigger in every normal man's brain, and when it switched over they suddenly stopped seeing her as a savior, and started seeing her as a monster. She knew, even only seeing him peripherally, that she had crossed that point. She didn't let herself think about it though.

An arm came from the creature from nowhere, meld-ing into it on one side and jutting out on the other, its mas-sive three-fingered palm clutching around her wholly. It rose, taking her with it and holding her up like King Kong holding up Ann Darrow.

"Jesus!" Forrest yelled again, but with much less ex-citement. He took aim at the creature's legs and opened fire, trying to knock them out from under it.

The fire swirled around Aisli again, picking up speed

and churning until it all pushed forward at her mental command, blasting through the creature's head, neck, and bust. The blast lasted several seconds and roared like a lion, and neither man listening knew if the sound was from the fire or the creature itself.

It stopped not when she told it to but when the flames ran out, leaving nothing of the creature's upper body but the sizzling, steaming place where flesh had once been. She dropped to the ground as its arm flopped over, releasing her as its muscles un-tensed. She bent over, gasping air into her soot-covered face.

"Yes!" Forrest applauded, stepping forward and pulling back his boot to kick at the lump of flesh.

Crenshaw rose to his feet quickly and grabbed at the man's collar, pulling him back.

"What?"

"It's not dead," Aisli said, wiping her mouth. She coughed, trying to form spit but finding it hard. She forced herself off her knees and onto her feet. "As long as one cell of it remains, it's still alive."

Forrest stopped, then stepped back a pace.

She cocked her head at him. "Signal the chopper and get the containment unit."

He nodded and turned away immediately, helping Davies to his feet as he passed and taking him as well.

Crenshaw circled around the creature wide, staying out of reach of another surprise assault. He stepped up to her side, looking around at the steaming remains of the small military town, its fires finally out. "How'd this site even get this bad?" he said to her under his breath, whispering surreptitiously even though there was no one around to have heard it. "I thought it was stable."

"The Merger has everything fucked up," she hissed, taking the moment to un-jam her gun and then re-holster it.

"If it happened."

"It happened. Things are slipping through the cracks."

He nodded. After a moment he looked down at the rotting corpses in the fountain and the pile of black goo that seemed to still be rising and falling with breath and the charred remains of the town all around them. He pursed his lips. "I wonder what else fell through the cracks."

Aisli glared forward as the helicopter passed overhead toward their rally point, and the fire once again flared up behind her eyes.

CHAPTER 01

Victor stepped inside from the east balcony of his estate, the morning sun still hot on his broad shoulders. There was a thin layer of sweat across his brow and despite his good shape, his cheeks were red with burst capillaries.

It had rained in Payson, Arizona the week before. That was not to say that it had rained at some point in the preceding one hundred and sixty-eight hours: it had, in actuality, rained for that entire time. The skies had cracked open and birthed their wrath open the earth, dousing it in not a light drizzle but in a heavy, torrential downpour for the entire seven days. It was the type of rain that kept even those climatized to it inside, running only from the car to the nearest building and back in quick bursts that left cheeks feeling raw and bruised from it.

Payson wasn't used to that kind of rain, and it showed. That kind of cleansing from the heavens revealed the cracks in the system: it showed where things had been left untidy and unkempt. Complacent. Storm drains that had been left with too much debris for too long overflowed. Areas that were deforested past the breaking point washed away and caused landslides. Earth that had been left arid and cracked broke away, revealing harsh stone beneath.

Victor had stood beneath the windows of his sunroom and watched it, slathering down over them like a hose had been turned on them full force. It had been unrelenting, and he had stayed in that space for hours watching it. It was meditative somehow, yet also disconcerting.

Abby and Alice had stepped into the room to join him at one point but had not sat down. They had stood in the gap between the kitchen and the sunroom, where the tile of the floor changed to hardwood. Abby had her hands rubbing each opposing arm as though she were cold, even though he had the temperature turned up to keep the house its normal toasty warm. It was as though the image of the rain itself had caused the reaction, a psychosomatic shiver.

"We've had the sun for so long I'd forgotten this could happen," he'd said in his gruff tone, leaning out and up and watching the water cascade down the sill. "We've had dry weather for... months."

"We'd been very *lucky* with the weather," Abby had responded, stressing the one word with barely concealed venom. "It's almost like our luck's run out."

He'd pursed his lips but not responded or even turned back to face them. After several minutes, they'd left and he had remained to watch the rain fall.

He had left things just as unprepared as the rest of Payson. The gutters along the east balcony had been blocked solid, had overflowed, and had caused flooding from that corner before they had found it and mended it.

Now the rain had stopped, and he had returned inside with what had caused the damage. There had been a bird's nest in the rain gutter, hidden from view. He'd gone up and pulled it out, now little more than mulch and dried leaves, coming out in small inky handfuls. He hadn't worn gloves and regretted it.

The nest had been empty, there were no eggs or even remnants of eggs in it. He had, however, reached in towards the last and found the corpse of an adult robin, its body stiff and cold, its feathers matted and torn. He'd pulled it out expecting more mulch and had dropped it in shock, sending it hurtling to the lawn below.

He held the frame of the nest under his arm now. The padding of it had come out in clumps, but the whole of its basin had been sturdy enough that it had gone in and come out whole. He brought it into the bathroom off of the east balcony and deposited it in the refuse bin, then washed his hands thoroughly.

He stepped back out into the main hall drying his hands with a soft towel before putting it in the bin, then turned and started down it. It looked long – longer than it had in years – so much so that it appeared to wind and twist like halls did in movies, aided by tricks of light and dolly-zooms and mirrors.

Victor sighed, rubbing the wrist of his left hand with the grip of his right, staring at the long line of shut doors before him as though it were a gauntlet. He started his march, his muscles returning to the firmness and rigidity of his military days as they always did during times of stress.

The first door on his right was open and the light was

on. There was no overhead light in the room: the switch powered an outlet, into which was connected a small but powerful book lamp. It was pointed at the bed – made with a soldier's precision – and fought the daylight to cast odd, graying shadows. The walls were lined with shelves, and on each shelf were small wooden figurines that the room's owner had carved himself. There were several small rabbits and gnomes, turtles, and bears.

The room had belonged to Jean-Claude Maximus, and Victor could see the ghost of him there even now: sitting on his bed cross-legged, a whittling knife held firmly in his hands. There was a small pile of shavings on the bed before him that he kept neat, like a tiny pyramid.

Victor regarded this apparition for a long moment, then reached out to grab at the doorknob and pull it shut. The visage of Maximus looked up as he did, his large eyes full of hurt.

The next room down the hall, by contrast, was a cluttered mess. There were paintings and paint supplies, but unlike Maximus' room, they were not so cleanly arranged. The bed was covered with them to the point that it was not even visible, hidden beneath canvasses of cadmium yellow and cornflower blue. They were piled high on the bed and packed tight in the space between the bed and the dresser, each of them standing upright and leaning against the next.

The paintings had been in Theo Flaherty's studio. Abby had since taken the studio for her own and moved his painting to his vacant room – most of them. She had kept several he'd done of her, and one other: an unfinished impressionist piece that she'd propped up in the corner of the storey against a toolbox. It stared at her no matter where she went in the room.

She'd kept his easel and most of his paints, but the paintings she'd stacked away in his room.

There were still clothes in Theo's dressers. He could see them now, packed tight and brimming with folded socks sticking out from between wedged-shut drawers.

Victor tried to close the door, but it was blocked with the paintings. He frowned and stepped past it.

The last room was Chad Matthews'. His was clean as well, with everything folded and tucked. There were no clothes in his drawers and his desk was free of the glut of papers that had been there every day he'd lived there. There were still photos on the wall: of his little sister Koy, of his friends from back home in Salt Lake City. The bed was made though – not to the same military precision that Maximus' had been, but well enough for civilian work.

Victor was about to step past it when he stopped and stepped back, lingering.

There was a dent in the sheets of Chad's bed. The rough shape of a human was there, curled atop the covers, as though someone had wanted to be on the bed but had not wanted to disturb the sheets. The same indent was on the pillow, he noticed now, along with tiny watermarks.

He frowned, sighed, then continued down into the kitchen.

His phone went off and when he fished it out of his pocket and looked at it. It said the name 'TASH' in large bold letters, then below it in thinner font (but still all upper case): COLD CASE. There was a link, and after he waited for it to buffer, a photo of a young woman appeared on the screen. She had hair that was that mix of blonde and brunette before age decided which it wanted to be, and her face was heart shaped. She was smiling into the camera in front of a big box store background that dated the photo almost instantly.

Victor regarded this for a moment, then squeezed the phone off without clicking the link.

The kitchen was a debris field, left over from the battle that was Abby and Alice's breakfast. There were three different cereal boxes on the island in its centre, each pried open and the plastic bag of its intestines eviscerated out and displayed like a warning to the other boxes. There was an empty carton of milk tipped upside-down open in the sink, draining of the last of its fatty fluid so that it would not stink up the recycling. The plates in the sink were stacked high, brought down from their private areas covered in the remnants of midnight snacks. The garbage was full, but not taken out.

This was uncommon but not unheard of. It was a clear indicator that they had gone out to enjoy some of the newly returned sunshine; sunshine only lasted a few hours a day and was only at its best for a very short window, so one had to seize the day: dishes could wait, the morning star would not.

He went through the boxes of sugary crunch they'd left out on the island, examining each of their pouches as if unfamiliar with what they were based on the box. He found neither appetizing and went to the cupboard to produce a box of off-brand wheat cereal.

It was the sort with no sugar and came out of the box as just a solid block of wheat. He placed it in his bowl, and it looked like something you would heat up to turn into a meal in a science fiction movie. He added milk to it and got a spoon and sat at the table. He wielded the spoon like a tiny shovel, breaking off chunks of the main brick into slivers that then got soaked and made palatable by the milk.

As he chewed his first crunchy bites, he reached out and grabbed the fruit bowl, dragging it forward. He did not take out any of the fruit. He took out his phone, opened it to YouTube, and balanced it on two oranges, propped up to his viewing angle on loose bananas.

After several minutes of scrolling without respite, he clicked on an infotainment essay deriding the 'Nonsense Politics' of someone the essayist disagreed with. The presenter was well spoken and well-reasoned, so he continued to watch.

A minute into the nine-minute video, a second text notification came in from Tash. It lingered on the top of his screen, blocking the top third of the video. The essayist's eyes were covered, as though his identity were being protected by documentarians.

Victor frowned. When the alert would not go away, he flicked it up with his finger, sending it into the ether wherever notifications went once dismissed.

At the three-minute mark another came, and he did the same. At the five-minute mark there was a third. He had finished his wheat and closed the video, opening his messages with a huffed sigh.

The link opened to a news article about the state of the missing girl, Lauryn Houle. It was an update to a cold case from several years back. Lauryn had gone missing from the third floor of her Rhode Island home, with no evidence of kidnapping or estrangement from her family. One night she had gone up to her room with a sandwich and some potato chips emptied out onto the plate as though they were french fries, and they'd never seen her again. They'd found the pastrami on rye the next morning with the chips next to it, but never her.

He sighed. She'd been bright, according to the article; though he couldn't recall having ever seen an article about a missing youth that didn't lament about how smart they were. In that way the missing were like the dead: they could do no wrong. Unlike the dead though, there was always a chance the missing could show up and prove to disappoint.

He read the next message from Tash: 'I don't think there's anything cultish about this one, but I'm looking into that.' That would seem like an odd statement to anyone reading through his phone without context, but they'd dealt with two such instances in the past several months: people who took vulnerable youth and brainwashed them with corrupted ideals, turning them into weapons against their own self interests.

Even the phrasing of her statement against that made him consider it and linger on that consideration for longer than was probably necessary.

The last text from Tash, the one that prompted him to stop his video, read: 'I've been looking into it remotely. Been thinking about making the trip to check it out.' There was a hard break then, a new paragraph within the same text. 'I could use some help. Care to join me?'

He stared at that for a long moment, dribbles of milk

caught in his beard. What was left of his wheat brick took on more and more milk, like a lifeboat with a leak in its centre, eventually becoming a sopping, soggy mess.

He stood and turned, stepping from the mess of the kitchen at out into the main hall, looking out into the empty living room. The television was off and looked as though it hadn't been on for some time, the dust that its electricity collected having settled on the ledge in front of it. The couch had that stale, unused look. He had never been able to articulate what about a piece of furniture made it obvious that it hadn't been utilized in some time, but he knew it when he saw it. He'd first seen it while visiting his grandmother in his youth: she'd gotten arthritis in both knees and been unable to get up from the couches if she sat on them, and so elected not to do it at all. When he arrived for their summerly visits, he had always looked at the couches and known that the last ass to have sat on them was his own.

All of the furniture in the house had that look now, except for the kitchen. It dawned on him, suddenly, that he could not remember the last time he, Abby, and Alice had sat down and had a meal together. Or watched television. Or debated around the fireplace.

He watched that empty room as if expecting it to do something. Waiting for it to do *something*. But it did not. He let out a long, full-lunged sigh, then turned and went back to the kitchen. He scraped what was left of his cereal into the trash and rinsed the bowl, then took a single sheet of lined paper and a pen out of the junk drawer and wrote a note to Abby and Alice.

Victor picked up his phone and finally texted Tash back with one simple, direct statement: 'I'm on my way.'

CHAPTER 02

The El Dorado lurched forward and Abby lurched with it, pushing her hand against the glove compartment to halt her forward momentum. Alice turned to her suddenly, her black hair whipping around and striking her cheek as she did, face painted in panic.

"Eyes on the road!" Abby both yelled and laughed, pointing with her full arm extended out the windshield. The car lurched again, and she grabbed her seatbelt from its shoulder, pulling it down and snapping it into place.

Alice turned back to the road quickly, then pulled the car into the alley besides Williams's Convenience. It was spelled that way on the sign, with an apostrophe and an S after the first S. She pulled in and through with a few feet on either side of the car, emptying in a large, sloped parking lot behind it. The parking lot existed between the streets and sloped down on grassy knolls to fences on three sides.

Alice had never learned to drive. She had grown up cloistered and reclusive at the Black Springs Hospital in Los Angeles, though she didn't consider herself an Angelino. She hadn't gotten enough of the culture while she'd been there, enough of the flavour that made a place a place. She didn't speak with an Angelino accent, and her olive skin was no more accustomed to the sun than anyone else currently living in the flyover states.

Abby had learned to drive at age twelve. Her father had taken her out to the backroads behind their town and taught her how to drive stick around garbage dumps with potholes large enough to swallow the wheel of a car whole if one got too close to them. That old truck hadn't had good shocks in the twenty years prior, and she'd bumped and volleyed on the seat, clutching onto the wheel to stay oriented as she'd figured out the clutch. That clutch had been the bane of her existence that day: large and too poorly shaped for her tiny fingers to grasp. But she'd done it, and by the end of that day she had driven home on the main road, smiling from ear to ear as she pulled into her driveway.

The parking lot behind Williams's Convenience was largely empty, as it usually was this time of day. It was used for overflow parking downtown, but nobody in Payson liked the hustle and hassle of lining up to escape it through that slender alleyway come rush hour. Alice pulled into its centre and pressed on the break, with that sort of too-hard energy that people did when they weren't used to driving. The car lurched forward, and Abby caught herself on the dash again, even though her seatbelt would have saved her.

"I'm sorry," Alice spat, leaning forward and resting her forehead on the wheel. "That was bad. I'm so —"

"It's okay," Abby laughed. "You did fine. Really."

The car started to pull forward slightly. Alice jolted back to a ninety-degree angle, unsure of what was happening. Abby quickly shifted the car into park.

Alice sighed, and it became a resigned, hysterical laughter after a moment.

"Okay," Abby said, placing both her hands out in front of her with her thumbs facing each other, fingers at ninety-degree angles to them. It looked like she had made a little screen for herself. "Here's the game plan. We're going to practice parking."

"I'm not sure this is a great plan."

"Stop it," Abby said, breaking her screen to point a finger in her face. She moved it back, took a breath, then centred herself. "We're going to practice parking by taking the car in a big loop. If you turn the wheel as far as it'll go, it makes this perfect circle. You're going to drive around a bit, then pull up into one of the slots and try to get yourself centred between the yellow lines. After that we'll try it in reverse and then parallel."

"I'm not planning on ever parallel parking, thanks."

"You'll need it for the driving test." She splayed her hands forward, like a Price Is Right model displaying the next item up for bids. "Let's go."

"See, I'm not quite sure this is the best—

Abby repeated the motion, splaying her hands out before her again.

Alice sighed, nodded, then pushed the car into Drive.

"I think Victor should be here for this," Alice cautioned.

"We don't need Victor."

The El Dorado moved evenly around the parking lot,

just as Abby had said it would. It was a large and sturdy, much like the man who owned it. Its presence had become so closely associated with Victor that – on the rare times she saw an El Dorado on the –street – she'd begun to think of it as 'Victor's Car.' He kept it clean and he kept it well running: no part on it at this point was original, but the whole was the same. There was continuity to it, in the same way the cells in all the organs of a human could divide and change, but the whole still be the same human.

Abby's head tilted to one side. "Do your cells divide?" she asked, rolling her tongue around her mouth.

Alice turned to her, then quickly back to the road. "What?"

"Your cells." She cupped one hand over the fist of the other, then separated them into two fists, as if illustration were the reason behind the confusion. "If you don't die, do your cells die? How far down does that go?"

"This isn't... this isn't the time for a Death Twins Debate."

Abby shrugged as Alice pulled back around to the parking space, sliding the El Dorado snugly between the lines. "See? That's all it takes."

Alice smiled happily to itself, and the car continued forward.

"You can stop now, though."

The El Dorado continued forward on the flat lot. It rolled as if by its own impulse power, with no pressure on the gas at all. Alice reached and grabbed at the clutch, and the car continued forward.

At the far end of the lot was a foot-high concrete divider with tapered edges. It loomed closer and closer as the car continued to roll.

"Seriously, Alice. You can stop."

Alice turned to her, face flushed. "I am stopped!"

Abby cocked an eyebrow, rising in her seat. "Reality begs to differ!"

The wheels hit the divider, lightly enough that it did not damage the car but with enough momentum behind it that rolled over it. The Ed Dorado slid down the grassy slope toward the wooden planks of the fence at its end, coming to a stop just before it as the back wheels became caught on the same divider, not having the momentum to overcome it now.

The El Dorado teetered like that, like a teeter-totter, neither having the thrust to keep going nor the traction to back up.

Alice clutched the wheel, her hair down in front of her face and clinging to it.

Abby bubbled over in laughter, snorting as more and more waves of it came.

∞

They'd tried to back up the car several times but had failed to get enough traction to budge it. In the end they had called a tow truck, which had had a monstrously difficult time getting through the small alley that led to Williams's Convenience, but had done so nonetheless. It was now sliding a metal pan beneath the car and was in the process of hoisting it up.

"Why do cars still have clutches anyway?" Alice grumbled, her arms folded in front of her.

"I mean, most people don't confuse the break and the

gas, so..."

"If there wasn't a third lever there, I wouldn't have gotten confused."

Abby nodded even as the woman driving the tow truck started to pull forward. Her truck let out a series of beeps as it proceeded, slowly. They were the same sharp chimes that usually rang out whenever a vehicle that large was backing up, but this one did it going forward as well. Abby supposed that it was so that people would be cautious: there was a non-zero chance that the car was improperly secured to the truck and would slide off, damaging itself and anyone caught unawares.

She pictured the El Dorado doing that now, lobbing slowly to one side in a way that just tricked the mind into thinking it was a figment of its own imagination, then speeding up as gravity took firm hold and banishing the thought. She pictured Alice jumping out of the way as it went up onto its side, smashing in the side-view mirror and collapsing in the door.

"It looks fine," said the tow truck driver, shining a flashlight up underneath the car while it was still elevated. The name 'Sam' was embroidered in red cursive along the right breast of her coveralls.

Abby assumed it stood for Samantha but did not ask, snapped out of her daydream by Sam's diagnosis.

"There's a little scraping to the bottom of the chassis, but you'll never notice. None of the parts got whacked."

Alice breathed a sigh of relief. Her shoulders let go of tension she hadn't been aware she'd been carrying.

Sam pulled a long sheet of paper from the inside pocket of the coveralls and started filling out blank spaces in

it. She looked thoughtful, turning to the slight alley she'd
traversed but then also back to Abby and Alice, then went
back to the job of filling out the form.

"I assume this isn't going to help my insurance," Abby
grumbled, her mouth warbling.

"I'd pay it out of pocket, honestly. It won't be much."
Sam turned the page and continued to write. "I have a
debit machine if you need."

Abby nodded.

"Why do cars still come in standard, anyway?" Alice
asked, stepping around the vehicle now and examining
it.

Sam paused, looking up from her paperwork.

"Seriously? We didn't keep lamp lighters around once
streetlights were invented. We didn't keep using dial-up
once we could get broadband... why this? Why have we
been clinging to this old tech for... one hundred years or
more, now?"

"You can shift better," Abby mumbled, pushing her
hand forward as if it were a small car to illustrate. "And
you get better miles to the gallon once you get used to
it."

"You want the real reason?" Sam asked suddenly,
snapping the form she'd been filling off of its carbon copy
with one quick tug.

Alice nodded.

"The real reason's the same as everything – some new
fangled thing was invented, and old white men didn't
want to change and didn't see a reason to change. So, they
made up reasons why the old thing was better all along:
better shifting. Miles to the gallon."

Abby stiffened.

Alice bobbed her head in a big exaggerated motion, turning to look at Abby as she did so. "Really? Good to know."

Abby rolled her eyes and took the paper from Sam.

Sam fished into her pocket again, withdrawing a business card and offering it to Abby at the end of a fully extended arm. "If you're worried about insurance, you should check out Demeter. All female insurance company. They'll give you a good rate."

"All female?" Alice said, taking the card before Alice could and flipping it through her fingers.

Sam nodded. "Keeps the rates low, smaller pool of insured. You'd think the rate would be higher, but... well, you know who thought that."

Alice snorted, looking over the card. The name was in raised gold font, and below it the slogan: 'Don't Pay for Man's Mistakes.'

Abby folded her arms and shifted on her heels. "You said the machine's in the truck?"

Once the car was down, they decided to leave it in the parking lot and walk. There was only so much they could tempt fate in one day, they reasoned.

They'd stopped into Williams's Convenience, and resisted the urge to educate the man behind the counter about the grammatical flaw in the name. They were sure he'd heard it before.

It was a hodge-podge of different items all crammed together, like a store comprised of unused aisles from other, better stores. It bothered Abby in a way she couldn't fully articulate.

The aisle that faced the window was lined with DVDs and old sun-faded VHS tapes that could be rented. The newest release there was over three years old and had been replaced by a Red Box terminal that stood next to the ATM at the end of the row. There were chairs and tables set up across from them under the window, for those 'dining in' at this convenience store.

The aisle opposite it was candy and confectionary, with popcorn and large bags of potato chips. At the end, and very out of place, was a small cooler packed with cheese and vegetables that needed to be cooled and the sandwiches that the owner made and wrapped by hand.

Other items included all the standard things one would find at a large chain grocery store, but without the variety present in one. There were cookies and soft drinks, but there was only the one brand of each. Despite the eclecticism of the rest of the store's variety, in options they were limited.

The front wall was a deli and bakery, with long glass cases on either side of the cash that displayed the various meats and pastries on either side. It was filled with eclairs, donuts, and cream-filled treats. The back was selling bad handmade wood carvings, all of which looked too phallic to be a coincidence. There were several superhero toys lined up on peg boards next to them, almost as an afterthought.

The cashier had faced them and their purchases of confectionary, eyeing them with a hairy eyebrow that said: 'I know what happened in the back,' but instead just said,

"Anything else?" in a gravelly voice.

Now they were walking down the main arterial of Payson with a soda each and a large pack of Twizzlers shoved into Abby's purse, their red lines sticking out from the pocket just enough that they could be grabbed without trouble. Alice had bitten off the ends of hers and was using it as a straw for her cherry cola.

"Doesn't that... make it fizz?" Abby asked, scrunching up her nose as Alice took another drink.

"Hm?"

"You know, like when you're a kid and you put sugar in a soft drink, and it fizzes up. Doesn't the sugar in the Twizzler like... I don't know... activate it?"

"Nope," she smiled. She took another sip. She contemplated after taking it, as though now analyzing the taste and sensation for the first time. She clicked her tongue against the roof of her mouth. "It does tickle the nose a little, though."

They passed by a small restaurant, one so small there were no seats inside – only the kitchen. The entire seating area was on its deck. It was beautiful but limiting in the problematic seasonal weather of Payson.

Payson was a township built around the airstrip, in the way some towns were built around produce or others built around a university. Payson had an airfield that brought it outside travel going to and from other places, and as such had amenities that a normal town of this size would not, and a population that served those amenities. The result was a town that was every bit the hodge-podge that Williams's Convenience had been: things thrown together without theme or reason, just because they could be.

There was an ice cream parlor across the street from the restaurant, and beyond it a motel. On the street corner there was a mime that was dressed like Charlie Chaplin, if Charlie Chaplin had been painted silver from head to toe. Abby had stared at it for a long moment before recognizing it from the Tramp that it was – the tiny mustache having taken on a far more sinister connotation when the silver paint had stripped it of context.

Alice stopped and smiled at the man, who pretended to bow for her but did a prat fall over himself. When she laughed, he got up on one knee in a proposing gesture, which culminated in another prat fall. She laughed until her cheeks were red and left him money.

Abby had walked on while she'd been there, and Alice jogged to catch up.

"I don't know why you encourage them," Abby tisked, shaking her head in a playful sneer.

"That was amazing! Did you see what that guy could do?"

"You act like you've never seen a mime before."

"I haven't."

Abby's head snapped toward her, and then she relented. She turned back to the light pole she'd been waiting in front of; on it were flyers and ads that were ripped down and re-posted every week or so, advertising bands and sales and public appearances.

Flapping in the scant breeze coming down main street was a 'Help Wanted' flyer, the kind with the phone number cut into tabs at the bottom. All but two of the tabs were gone.

Alice eyed the flyer, then Abby, then the flyer again. "You thinking of taking that?"

Abby pursed her lips and sighed.

∞

Abby and Alice retrieved the El Dorado after they'd walked in the summer sun enough. By the time they were done, it had gotten low enough in the sky that the buildings of main street blocked the majority of it anyway. They'd turned the car over praying that the tow truck driver had been right, and she had been. The car roared to life and had given them no trouble on the drive out of town.

They came into the kitchen and at once, Abby began clearing away the packages of cereal they'd left about before going on their adventure. She piled the dishes into the sink – took note of Victor's, still in the drip tray – and got to the business of the day.

Alice sat at the table and started her laptop, the loading screen spinning.

There was a note in the fruit bowl, held down by an orange. She picked it up and pulled it out of the unsealed envelope it had been tucked into and read it.

"Abby," she said, her brow scrunched together as she held out the paper.

Abby furrowed her brow, stepped over, and took the paper from her. Her moist hands soaked into the page as she read.

She frowned, rested the page on the island, then went back to the dishes. "I guess we're on our own for a while."

CHAPTER 03

Aisli sat in her loft with her legs crossed, each hand resting lazily on either of her knees. There was incense burning a few feet away, the calming scent of jasmine curling through the air in tangles of smoke.

She took a deep breath, in through her nose – the smoke from the incense jerking toward her – then out through her mouth. Her chest rose and fell. She was wearing a black top and gray jogging pants, two of the most comfortable items she owed. There was a yoga mat below her, a new one. Her hair had been wrapped into a ponytail and pulled back, but the bangs had gotten loose and still fell over her brow. All of it clung to her though, damp from the heat of the shower and the humidity of her loft. The desert air should have dried her off, but she refused to let it, fighting nature to stay lubricous.

Her loft stood atop the CO-93 bunker. Not as the top floor of it, but literally: above it. The bunker was long and flat, the sort of facility you build when you have enough ground that there's no need to conserve space. It was two floors high with several separate sub-basements, jutting down like feet from the schematics but invisible to the naked eye. There were no elevators in the building, only travelators that ran between sections of the facility for faster, unencumbered travel. They were also used to deliver hot meals on occasion, but had not been designed as such and there were periodic signs advising not to do exactly that. They were ignored.

When she'd arrived, she had been given quarters. They were actually still vacant. They had been nice quarters – had even had a faux window that glowed like real sunlight – but no matter how nice the quarters in a place like this got, they were still just rooms in a bunker. As soon as she'd stepped in, she'd felt the walls start to tug in at her.

It had taken her most of her teens to recognize that feeling as claustrophobic in nature, because it felt so little like the way they described it in popular media. It did not – for her – present as a feeling that the 'walls were closing in,' but instead it felt like every room had needles attached to them, and they were always pointed at her. The smaller, the more enclosed the room, the closer the needles got to her. In those still-empty quarters in corridor C, the needles were close enough that she'd felt them pierce her flesh when she'd walked in. She hadn't even taken the whole tour.

The roof of the building was large and flat and well built. It was covered in yellow roofing dust that reflected the heat and made the facility harder to see from the air. It was meant to look like sand, and from far away did, but up close it looked more like the golden flavour powder that came with ramen noodles. It stuck to your boots and the cuffs of your pants and was impossibly hard to get off.

There was one entrance to the main building that popped up out of the southwest corner like an outhouse.

She had gone up there to get air on that first day, and having done so, had found where she'd wanted to stay in substitute.

Her loft was large and also a single storey. From the outside it looked like a log cabin, held apart from the roof of CO-93 by a foundation of wooden feet. They kept enough distance from the roofing dust and her door that very little of it got inside. Awning windows were large and on all four sides and were usually open, letting in the desert air and scant breeze that came over it. From the view of each, she could see the dust of the roof and the sand out beyond it and was able to convince herself that she wasn't exactly where she was.

The inside was more modern – sleek tile and ceramics – but from the outside it looked as though a wild man had set up shop in the northeast corner of the bunker's roof, like a nest of crows.

She took another deep breath in and then exhaled it, slowly, emptying herself. "What do you want?" she said finally.

Crenshaw stepped back a pace, taken aback by her abrupt address. She had yet to open her eyes, and as much as he'd seen her do incredible things, telepathy was not yet one of them. "How'd you know I was here?"

"The roofing dust," she signed, letting her eyes open. "I can hear it when it settles."

He nodded.

She sighed, her shoulders falling forward. It was a small thing – not exaggerated or childish – but communicated disappointment and exhaustion all at the same time. She rolled her head, first in clockwise and then counter, and got to her feet. She licked her fingers and put out the incense between them, lingering by it to make sure that it worked.

Crenshaw watched her as she made her way from the main body of the room into her kitchenette. He watched the way she moved, light, as though gravity's grasp on her was tenuous at best. She walked on her toes, the smallest amount of her catching the ground possible, with a swiftness and a fluidity of motion that was uncanny to the eye.

He watched her and felt guilty for watching her. There was no sinister intent behind it, no lust or desire. When she moved like this, he found his eye drawn to it, no matter how much he tried to force himself to look away. It was not, after all, professional.

She caught his gaze lingering out of the corner of her eye and turned to him. Her mouth became a thin line across the lower rung of her face.

In profile now, her hair pulled back, her ears caught his attention: slanted up, slightly, less a circle than a warped parallelogram. They were just different enough from the norm to be noticed, but normal enough that when you lingered on them you had to convince yourself you'd seen anything different at all. That you weren't hallucinating.

Aisli scooped loose tea into a French Press and started an electric kettle made of glass. He could see the mechanism inside it start to heat the moment she turned it on and wondered, privately, if they were all like that, or if it was something specific to her.

"There's a new job," he said, straightening and righting his train of thought.

She watched him do this with interest. It was a skill she didn't have: compartmentalization. She could see his body language shift from his relaxed frame of mind into the soldier. He stood a little straighter, his chin a little higher. His voice changed, too.

"It's up north, dangerous. They said it was Alaskan, but the coordinates look more like the Territories to me. I think they're fudging the name on the report so they don't have to answer any questions."

She nodded. She added sugar to the currently dry leaves in the press and didn't ask him if he took any, making it clear that it was not being made out of hospitality.

He waited for her to respond. When she didn't, his stance loosened again, feeling trepidation. "I have the details if you—"

"I'm not going on another mission. Not yet."

He stopped in mid-sentence, shocked. She said 'I'm' with the same sort of connotation as a Royal We, and he caught it. He regained himself. "You can't decide what missions you go on and what ones you don't. That's not how anything works."

She raised her eyebrows and bobbed her head from side to side, mockingly. "It is for me."

His mouth creased down at the sides.

"I'm still PC, and I'm staying that way. None of this 'how high' bullshit for me. They try and force me, they aren't going to get one more agent, they're getting one less PC."

She shot him a look as the kettle began to boil that told

him to get that frown off his face, and he did so as if commanded to. She stopped the kettle before it could whistle and poured the hot water over the leaves and sugar, then put the top over it and waited. The liquid was already changing colour, infusing it.

He sighed. Despite her presence here, all but living in an apartment atop their facility, she was still a Professional Consultant and had insisted on keeping it that way. "Church and State," she'd called it once while celebrating after a particularly dangerous op. He'd asked her what she'd met but she'd refused to clarify her stance further.

"I can't be deciding which jobs you want and which ones you don't."

"As we've discussed, I *can*—"

"I know, *technically*, you *can*," he interrupted, putting both hands in front of himself for emphasis. It was the motion you did when you were trying to calm a dangerous animal and was usually accompanied by a series of low clicking sounds. "You are able to, yes. Yes. But have you ever stopped to think that through to its logical conclusion?"

She smiled with thinned lips, the sort of smile that was a contemptuous reflex, not a joyous one. "That's the kind of circular thinking most men use when they're trying to get you into bed." She held her spoon out toward him like a weapon.

He sighed. "What would have happened if you hadn't been there on the Stapleton Op? What if you'd decided, 'Nah, I'm going to sit this one out' and that... thing... had gotten out into GP?" General Public. "How would you feel then?"

"I would feel a great swell of anger towards the person who sent it in there to begin with," she said, each of her words clipped. "By your logic if the police don't stop a domestic abuse, is that abuse then their fault?"

"Maybe if they were told about it, yeah."

She stopped, standing up straighter, the firm walls of her belief system finally scraping up against the walls of his, like two ships in the night on a collision course. She turned back to her tea and watched it steep. "That kind of hero complex talk is exactly why I have to be PC."

Crenshaw laughed, shaking his head. "Alright, have it that way. But what if you hadn't been there and Forrest or Davies hadn't made it out? That thing could have easily ripped Forrest in half if you hadn't stopped it. What would you feel like then, if they sent the rest of the team in without you?"

"A great swell of anger for the people who sent you in." She shot him a look. "Which is why they don't, by the way."

He shook his head. "No responsibility for you, huh?"

Her head spun towards him, so fast her ponytail shifted around from one shoulder to the other. "I have been taking responsibility for the mistakes of men for most of my life, thank you. I won't do it anymore. I do what I do, and the responsibility for men's mistakes is their own." She pressed down on the press' plunger, squeezing all the loose leaves into the bottom of the pot.

She opened a small drawer next to her. It wasn't nailed down and looked as though it were supposed to be a bread box, but she didn't need a large cupboard. It was just her, and it sufficed. There was enough room inside for two China teacups on the top level, and two small plates on the lower. She took out one cup, then lingered, her fingers dancing in mid-air without closing the box.

She turned and looked at him over her shoulder, narrowing her eyes at him. She withdrew the second teacup, poured sugary liquid from the pot into both, and handed him one. He nodded graciously and took it, taking a sip of the sugary tea into his mouth and liking it.

They moved to the half-table in the corner. It looked like something out of an 80s home, but it saved space and she liked it. They sipped their tea, her leaning forward and sitting comfortably and him bunched into his gear, barely able to fit behind the seat.

When their tea was half done, he looked over the edge of the cup at her. "It's an old Engen test site, we think." He paused. "The Alaska job, I mean. Could take weeks."

Aisli stared at him for a long, pregnant pause. She pursed her lips, rolling her tongue around the inside of her gums. Finally she spoke, snapping her lips together.

"When do we leave?"

CHAPTER 04

Abby sat on the couch in the living room, her head and shoulders sunken until the cushions were up on either side of her head. Her arms were up at odd angles that should have been uncomfortable, traveling the full length of the armrests and strumming her fingers along their edges.

Alice looked at her from the archway into the main hall. She was leaned against it with one foot kicked up, looking for the world like a character that an 80s film director desperately wanted to introduce as 'cool.'

Abby watched the analog clock on the wall as it ticked through each second in its circumference, pecking away at time itself. It was 3:13 in the morning.

"You sure they meant in the morning?" Alice started, yawning as looked out the window. The forest surrounding the house was deep and black, like something out of a Disney matte painting. "Because this seems a bit—"

Abby held up her finger for silence. There was a phone clutched in the hand – not an expensive smartphone, but an old model flip phone. It had a purple ring around its face from the days when you picked the colour of your phone when you bought it and that was that. It had a colour screen from back in a time when that would have been considered a selling point.

Abby opened the phone and rested her thumb on the eight key without depressing it, waiting as the second hand of the clock completed its rotation and brought 3:14.

She pressed and held the button. Dial tone sprung over the speaker for a moment and then a number automatically dialed and started to ring. Abby turned up the volume via the rocker on the side and rested it on the arm of the chair, sitting up straight.

The third ring came and there was no answer.

"Are we sure that clock's right?" Alice asked, stepping over to hover around the phone.

"Shh!" Abby waved, nodding.

On the eighth ring the call connected, and a low voice with the deep twang of a New Orleans accent drawled onto the line. It came on as though it had materialized out of the eighth ring – there had been no telltale click of connection, no pause or chipper hello; the eighth ring had morphed as though on a mixing board and become, "We've got to revisit this time. This is not savvy with this time zone."

"Don't hang up," Abby said, quickly.

There was a stuttered pause on the other end of the line – not much, but enough to register. When the voice came back all trace of its Creole was gone, replaced with something that was the middle ground between posh Bostonian and lower-class English. "How'd you get this number?"

"Please Simon, just—"

"I'm hanging up. This number won't work ag—"

"Three daffodils live in Waverly place, but thirty more live in Roxford with shells."

There was another pause at the end of the line, this one long enough that the women started to wonder if he had hung up after all. "What did you just say?" he said, finally.

"Three daffodils live in Waverly place... but thirty more live in Roxford, with shells."

"... five more in the morning than the afternoon, at tea," he said, in a resigned voice. "How did you get this number?"

"Victor showed me once." She paused. "If I ever needed help."

There was another long pause on the other end of the line. "Is this an emergency?"

A lump formed in Abby's throat. She turned to Alice, who shrugged. "No?"

"He should have told you it was for emergencies," he grumbled. There were sounds of shifting blankets and springs, and she imagined him rising out of bed. There was a sound in the distance, a different voice, by Abby knew not to comment on it.

"This is Abby."

"I know who this is," he said, annoyed. She could almost hear him rubbing the bridge of his nose. "What do you need?"

Abby opened her mouth to speak, then closed it again, hesitating.

Alice pushed off from the doorframe and stepped over next to Abby, resting a respectful and reassuring hand on her shoulder. She mouthed, "You've got this."

There was a shuffle on the other end of the line, and a series of grunts, as the phone was switched from one ear to the other and jeans pulled on. "Do you have me on *speakerphone*?" he chided, harshly.

Abby grimaced and Alice backed up again, her hands in the air. "I'm calling because I need work," she said finally. She spoke with slight hesitation, but then when she clarified, she regained her typical composure. "Victor's gone, and we need work."

"Go read a Want Ad then," Simon barked. "I'm not your Guidance Counselor."

"No, I mean... I need documents. Fake identities to apply with."

There was a long pause on the other end of the line. At the end of it there was a resigned sigh, and when he spoke again much of the gristle had gone from his voice. "Now why would you think you needed that?"

His question wasn't a denial that they'd need it, and that came across in his tone. In her brief dealings with him in the past, Abby had been amazed with how much Simon was able to convey in a tone. Some days she felt like she only had two modes, two settings, but Simon – Simon seemed to have hundreds.

"We're—" she paused, turning to Alice. "There are still people looking for us, we think. We're never sure. The people who tried to keep her at Black Springs, the people who came after me at Port Haven... that's never really been resolved. I assume that if we put our names on socials out there on the grid, it'll trigger something, somewhere." She paused. "I assume they'd come looking again."

Simon frowned. It was audible. "That's... probably true, yeah." There was a sound in the immediate distance of a whistling kettle, and somewhere in the background, a female voice chided him. Abby couldn't hear what was said but recognized the tone and the sentiment.

"Are you making coffee?" Alice asked incredulously, forgetting herself. She checked her watch. "It's got to be past midnight there."

"Too long in Turkey, kid," he said. There was a pouring sound. "You get up when they say to get up and you stay that way. It's been years, and I still can't be risen from a sleep and go back down."

Abby winced. "I'm sorry."

"I picked the time." He slurped his coffee. "And it's one group, by the way."

She scrunched her face and looked at Alice, who shrugged. "What?"

"The people looking for you and the people looking for her, that's one group of people, not two." He paused and sipped again. "At the parent level, anyway."

She turned to Alice, mouth slack. "I—"

"I can get them for you, yes," the mike of the phone picked up fabric in motion. He was nodding. "New socials, new names, birth certificates... a few references. I can get that into the system, customize it for what you're applying for."

"It's—"

"Do not say it over this line," he cut off again, just a tinge of his original bitter exasperation present.

She caught the words in her throat and swallowed them. "Will they be secure?"

There was a balking sound on the other end of the line, and Abby thought she could hear Simon spitting out his coffee. "I cannot believe you just asked me that."

"Will they be traceable? Will anyone be able to find us?"

"No." He paused. "*No*. It's me." He paused again. "They'll be texted encrypted to your cells within the hour. When you get them, download them immediately and get them off the device. They won't be readable on it after thirty minutes."

"Yes," Abby nodded. "Thank you."

"Next time you use this line, something had better be *on fire*," he snapped.

"Okay. Thank you."

He paused. "That was a metaphor, by the way. A fire isn't actually a good enough reason to call me."

"I know."

He made a dismissive, tired grunt – then the line went dead.

Abby turned to Alice, who grinned. The tension became too much, and suddenly bubbled over into laughter. "It could have been worse," she smirked, making sure the volume rocker on her phone was set to the on position.

CHAPTER 05

The whirl of the helicopter blades pushed back snow dunes that had drifted into peaking, arching waves north of the sixty-degree north latitude. The skies were clear. The first time she'd been this close to the top of the world, Aisli had been shocked at how blue and clear the skies were – she had expected it to snow constantly. But in fact it rarely snowed; the mounds of loose white powder came from the fact that the snow never *melted* once it did fall.

But this was not her first time north of sixty.

The chopper didn't land, it hovered inches from the ground. She dropped out with her rucksack strapped to her back and her scarf pressed tight against her face. When her feet hit the ground, the snow poofed up as though it were dust – that was another thing that had shocked her about being this far north: the snow was dry and devoid of moisture. It couldn't be packed into balls or rolled into boulders from making snowmen. It rode the skim of the ice like dust, slave to every whim of the wind.

She peeled back her scarf as Crenshaw, Davies, and Forrest exited the chopper behind her. Theirs were kept clamped tight around their faces, pinched at the jaws. Her breath churned out from her lips in big, curling trails. Usually after several breaths the lungs became climatized and exhaled in shorter, wispier puffs, but hers did not.

Her breath fogged her goggles, so she pulled them back, resting them atop her brow.

"You'll get bit without that on," Davies said as he disembarked, referring to her scarf.

"No, I won't."

He pursed his lips then turned forward toward the horizon. The three men of her team had their guns drawn – automatic weapons that (if she was right about their true location) couldn't be gotten here – but she did not. She had a pistol strapped to her lip, but the safety was on and the leather flap that held it down was clasped shut.

Crenshaw checked his compass, then the horizon, as if to compare one the other. "The settlement's that way," he said, motioning to their noon.

They started walking. Every so often the snow slipped beneath Aisli's feet, as though she were melting through it. She did not break stride.

∞

Abby laid one of Theo's unfinished canvasses onto his easel. It would always be his easel on some level, he had done too much to personalize it. He had been prone to tapping it with his palette knife when he was thinking, and as a result had left a line of chips and chunks missing from its legs, like the first hesitant chops of a logger attacking a great oak.

The painting was loose and unfinished. It was a front

on view of an opened medicine cabinet – the medicine cabinet near the back of the ground floor, actually – the frame of the cabinet perfectly mirroring the frame of the canvas. Inside there were pill bottles on the topmost and lowermost shelves, but between there were loose pills and tablets and capsules, each one catching the light from the unseen source a different way. It looked like a Damien Hirst photograph, although composed differently.

Most of the pills and all of the bottles only had washed out, flat colours down, currently. The lower right corner of the canvas was bare save for Theo's scratched lines of graphite. Three pills were painted in though, and they looked like photographs instead of illustrations: light passing through the flesh of a jade capsule and projecting it onto the back of the cabinet, light reflecting off its apex and going through it all the same, like an eye. It provided a road map for what he'd meant to do with the rest, and as she let her gaze fall over the soft pastels of the rest of the flats, she could see it for what it had been intended to be.

She turned. Alice was in the studio's window behind her, caught in a beam of sunlight. Her hair was pulled back and she sat cross-legged in sweats. There was a driving manual she'd printed off from the internet on her lap, and next to her was a laminated guide that Demeter had sent her, outlining their different packages and plans.

Alice looked up through the loose strands of her bangs and met Abby's eye. She nodded, and Abby nodded back before she turned back towards the canvas.

She dipped her brush into the cadmium yellow.

Atlanta, Georgia

Victor got out of the taxi and slung his valise bag over his shoulder. He pulled some cash from his pocket and handed it through the driver's window. "Keep the change."

The driver thanked him, then looked at the bills presented. "There isn't any."

"That should tell you something."

He stepped up towards the expansive house and the driver pulled away with a screech of tires. He looked up at it, and the sun caught in the rafters of the house like something from a painting. The air smelled fresh and clean and crisp, so he took a moment to close his eyes and breathe it in.

"You'd think you'd been in self isolation, the way you breathe when you get out of a car," Tash said. "It's hilarious."

When he opened his eyes, she was standing at the edge of the driveway in a beam of sunlight. Her arms were crossed but she opened them almost immediately, smile stretched from ear to ear, and she pulled him into a hug. He patted her on the back with his free hand, and when she did not let him go, he squeezed in an honest moment that seemed to drain something from him.

"I think I needed that," he said as they disembarked.

He looked up from her. There were several youths in the backyard throwing a ball back and forth, and one girl on the front stoop reading a battered copy of *Why Nations Fail*. She didn't appear to be any more than twelve. Victor didn't recognize any of them and could hear the sounds of many more.

"You've been busy," he said, even as a teen bolted around the corner of the building and ran to the opposite corner before disappearing behind it, running laps.

She kissed his cheek. "Your loft is soundproofed."

"Oh, thank God," he laughed, more tension draining from him.

They stepped forward into towards the house. "Did you give Maurice a hard time?" she asked, eyeing the cab as it pulled out of the driveway with a squeal of the tires.

"Who?"

"The driver. Maurice."

"He overcharged. You should use a different company."

Tash nodded. "I will then." Silently, she took out her phone and transferred Maurice his tip, with an apology.

They stepped through the front doors and Victor let his bag fall from his shoulder into a clump, finally. He brought his arm up and around in its socket and heard it pop.

Nick and Kelly were sitting on the stairs. Before Victor had even gotten in through the foyer, Kelly was up and on her feet. She embraced him in a hug and, like Tash, did not let go until he returned her squeeze with appropriate measure. She was beaming from ear to ear. "You need a haircut," she laughed.

He smirked and brought his hand up, pinching the end of a shock of hair. "It's the same length as yours."

"That's kind of my point."

He stepped forward and extended a hand to Nick,

who took it and shook it. Victor pulled him to his feet as he did. Nick nodded, his lips a thin line in the centre of his face, then stepped past Victor to grab his bag.

Iseult appeared from the kitchen and came out, two youths following behind her. She smiled and nodded at him, and he nodded back as she vanished to the other side of the stairs.

Victor felt a smile slowly grow across his lips. "Okay..." he breathed. "Let's get to work."

Aisli stood at the property edge of a burned out building that looked like every other building on its quiet road. Paint had been peeling and vinyl edging before the place had even caught aflame. Other homes they'd stepped past had looked the same: all in varying stages of completion despite being, in fact, complete.

The burnt husk of a home in front of them was technically at 8 Side Road. There were few enough streets in the town that they all had common sense names. Main Road. Side Road. Cemetery Road. School Road. There were no streets named after politicians who had never heard of or stepped foot in the town. No streets named after larger cities to give a residual feeling of grandiosity. Just good, old fashioned, what-is-on-this-street street names.

She liked it. The bluntness of it.

The town was still alive but looked unlively. Three young girls started walking down the street towards Aisli and her team from the Main Street branch, then realized where they were and stopped in their tracks, turning down a side-road where the snow was ankle-high instead.

"We're freaking out the locals," Crenshaw said in a low voice, barely moving his lips.

"It's not us," Aisli corrected.

She stepped forward into the shell of the home. The furniture and appliances left here were just metal frames of what they had been, an artist's loose sketch of where the elements of a home would, eventually, go. There were gaps in the pattern of the smoke damage on the wall where chairs and tables had been ripped out during the dousing of it – an act taken to prevent flare-ups. When she stepped into the living room, all of the smoke and fire patterning seems to point back at her.

"We're looking for a pyro, then?" Crenshaw asked, cocking an eyebrow. Then, in a lower voice. "Someone like you?"

"No, I don't think so," she said, her voice far away and contemplative. She motioned toward the pattern of destruction on the walls, swirling her fingers and then pointing back out the door she was in front of. "The directionality of the blaze takes it back towards the bedroom as a point of origin."

"You know a lot about combustion."

She shot him a wry look.

Aisli stepped into the centre of the living room. The tile that had been down had been burned or stripped away, leaving only knotted wood behind. She knelt down amongst it, placing her palm flat against the charred board.

Davies walked into the room on his way to clear the bedrooms and rolled his eyes. "What're you, communing with the flames right now?"

"No," she said simply, but did not immediately offer an explanation of what she *was* doing.

Davies tutted and stepped past Crenshaw down the hall, back towards the source point of the flame.

Crenshaw stepped forward. "What are you doing?"

She turned to watch him inch closer over her shoulder, then turned back to the floor. She pulled herself forward a little, examining the next chunk of the flooring. "When I was young, I had to hide a lot," she said, her voice a low hum.

"I know what happened when you were young."

"People think I'm good with fire, but really, I'm a good little rat." She smirked. "I know how to hide and how to hoard." She reached out suddenly and dug pressed her thumb into one of the knotholes in the wooden floor. She gripped by it and pulled it loose, and it came easily: a hidden compartment.

She tossed the wooden cover aside back behind her, banishing it from view, then reached into the compartment she'd uncovered. She pulled out a small wooden box, a little larger than a glasses case. It was sealed shut from the heat, but she pried it open carefully and eventually it let out a firm, audible 'pop' and cracked open, like a nut.

She looked inside and smiled, then held the contents out for Crenshaw to see.

Nestled in a bed of velvet were the melted remains of a glass syringe, its innards stained with black. A needlepoint protruded from its tip, still sharp and shimmering and deadly in the light from outside.

She smiled ruefully.

"Fuck me," Crenshaw huffed.

∞

Abby placed a new painting on the canvas. This one was dominated by deep, firm reds – at least the half of it that was in a post-concept stage of visualization. Cherry, garnet, crimson, blood; it seemed as though it had been Theo's intention to use only red and as many different reds as possible. Even the sketched, skeletal outline he'd drawn lightly on the as-yet-unpainted side of the canvas had been laid down in a red colouring pencil.

Behind her, Alice was sitting in the window frame with her legs curled up around her and a quilt around them. It was raining in sheets again outside. The sky had opened around noon and hadn't stopped since, now in the wind-down of post dinner. She had a manual in front of her, one that was splayed out across her knees and flopped to either side. It was one of the workplace manuals that was printed long for reasons that were not clear: eleven inches by five inches and bound on the five-inch side. It was an employee training handbook and had the name and logo of Demeter emblazoned across its glossy cover.

Alice's hair was purple, so brightly so that it caught even the meager diffused light coming in from the stormy window and seemed to glow with it. It looked radioactive. The dye job was so fresh that the ends of her hair drew scant lines against her bare shoulders, marking her with each bob or turn of her head. She looked up from her work and saw that Abby was looking at her, and smiled. "What's this one?"

Abby turned back to the canvas. She stepped back from

it a pace and tilted her head. "It's a phoenix, I think."

Alice tilted her head in the same direction, newly purple hair falling like a psychedelic curtain to that side. "Yeah. Yeah, I see that."

The wing was all that was done, and the outline of a torso. Theo sometimes had had an odd style of painting – rather than painting the whole work and adding layers, or painting the background then the mid-ground then the foreground, sometimes he would paint from left to right: like the way a printer printed. This was one of those canvases, and while some of his work had bled out to a little beyond the middle of the canvas, it still gave the work an odd, unrealized feeling.

Abby squinted. "It looks like one of the first paintings I ever watched him do, start to finish. Back when we were in Port Haven together." She paused, lingering on the memory. "It was of me. I hadn't figured out I had powers at the time and he painted me using them to kind of... wake me up, I guess. He'd seen the memories of me using them when I dreamed."

Alice gave her a droll look. "You didn't realize you had powers?"

Abby laughed, then stuck out her tongue at her. "All of this was alien to me. I grew up in a normal house. Don't give me a hard time." She paused. "Chad didn't realize either."

"Chad's power is that if he buys a lotto ticket, he'll win a few more times than you would have." She paused for effect. "You *explode*."

Abby stuck out her tongue again, then they both smiled and went back to their work.

Victor sipped tea from his cup, holding its slender handle gently between his thumb and forefinger. Small droplets of the sweet liquid remained caught in the blonde scruff of his mustache and he tapped them away, lowering the teacup to its saucer and then lowering them both back to the table.

He turned the saucer on its side, examining the intricate pattern. There was a rose on either side, painted in pastel hues with its four major bulbs in the centre. Bright green leaves came out from its peak. He picked up the cup and brought it to his lips again, taking a small careful sip. He could almost taste it.

The tearoom was a thing of beauty. Tash's bedroom was on the top floor of the house and had, previously, opened up to a flat roof that most people would have used for a garden or a place to lounge in the sun. She, instead, had built a greenhouse there. It was round, made of clear glass panes that went all the way around, separated only by the wooden frame that kept it all together. It came up to an open point at the top, which she'd covered in long, dry palm leaves. All around the base were violets and irises, their purples and greens smiling at him warmly. Sunlight glistened in and was trapped in the thick, moist air of the room and seemed to hang in the air forever. It was always summer here.

There was a missing person's report laid flat on the table in front of him for Lauryn Houle, a Rhode Islander from Duch. The section he was reading was plodding and pedantic – most police reports were – divulging the methods and results of their search for the girl. Making grids to check the countryside, making sure no one person or connected persons checked the same grid twice, making sure unrestrained sheds were checked and that the owners of restrained sheds were contacted and permission requested of them. Those who were resistant were noted, but no one had been. In a rare moment of clarity, the welfare of the missing girl had been put above civil liberty.

Victor considered, briefly, the idea of moving to Rhode Island when he retired.

Iseult appeared in the doorway that led from Tash's bedroom into the greenhouse and stopped short. "I'm sorry," she said, backing up a pace and starting to turn. "I didn't know you were here..." She started to step back out towards the main house.

"Stop," Victor said, loudly but kindly. His voice travelled after her and gently took her by the arm. "Come in, it's fine."

Iseult frozen, watching him hesitantly, then stepped back through the divide and onto the scant walkway that led to the greenhouse. She lingered near the chair across from him for a moment, unsure of what to do. He motioned to the chair with all the fingers of his right hand and she nodded, then sat.

A twist of his wrist changed the direction of his gesture to address the rose-printed teapot between them. "Strawberry tea?"

She nodded. He turned over a cup – Tash's cup – onto its saucer and poured out the liquid. It had so much red colour that it was almost not transparent, dark and thick like blood. When it had been filled the appropriate amount, he laid down the kettle and picked the cup up by its saucer and extended it to her. His rough, large fingers had trouble grasping the dainty implement and made it shook, so she took it quickly and placed it in front of her.

She sat with her lips pursed, turning and looking all around the greenhouse and tapping her fingers against the rim of the saucer. She looked everywhere except at eyelevel with Victor.

He made a note on the file he was reading, then smirked and watched her. "I didn't realize anyone used this space except Tasha."

Iseult turned her head to one side, her train of thought temporarily disrupted by the use of Tash's name that way. She was tempted to draw attention to it, but then decided against it. "It used to be no one was allowed up here," she nodded. "Now it's just the new kids that aren't allowed up here."

Victor nodded in a big, exaggerated motion. "I see. I've invaded your teacher's lounge then, I apologize."

"No, no it's fine. It's fine, I just—"

"Relax," he said; and she treated it as a command to be obeyed, and did.

She took a sip of the tea she'd been offered, her first. Her eyes widened. "This is good. It's like an Italian Soda."

He nodded, taking a sip of his own.

"What's this called?"

"My own blend. Some apple, some hibiscus blossoms, lemongrass... strawberry, of course, but some orange as well. Orange helps it all stay together. We're used to tea tasting vaguely of orange."

She nodded, taking another healthy sip. When she

took the cup away, the dark red liquid had stained her lips crimson, making it look as though she'd applied makeup between mouthfuls. He smiled at it.

"I hear you've been taking to looking after the youth," Victor said, his voice changing from paternal to one with more of a twinge of the military man in it.

He wasn't aware of the change in his tone, Iseult decided, and tried to force herself to ignore it. "I do. They've had it rough."

"I hear *you've* had it rough."

She paused, suddenly aware that this had stopped being a conversation and had started being an interview, and bristled. "We've all had it rough."

His lips became a thin line at the lower extreme of his face, and he nodded. He took a sip of his tea. "Tasha told me about what happened on the offshore rig."

"I'm sorry – *Tasha*?"

"How have you been coping, since?"

She turned from his gaze, again looking anywhere but at his eyeline. She waited for him to move on to his next line of inquiry, and when he didn't, she turned back to him and sighed. "It's a good thing that I'm enjoying helping with the new kids. Because if I didn't, being confined to the property for fear of legal repercussions would *suck*."

He smirked, nodded, then took a sip of his tea. "I'm sure that will work itself out."

Something about the way he said that did not put Iseult at ease, although she knew it was meant to. She bristled again, gooseflesh appearing over her arms.

Tasha – *Tash* – appeared in the archway between her

room and the greenhouse, a watering can in one hand and several more file folders for Victor under the arm of the other. She stopped next to the table and lay the folder down between them, turned to Victor, then to Iseult, then back to Victor again.

Tash frowned. "If you're interrogating my children, I'll confine you to your quarters," she said flatly.

Victor looked at her, the barest hint of surprise in his eye, then nodded and went back to his work.

Iseult sipped her tea in peace, eventually taking out a sudoku puzzle.

There was an ice cave far off into the barren tundra the likes of which neither Aisli nor her crew had ever seen before. It rose up from the dunes of snow like a maw, pushing up in a corkscrew swirl. There was no surrounding infrastructure of ice or rock, only barren nothingness. It appeared from nowhere and plummeted deep, light finding its blue shards only nominally before all illumination was lost.

"Fuck, that is a creepy cave," Crenshaw sighed, eyeing the expanse.

Aisli turned to look at him, slowly. She clicked her tongue against the roof of her mouth but said nothing. She withdrew her pistol, raised it to half height, then stepped through the mouth of the cave.

The soft hues of the barely risen sun glistened off the ice crystals on all sides of the cave, playing tricks with shape and shadow as they stepped down. Vaguely humanoid shapes appeared in the darkness as the light became less and less, but were gone when they turned their focus on them.

Davies was the first to turn on his light.

Forrest reached out and touched the ice wall. It didn't even look like ice, it looked more like clear, refined quartz; but when he broke off a piece from it, cold shot through the fingers of his gloves and brought frigid pain through it. He hissed and dropped it.

Aisli hushed him, but continued forward without turning back.

"I don't get it," he said, shaking his hand and holding it up in the light from Davies' scoped flashlight. "Why would he be in an ice cave if he had developed fire abilities? Wouldn't this be the worst spot for him? He'd melt the place and cave in or drown or... something."

"There fires weren't coming from him, that's why the directionality was wrong," Aisli clarified, under her breath. "The fires were meant to end him."

Crenshaw cocked an eyebrow. "Murder?"

"Or suicide," she corrected. "Maybe he couldn't take what he'd become anymore."

Crenshaw's gaze lingered on her at that, but he made nothing of it. "We should find him soon for his own good. The Eden will have worn off by now... he'll freeze to death down here."

There was a sharp sound of glass snapping, and all four of them stopped. Aisli raised her boot and revealed another needle crushed beneath it, its black content half spent and half leaking out onto the crystalline floor.

She shot Crenshaw a look that said 'you had to say it, didn't you' without actually saying it, just as a blast of ice erupted from the dark and struck her pistol. It froze immediately, and when she tried to fire it into the dark it would not discharge, the blazing white-blue of the frost continuing to travel up it and onto her glove.

"Fuck!" she screamed, trying to drop the weapon. It refused to close loose from the glove, so she peeled the glove off as well, and when she turned back up to the mouth of the cave it had emerged from the dark bleakness of its depths.

It came out of the darkness then, the same sort of crystalline structure as the walls around it. It lumbered, its every move bringing the grinds and clacks of ice coming up solid against ice. It reminded Aisli of ice flows, of the way they would pack in tighter and tighter into a bay before finally pushing up against each other: that sound of the slow-moving car crash was what followed this thing's every motion.

"What the holy fuck," Forrest said in a shocked, hushed voice. He said it in the tone of someone about to cross themselves having just seen sacrilege.

The creature opened its mouth to speak. It moved its lips as though it were speaking, but there was something about the process that had made its tongue incapable of making the tones and frictions associated with speech. Was his tongue frozen... or had the cold made its throat too dry to produce the sound?

Aisli reached for her backup weapon while keeping her eyes trained on the unwieldy form staggering towards her, fumbling with its clip. "You stay back there, that's close enough."

The creature pushed forward, steam rising off of it as

the cold of his icy skin met the sun. It opened its mouth again, letting out a long, strained H-sound that was not quite a hiss, but almost.

"I said stop where you are," Aisli said again, firmer.

Crenshaw raised his weapon and the other two followed suit. When it did not stop, they opened fire. The bullets ricocheted off of it, and then off of the ice cavern walls all around, the echoing sounds of gunfire in the enclosed space making them clutch at their ears. Crenshaw raised his weapon again, taking aim near the creature's eye.

"Hold fire!" Aisli yelled, giving up the battle with her frozen holster and raising her arms to either side of her face, like a boxer. The creature lunged forward one last time and grabbed at her by both wrists and she screamed... they both did, and it was the first sound it made that had sounded human.

Steam shot out from between the creature's fingers where they touched, filling the cavern with it until the air was as thick as a sauna. It was close enough that she could see that its eyes were not completely frozen, there were just thin sheets over them... and that they were red. Not bloodshot, but the same glowing, bestial red of the monster she'd encountered at Stapleton.

She pushed it back, but her hands were blue now, that dark shade of the shadow of hypothermia.

The creature's fingers were stripped, melted down to clear icicle shards, yet somehow had not yet reached flesh. Aisli stared at that, her eyes wide with horror but not with fear.

"Stay. Where. You. Are," she ordered, hugging her

arms into her torso and building their heat again.

It lumbered forward again, arms outstretched and grabbing, as though it needed the heat of her.

She pushed her arm forward and let out a swirling blast of hot air, with such force that it pushed a large chunk free from its torso. There was a half-circle missing from its left side now, the entirety of where human anatomy said that half of its rib cage should have been gone. There was no flesh beneath, like with the fingers: only the horror of open air, and yet somehow it continued forward, the uncanny valley personified.

It lunged forward at Aisli again as she built her heat from the steam that surrounded them, cutting them off from the rest of her team. It grabbed at her, tripping and taking them both to the frigid ground with it atop.

Davies appeared out of the mist, his pistol drawn. He brought it squarely against the creature's glowing red eye, almost touching its lens with the barrel and fired a single shot.

The creature's head snapped away, and it landed on its back in the cave it itself had created.

"Works every time," Davies said, his lip curling into a snarl.

"Thanks," Aisli breathed. He did not offer her a hand up, nor did she request one. The steam was dissipating.

"That's it, then? Time to go back to base, finally?"

She squinted, looking back out towards the mouth of the cave as Crenshaw and Forrest came back into view, and the world behind them. "Not yet," she said, her lips pursed and warbling.

Crenshaw nodded at her, encouraging.

"If I know them, and I *know* them, there's a duck blind nearby. That's what we really need to take out." She leaned down and picked up the broken syringe, careful not to get any of its black contents on her. "That's where we'll find the rest of this and be done with it."

∞

Alice pushed her hair back behind her ear and out of her face as she hunched over her exam booklet like a gargoyle. The purple had faded to its final stasis now, no longer the radioactive neon it had been when she'd dyed it first but now the faded hue of a smoggy sunset.

She lingered long and hard at the question she was on, tapping her pen against her lips.

Abby watched her from the other side of the room as she came in, carrying another canvas in under her arm from where it had been, in storage in Theo's room. She watched contemplatively, turning back every second or so as she adjusted the canvas and mounted it to its pinchers. "You know you can look up the answers, right?" she said, finally.

Alice arched her head up, a confused look on it.

"Home tests, that's why you do them at home. They're not testing you on if you can rhyme off all that information off the tip of your tongue, they're trying to weed out people too stupid to look up the answer."

Alice lowered her eyebrows into a straight line across her face.

"No, not that you're stupid right now. I mean, out in the world if you had to look something up: would you find the wrong information in the book? Would you look it up wrong and quote the wrong price back or something."

Alice turned and looked at the textbooks stacked behind her near her bookbag. "They asked me to be a floor manager, though. They might want me to actually know this."

"They don't. They just want you to know how to look it up."

Alice pressed her lips back and forth, rocking the upper one against the lower as she thought. She turned back and looked at the stack of books again, then shook her head and went back to the test, selecting her answer from the multiple choice list.

Abby smirked at her, then went back to her painting. Only the very top left quadrant of this one was done, the rest not even sketched out or primer flats put down. It had the effect of turning that top corner into its own small painting, divorced from the eggshell of the rest of the canvas.

What was painted was a deep, swirling black.

It wasn't that he was laying down flats: she'd seen him do that and he always did so with a broad brush that covered as much of the canvas as possible. That part of the process had never been fun for Theo, and he'd approached it with the same lackadaisical enthusiasm as Tom Sawyer painting a fence.

No, these black were deep and layered and intentional. They were thick, creating a cliffside of black that rose up from the flat white of the rest of the canvas. It had been painted wet on dry when he had typically been a proponent of wet on wet, each layer building on the last and propping up some sections while others recessed in response.

It was like he'd been sculpting with paint.

The effect from afar had been strange to behold. It looked like nothing but deep blackness... it was only when one got up close that they saw the curves and ridges, the differences in elevations made with the thick paint. Light and shadow helped paint this piece as much as what was on the canvas: in dim light it would be nothing, but here in the light of the window in the studio it was made in, it was waves. The black, churning waves of an angry sea: light from the window making the foam at their peaks and shadows making the deep valleys of the ocean's depths.

Abby wished she could be as still as the waves, but inside her own waves were crashing.

She shuddered, a shock of chill ravaging its way down her spine, then dipped the edge of her painter's knife into the pool of Sherwin-Williams Caviar Black until it was thick on its ridge, and began to sculpt.

Victor sat on the couch in the living room, Tash's laptop in front of him and a *large* cup of coffee next to that. The cup was comedically large, and Victor had bypassed it several times in the cupboard thinking it was a cereal bowl.

Nick was behind him, his hands on the cushioned back of Victor's chair. His head was out of the view of the laptop's camera, but he could see its screen just fine.

On the screen in front of him was a live video-call feed of Officer Martin Danvers from Rhode Island. They had been on the line together for several minutes already.

"We checked the grounds, the home, everywhere," said the man, shaking his head. He was young. He was young now which meant he would have been *very* young when the Houle girl had vanished. It might have even been his first missing person case, Victor thought but did not say. "Within the first twenty-four we expanded the search out, started to look at other grounds, common grounds, other homes."

"People let you into their homes?" Victor snapped in. The comment was quick and clipped but not biting. It rode the line between to-the-point and rude.

"Everyone let us into their homes," Danvers clarified, raising his hands and letting them fall again.

Victor squinted, eyeing the man. Nick did the same, almost in unison, out of the camera's view.

"It's a small township. Everyone wanted to help, everyone wanted Lauryn found. Every person we asked let us trapse right through their home, check every room and every hole in the wall. Nobody said no to us taking a sample. A few people drew the line at us checking their computers until a boy from legal drew something up that said we wouldn't do anything about their porn preferences, and then nobody said no to that neither." He paused, running his tongue along the backs of his teeth. After a long, pregnant pause he continued, "It was almost too much. The whole town said they'd open their doors... you know how important the first forty-eight are."

"I do, sadly."

"Yeah. So, we're in the first forty-eight and suddenly everyone in town has opened up their doors. Way more than we have the manpower to search through in the first forty-eight, even if we pulled all the overtime we could."

"So now you have to be strategic."

Danvers nodded. "And we were. We looked at people she'd been close with, people in her orbit, and then we started expanding out, you know?" He paused for Victor to interject again, then continued when no interjection came. "We eventually did check all the houses offered. Which was eventually all the houses, but by that point we were looking for evidence of her, not for her herself, if you get me."

Victor clenched his jaw and nodded.

"We even checked show homes. You know, in case it was a runaway situation. Which none of us really thought it would be, but... you have to check."

"This is going to be a hard question, but... did anyone check on the police themselves?" He cleared his throat.

Nick's gaze fell from the screen to the back of Victor's neck, which Victor had begun to rub lightly. It was the first time his eyes had left the screen since the call had loaded.

"I've worked cases... before," Victor continued apprehensively. "When, as gross as it sounds, there was someone in the police that was responsible. Or someone who'd been volunteering with the search, even. Things like that. People... people in a position to steer the investigation on way or another the benefit them."

"I see what you're saying."

"Please don't be offended."

"Oh, no. I hear you. We tried to be cognoscente of that, best we could. After the first forty-eight. I was hard in the first forty-eight to put that kind of stuff into play... people are just doing they's jobs, trying to get things done." His drawl slipped in for a moment, and Victor realized that Danvers was hiding his accent for the city-folk call, but said nothing of it. "But after that, if you were working the Houle case you had a special partner. You had your regular partner most of the time, but on Houle you had a different one, and you watched each other. And nobody worked the Houle case alone. It's not perfect, mind, but it's—"

"The best it can be, yeah," Victor nodded solemnly. "Okay, well. Thank you for your time, Officer Danvers. It was much appreciated."

Danvers reciprocated respectfully, then reached towards the screen and the feed went dead.

Victor turned and leaned his arm other the back of the chair to face Nick. "You get anything?"

"Not from him, no. No pupil dilation unconnected to lighting changes, pores stayed the same dilation. No twitching at the mouth or aborted movements at the arms, no foot shuffling—"

"He was behind a desk."

Nick raised an eyebrow at him. "Try and move your feet without shifting the muscles in your back. I dare you. No stress of the larynx either... yeah, if I had to guess, I'd say this guy was telling the truth. If I had to bet my own money on it."

Nick reached into his pocket and withdrew a small case made of two circles, connected by a thin sheath of plastic. He opened it and withdrew his contacts, popping one into each eye with discomfort and giving each pale white orb the illusion of a pupil and iris.

"Why do you do that, when it's just us in the house?" Victor asked.

"I do it for people like you, actually," Nick grumbled. "People don't know where to look when they can't see your pupils. Their gaze just wanders all around your face. It's hard to carry on a conversation with them."

Victor straightened, wondered if he'd done that, then chose to just accept Nick's assessment of his own situation and move on. He turned back towards the branded conference call screen and motioned towards it. "So, you didn't see anything."

"I didn't say that. Clenched jaw, clipped comments, but especially that unconscious rubbing at the neck."

Victor squinted in confusion for a moment, then his face slackened into a stern poker face. "I beg your pardon?"

"You tensed up a lot, but especially when you were talking about that other case. You tensed up enough that you had to massage out some of it."

Victor glared at him for a long moment.

"You wanted my eyes. I see what I see."

He frowned, then nodded, and turned back to the screen and picked up his drink. "I can see why Tasha likes you."

Aisli fired her gun three times, striking two people aiming at her from the high balcony of the duck blind and sending them over the edge and into a tall mushroom-cloud plume of snow. She was back from it, having let her team with their more formal training go in first – this was where they excelled. Davies was covering flank right now, his weapon at the ready, while Crenshaw waited with his back pressed to the entrance's door frame, and Forrest was inside, clearing each room. They would go through the entire facility like this: one clearing, one guarding the clearers back, one taking a larger scan of the surrounding area.

Davies turned back to her with a quick cock of his head when the enemy target hit the snow. He nodded at her and she back, even as she stepped up around some rocks to get a better view of the blind.

It looked as though it came out of a snow drift, but she knew that that was wrong. Looking at the pattern of drifts now – the ebb and flow of them – it seemed clear that they'd built the sloped structure first and then created the drift around it. The white powder on the top looked slightly different than the rest, and heavier. The stiff breeze over the barrens didn't pick up what was on it the same way it did all the other loose snow around.

The drift it was constructed as had a sharp divot in it, like a slice taken out of the middle of a cake, where the entrance was. To one side of the slice was the duck blind, to the other a small bunker. The outer, exposed walls of each were a light, metallic blue that reflected the light around in a mirror shine. To the untrained eye and from most angles, it would have presented as a normal drift.

Her men made short work of the facility. It was lightly staffed – ten active operatives – and they took six of them alive. By the time she stepped through the facility, those six were bound with zip-ties in the facility's main room. She eyed each one of them carefully as she stepped past, knowing what she was looking for and yet not wanting to appear as though she were looking for it.

Aisli stepped through the winding, interconnected rooms of the facility, finally joining Crenshaw and Forrest in a computer lab. There was a large glass screen dividing one side of the room from the other, the first with terminals and the second with seats. It was scrolling through different residential camera feeds, and after a few she realized she was looking at live feeds from the town.

"Shut that down please," she said in a low, even tone. "Especially if it's broadcasting to their servers."

"It's coming in live from the homes," Davies frowned. "There must be some sort of remote Bluetooth system, or something like it."

Aisli frowned, stepped forward, and looked at the terminal he was at. "Is this your first Engen facility, Davies?"

"No."

"Then I don't know why you're acting like it." She stepped to the side of the machines and found a patch of tile floor with no dust or footprints on it. She slid her fingers along the sides and found purchase, then peeled them back, revealing a shallow shaft beneath. It was designed akin to a drop-safe, but housed a computer terminal, which from the indicator lights on it was active. "Shut it down, *please*."

Davies nodded, stepping away from the terminal he'd been at to address the other.

Crenshaw had his hand up to his earpiece as though he were listening to something, but Aisli heard nothing over hers. That meant a private call coming in, and she ignored it to step to the other side of the glass divider.

She stepped up to a desk that still had a spiral notepad on it, like the sort college students used. It was opened to the last page worked, and she rotated it along the desk with one finger until it faced her, and read.

Crenshaw stepped into the doorway between the two halves of the room, letting the shadow from the glass bisect him. He lingered there and watched her for a long moment before speaking. "A new lead came in over the wire. Someone tripped some fake IDs."

"I'm on a mission right now," she drawled. "I'm on a mission I didn't want to be on. I'm taking some time after this, no matter what they have."

"Two IDs. Both out in the world in a... small town." He glanced back at the still-active camera feeds from the community as he spoke. "Both former Shane."

Aisli hit her hand against the desk, leaving a glowing red mark in the otherwise low-lit room. She turned back to Crenshaw, forced a smile, then said, "Tell me the details."

CHAPTER 06

Victor sipped his tea on the balcony, holding the cup in such a way that it was uncomfortable. His fingers were too large and calloused and bulky to fit in through the thin swirl of china that was the cup's handle, and he feared that if he tried he would snap it in twain. It was filled with a translucent black tea that tasted of coffee and date squares, but was neither.

Tash sat across from him, her own cup of the same in front of her, untouched. Her chair was back from the tea table between them and there was an open folder of unkempt papers resting on her legs between them.

Victor watched her and took another sip of his drink, made a satisfied sound, then brought the cup back down to its saucer. His hands shook when he did, having difficulty with the tiny implement to the point that it seemed as though it were going to aggravate his carpel tunnel syndrome.

"You know, if you'd wanted something that taste like coffee and date squares, we could have just served coffee. Possibly with date squares," he drawled, picking up his phone and checking through his messages. He looked at the beverage as though it were traitorous.

Tash stopped moving her page mid-turn, looking at him from the top of her eyes and raising an eyebrow. "It's too late for coffee. You'd be up all night."

"Correcto, then. Mix it with a depressant. Works like a charm." He made several quick flips with his thumb, scrolling through several tabs he had open. "This is pointless."

She frowned, closed her folder, and laid it on the table to her immediate left. "There's a girl missing."

"She's been missing five years. Five years is enough that even you shouldn't be comfortable calling her 'girl' anymore." He made three more flips with his thumb, then brought the phone face-down onto the table, hard. Hard enough that it might have shattered the screen were it not for the case he kept on it. "There's nothing to go on. The police... the police did their job. They covered their asses, they searched in a logical pattern, they questioned everyone. There's nothing to dig into." He paused. "There's nothing to see here."

"If there was nothing to see, she'd have been found."

He paused halfway to picking up his tea again, aiming for the rim this time instead of the dainty handle. "I'm sorry, is your position that *every* missing person case is solvable? And that any unsolved rate is the result of some deficit or cognitive fault?"

"Yes." She spoke bluntly.

He raised his eyebrows comedically, in a way he wouldn't have in front of anyone else, nodding sarcastically. "That's quite a position, Tasha." He sipped his tea. "Can't imagine why law enforcement doesn't always like working with you."

"Police *love* working with me," she snorted. "They hate working with *you*."

He paused, then nodded.

"We haven't even been out to the location yet."

"That is a hell of a distance to go when we can't even find anything fishy about the investigation. Hell of a distance."

Her lips pursed to the point of disappearing, her mouth becoming a thin white line across the lower half of her face. She reached out and plucked up the edge of the folder again, scanning through the top page of her notes. "Are we sure it's not one of the cults?"

Victor put down his teacup with conviction. "You've got to be kidding me."

""When you eliminate the impossible, whatever's left over – no matter how unlikely – must be the truth."

"Don't quote Doyle to me."

She shrugged half-heartedly, turning her attention down towards the back yard. There was a field of green that grew out of the back of the house so broad and long that it seemed to house the curvature of the earth. On it, Nick, Kelly and Iseult were playing catch with several of the newer children.

It looked as though they had tried in vain to mark out a rudimentary baseball diamond into the centre of the field, dragging their feet along the damp blades to illustrate where the path would go and maneuvering stones into the spaces plates would be. Despite being done so lackadaisically, the diamond looked to be within a hair of geometrically sound, which made her suspect that Nick had been the one who'd traced it out.

The diamond was complete, and it was clear from above what it had been intended to be, but the lot of them were merely throwing the ball around, not playing any sort of game around it. She suspected that they'd gotten the balls and the diamond, only to then realize too late that they didn't have any bats.

She smirked to herself and decided to order some.

At the moment she looked, Nick was encouraging someone younger than him to throw the ball as hard as he could to him. He had little fear of missing it or not seeing it coming. Iseult had a small group of the youngest in the house around her, and Kelly was racing one child in particular back and forth as though she were running drills.

"I haven't heard you take a call from your team since you've been here," Tash said, still looking down at the games taking place in the warmth of the sun.

"My team is self-sufficient," he said. He clipped his words when he spoke, like someone shutting a door. "They're adults."

"Mm." Tash hummed. She picked up her mug, strummed her fingers along its edge, then took a long sip. "That must be it."

He lowered his eyes at her, giving her a droll, unamused look. "I can see what you're doing, you know. Like, I can literally see it. So if perhaps you could just skip ahead and arrive at your point, that'd be great."

"I'm just saying... you're the one who is always saying he can do the math."

"I don't *always* say that."

It was her turn to shoot him a droll, unamused look with slanted eyes. "You're kidding, right? Like you're... yeah, you're kidding. Anyway. You're the one who is *al-*

ways saying he can 'do the math.' Why can't everyone else just put it together? And if they can't put it together, why can't they understand that there's something they're missing?"

"This isn't the equivalent of some arithmetic equation, Tasha." He smacked the folder with the back of his hand. "This isn't being given the answer but the data doesn't make sense, so you don't know what part of the equation you missed, solve for X. This is two plus two equals four, and you're sitting there like you're trying to tell me that no, it's not actually four, it's seventeen thousand and I've missed a dozen steps." He leaned back away from the table, covering his mouth in frustration.

Tash turned and watched the kids play for another long moment, took a deep breath in, then sighed. She picked up her folder and moved it to be in the centre of the table between them, fumbling through its pages until she found a particular one. It was a grainy black and white photo, taken at a long distance and artificially zoomed in. It showed a largish man stepping into a quaint, suburban home from a profile view. There was a flight itinerary pinned to the upper corner of the photo that Victor did not need to look at in order to know who it was in the photo.

"Jona visited the family not long after the police gave up on the investigation," she said, in a matter of fact tone.

Victor stared at the picture with furrowed brows, turning it toward his point of view. The profile was grainy and pixilated, zoomed in after the fact in photoshop, but still clearly Jona. He'd have recognized the man anywhere. "When do we leave?"

CHAPTER 07

The Demeter Insurance offices were one large flat floor in downtown Payson, taking up the entirety of the second floor of the Howse building. The first floor was a used bookstore and nick-knack shop that Alice often found herself disappearing into on breaks and lunches – sometimes with company, and sometimes without.

Both businesses had a shared foyer where people could post flyers and pickup free 'zines and local papers. There was a thin door next to the entrance into Athenan Books that most people thought – based on the layout of the building and the structure of the bookstore – was a storage room. In fact, it opened immediately into a long stairwell that went all the way up and to the back of the building, terminating in a fire exit to its front and a door to Demeter Insurance at its right.

The hallway was long and dark, as any effort to light it seemed to be in vain. Artificial light was drowned out by the natural glow that always seemed to pour in from the fire escape at the apex of the stairwell. No matter what they did, raising through the thin hallway to Demeter always looked like ascending towards the light at the end of the tunnel, then taking a hard right and the last possible second.

The office itself was a stark difference, and it was hard to believe when one opened the door that the two worlds were connected. Either side of the office – the street-facing east side or the lot-facing west side – had large bay windows that looked down on the street below. They were thick and shatterproof and covered the wall from top to bottom on either side, filling the room with natural light. Both floor and floating ceiling were the same shade of Winter Mood White, while the walls were a perfect, inoffensive Iceberg Blue. The space was open concept, with a large waiting area with comfortable chairs and a television mounted over a roaring fire and coffee, while the rest of the space was divided into thirty or so equal cubicles, each with walls low enough that they could be circumvented by merely standing up and leaning over into your neighbors' space.

Alice's floor manager cubicle was the same height and space as the rest of them but was against that far east wall so that she could turn and look out onto the busy streets of downtown Payson. It was bathed in sunlight that reflected off the windows, making it easy for her to see out but hard for others to see in. She turned during slow moments and watched them walk from one side of her domain to the other, oblivious to her as they went about their days.

She ran her pen along the inside of her cheek, chewing it aimlessly and leaning back in her chair as she watched them. There was a marketing pitch on her desk made up of stats and news articles about the confirmation bias that informed people's opinions on female drivers that she was trying to motivate the agents under her to work into their calls and sales pitches, unsuccessfully. She preferred face-to-face sale anyway, calling a client into the office and having a coffee with them, perhaps even bringing them down to Athenan Books to get away from the hustle of the office. That was how she'd been pitched by Sam, and it was how she preferred to close her pitches now. There was a confidence in knowing how it felt to speak to someone with conviction, because she'd felt it.

Deidre slung her arm over Alice's cubicle, startling her. "Almost quitting time," she grinned.

Alice looked at the clock on her computer screen, then at her watch, as if not believing Deidre or the screen and needed to check her personal time against both. "...Yeah," she said, absently. "Yeah."

"Daydreaming again, huh?" Deidre said, stepping over to the window with both hands clasped behind her back and staring down at the people below. "I get that. End of the week. It's why we don't put the front-line workers against the windows, if we're being honest."

"End of the week?"

"Yeah. Friday. You know, TGIF, Thank God It's Friday?"

Deidre was a tall woman who wore blazers and matching skirts every day. She wore them as though there were some patriarch making her wear them, the idea that that was what business attire was for her so engrained into how she thought of the world. It was burgundy today and her hair was pulled back into a bun so tight that Alice thought it would have given her a headache. She had small, pressed lips that were typically a tiny bow in the lower middle of her face, but now wore what passed for a smile on her. It was disarming; Alice wasn't sure she'd ever seen the woman smile.

"Yeah, right... Friday," Alice said below her breath, checking the clock on the computer and then her Word of the Day calendar against it. Algid. That was the word for today. It meant simply cold, and she found herself wondering why someone wouldn't simply use the word 'cold.'

Deidre usually felt algid, but today had a looser, more relaxed feel. Alice expected her to let her hair down at any moment.

"The gang was wondering if you wanted to head down to the karaoke bar for a drink once the clock hits," Deidre asked, looking down at the street below as she spoke.

"The Gang?" Alice asked, incredulously.

Deidre nodded.

Alice lifted herself up in her chair by pressing her palms flat against her arm rests, gaining just enough altitude to peek over the tops of her cubicle walls. Sure enough, there was a cadre of people all going about the business of ending their work week with lazy energy, each one of them keeping one weather eye on she and Deidre's conversation.

"Hm," Alice hummed, allowing herself to plop back down into her chair. "I drove here, so..."

"So did we all. Drinking isn't a prerequisite. But even if you had one, you'd be fine a few hours later."

Alice stiffened slightly, but said nothing. That, she kept inside, was the worry. That she'd go somewhere with a group of people she worked with but didn't know very well and have just that one drink, then discover that she was uncomfortable there and be trapped there for several hours, waiting for the effects of that one drink to wear off, anxiety building.

"I never have a drink when I'm driving," she responded after a long moment, finding the inner peace to be friendly when she did.

Deidre smiled. "That's great. That's smart, especially for a newer driver. But... really, it is just about winding down."

Alice raised herself up to look over the cubicles again, saw the faces staring back at her, and sighed.

Carol's Crooners was the sort of karaoke bar that large groups ended up at after a long night downtown, when they'd exhausted every other group member's suggestion during a pub crawl. It was unkempt and dark to hide its unkemptness, the dust in the corners disguised only by the shadows. Post-midnight it would become a haven for men's men and woo-girls who'd had too much and were now convinced they could sing, but just after quitting time it was still filled with people more interested in the pub food than the drink.

There was a wide range of ages in attendance: people so old they looked like they were reliving some long-lost dream of stardom and validation, and others that looked so young they looked like someone had let them in without checking their ID on the promise that they were only there to sing, not to drink, and that they'd be out before the heavy drinkers came. Those ones wore hoodies that hid their face even when they got up to sing, and Alice empathized with them. Her gaze followed them when they got down from the stage and went back to their table, and every time she couldn't shake the feeling that she was at the wrong one.

Sam arrived late, with a big smile and cheers from the group. She approached with a long "A" sound, as though she were some modern gender swapped Fonzie, and clapped hands with the rest of the Demeter employees. When she got to Alice her arms spread wide in shock and her smile widened. "You came!" she said, before pulling her into an un-telegraphed hug. "Your hair! I love the hair!"

"Thanks," Alice said, sure that she was blushing.

"What're you drinking?" Sam said, gesturing to the empty space where a glass would go in front of Alice. "Let me get you a drink. What're you drinking?"

Alice let her fingers splay over the table. She opened her mouth to respond, then stopped.

Sam nodded. "Let me get a round for everyone. Alice, can you help me carry?"

Alice nodded and got out from around the others that were crowded around her. Sam put an avuncular arm around her shoulder and squeezed it as they stepped away, and at once Alice felt more at ease. Some people had that ability: a tone of voice and an ease of touch that could just melt tension away.

"I'm not having anything," Alice said. "I'm not a prude, I just... I don't want to be stuck here if I want to go."

Sam nodded empathetically as they reached the bar. "I feel you. I do." The bartender came up to them and saw Sam's arm around Alice and shot her a wry look. He had a dopey grin plastered over his face, the sort all men of a certain stripe had when they saw two women with their arms around each other and thought the world didn't notice. Sam ignored him and ordered everyone's drink from memory. "And two Virgin Screwdrivers," she said at the end, almost as an addendum.

Alice cocked an eyebrow in her direction. "Virgin Screwdriver? Sounds nasty."

Sam laughed. "Yeah... yeah I guess it does a little, yeah."

"Like it sounds like something you'd give to virgins to let you drive your screw into them. Or like, the title given to the frat guy who deflowers the most freshmen, or something."

Sam laughed so hard at that that she bent over, taking her hand out from around Alice and losing her legs. "Yeah, it ah..." she wiped her face, chuckling. "I guess it does sound like that, yeah."

The bartender brought those two drinks first: they were tall and the orange of them seemed to glow neon in the dim light of the bar. They had orange slices sticking out of their tops and twisting coloured straws, and they fizzed.

It looked appetizing, but the fizz jumped out of the glass and hit Alice's hand like a mad scientist's elixir in an old 70s B-movie, and it made her apprehensive again.

"It's Sprite and orange juice," pointing between the two to indicate that Alice herself could choose, the green straw or the red straw. She gestured toward the green straw, so Sam took the red and sucked back a sip. "It'll keep you sober but there's something about the fizz and the way it tastes that... *feels* like a vodka and orange. It tastes like a Screwdriver; it just doesn't have the effects of one. I find it can trick your brain into going into relax mode like you do after a drink, but you can shrug it off if you need to."

Alice looked at the drink, wary of a sales pitch that sounded too good to be true, then grabbed it around its thick base and took a sip. As promised, it tasted exactly as a vodka and orange should, the Sprite sending tickles up her nasal cavity and into her nostrils. The orange juice was fresh and non-pulpy, and it set the part of her brain that craved sugar and vitamins ablaze, wanting more. "This is *good*."

Sam smiled and nodded, taking a sip of her own and then placing it on the tray the bartender brought with the rest of the drinks on it. She picked up one tray and nodded for Alice to pick up the other, and the two of them started back towards their table.

"But like... are you not having one because of me?" she asked, the realization of the order hitting her half-way back to the rest of the group.

"I never drink," Sam smirked, looking back over her shoulder. "Never know when some fool's gonna need a tow." She winked at her.

Alice smiled, then stepped back to the table with the drinks to cheers of thanks.

After that round Alice loosened, and so did everyone else around her. Tongues began to loosen too, and it wasn't long before one of them got up and decided to try a song.

Amanda from the accounting department had gotten up, writing her name on the slip as 'Mandi' and strutting up onto the stage when the showman had called her name with her hair down and the top two buttons of her blouse undone, all of which made Alice stare with a slack-jawed reverence. She sang a song called 'Party in the USA' that the rest of the office had sung along to when she'd started to fumble the words in the second verse, except Alice. Alice had never heard the song before and could only stare at the monitor blindly, seeing the words but unable to predict how they matched the changes in tune. Still she laughed along and smiled at 'Mandi,' hands on her hips and hair swinging back and forth to the bass riff, forgetting every few words that this was karaoke and not a lip synch.

Two sales reps – Nikki and Carla – got up with arms around each other to sing 'I Want It That Way,' and once again Alice smiled and marveled at how everyone knew the words. The rest of the bar – and her table especially – seemed incapable of getting through the chorus without chiming in, although they all seemed to instinctively pronounce the end of the title line 'That Ah-Way' instead of how it appeared on the monitor.

More people had entered the bar, now. Some of the younger-looking of the patrons had filtered out and there was at least one table of college-age men. They got up collectively and sang 'Man, I Feel like a Woman' but got most of the words wrong, making a joke of it. There was a trio in their thirties that looked to just be enjoying their drinks, as though to them this was just their Friday night bar, not 'The Karaoke Bar' and that everyone else was the entertainment. And there was a woman with shocking red hair that sat alone in the corner booth, watching the Demeter table every time someone got up to sing and sipping sweet vermouth.

Sarah from marketing got up twice in a row, once to sing a song called 'Betty Davis Eyes' and again to sing 'Son of a Preacher.' Alice hadn't known either, but Sarah hadn't even needed to look at the monitor, and during the second chorus of the second song had actually turned it off: it had been lagging behind her rhythm and throwing her off her game. The table – and most of the bar – seemed to be familiar not only with both of the songs but with Sarah's performance in particular, leaving Alice to watch in slowly ebbing excitement as several of them got up and moved to the music.

Sam looked over at Alice just as she finished the last of her second Virgin Screwdriver, noticing that what had started as a bewildered smile had slowly faded into a sad, null expression. At some point during the last song, she had ceased making eye contact with people and had found an imperfection on the floor to stare at.

Three coworkers, Deidre included, tried to pull Sam up onto the stage to sing a song called 'Don't Stop Believing,' even though it was unnecessary. The entire bar had erupted when the opening notes had started to play, and everyone had started to sing along with them. Sam refused to get up, instead retrieving another drink for herself and Alice and sliding into the booth next to her with the song selection book.

"Religious parents?" she asked, above the din and bass of the music and yelled lyrics.

Alice raised an eyebrow high, the oddly phrased question shaking her out of her trance. "Pardon?"

"I knew a girl in high school, deeply religious parents. Not that there's anything wrong with that," she clarified, raising her hands in defense to an attack that did not come. "She got fed up in her twenties and moved out to the city. She was fine mostly but... her parents didn't like rock and roll. Devil's music. All music except hymn, actually. So she hadn't heard any of it, and when she came out to a place like this... she just felt different."

Alice leaned away, slightly. Unconsciously. "I'm not religious," she said, low enough that Sam had to read her lips to grasp what was said. "And I wasn't raised that way."

Sam nodded and opened the book, its laminated pages crinkling with the motion of use. She stuck her finger in one of the tabs along the fore edge and pulled it open to the country section. They ran the gambit through the titles: Friends in Low Places and Before He Cheats, all the way to Jolene: Alice knew none of them.

"You've heard Jolene though, right?" Sam questioned, trying to keep any judgment out of her voice. "It's been covered by everyone."

Alice shook her head, shrugging slightly. Sam's eyebrows raised and her mouth warbled in almost disbelief.

She flipped the genre over to Rock, assuming that the small collection of titles she'd heard sung so far just wasn't ringing any bells. They went through Livin' on a Prayer and Pour Some Sugar On Me all the way to Sweet Child of Mine without a single hit. When they'd gone through all the hits, Sam turned to the Religious music section: just because she didn't *think* she'd been raised religious, didn't mean she hadn't been. They went through You Raise Me Up, I'll Fly Away, and Jesus Take the Wheel: none of them hit a mark and all seemed foreign to her.

That was what had given Sam the idea to try Foreign music, even as the gang returned and Deidre got up for her customary solo presentation of the 'My Heart will Go On' techno remix. She switched to the Foreign section and tried to get a handle on where this too-perfect-English co-worker might have hailed from, but failed to find matches in Asian, Russian, African, Canadian, or German music. She ran her fingers through her hair and finished her drink, lamenting that it was not vodka for the first time.

Alice took the book and started to flick through it herself, speed-reading through each page by placing her finger down it, not recognizing any songs or even most artists. A few she knew through the snippets of cultural context she'd assimilated, but most were just words on a page and even worse, some seemed to be purposefully engineered to cause confusion.

She started skipping pages, then dozens of them at a time, her heart rate raising red into her cheeks. Finally, she reached the last page, a list of 'New Additions' that had not yet made their way into reprinted pages of their respective genres. She smiled excitedly, tapping Sam on the shoulder. "I know these ones!"

Sam raised an eyebrow and turned to lean back in apprehensively. "These are Top Forty hits." She paused a beat. "These are *current* Top Forty hits."

"Yeah, I hear them on the radio on the way in to work." She paused. "How do I put in a request?"

Wincing hesitantly, Sam got an entry slip and a stubbed pencil with no eraser and gave it to Alice, who filled out the ballot and put it in. Two songs later she was called to the stage and started to sing. Her tone was off and her voice wavered, but she got all the words right and was just as competent as most of the other singers from the office had been. Still, nobody sang along. She didn't even have to look at the screen she knew the song so well, and on the second chorus the rest of her tribe tried to sing along with the screen but found it just as hard to follow the rhythm as she had.

She got down from the stage before the instrumental outro had even really revved up. The bar applauded her, and especially her team, yet she still returned to Sam and the rest of the Demeter table deflated.

Alice stepped around to the parking lot behind Demeter alone. Sam and Deidre had both offered to walk her back, but she'd refused, saying she was safe. And she *was* safe. From the things they were afraid of happening, Alice was typically... safe.

The sun had gone down, and the light of the back-alley lot was dim, illuminated by a single bulb that hovered on the back of the Demeter building. The walls surrounding her felt like they were closing in in the moonlight, bending and hovering over, judging. The vehicles of her coworkers glared at her as she stepped by, their chassis broad shoulders and their headlights deducing their way into her thoughts with their eyes.

Despite herself she clutched her hands a little closer to her body as she found her car, got in, put the key in the ignition and started the engine. The car roared to life and its headlights and dash came on, and only then did she see the red spray smattered across her windshield.

There was a dead rat on her hood, trapped beneath the driver's side wiper.

It was white and small, only about the size of her hand. It had blood red eyes and sharp teeth that came down from too-pink gums in a wedged-open mouth, all of which was staring right at her.

She jumped and made a sound she was embarrassed of; in her time she had stood firm against bullet fire and people trying to keep her in confinement, she was not prepared to be startled by a dead rat, even one that had emptied its veins all across her windshield.

She got out and stepped to the back of the car, getting some rubber gloves and her squeegee out of the trunk. Carefully, she pulled up the wiper and removed the small white rat from beneath it. It stuck to the wiper and made a sickening sound as it let go, the blood having dried and fused the two together. She made a gagging sound but got it free, cradling it for a moment in both cupped blue hands.

Alice brought it to the garbage can along the back wall of the lot, but before putting it in, she lingered her gaze on it. It was thin, its eyes frozen open. She hadn't thought of how it had gotten there: she had assumed at first it had pinned itself under the wiper and hurt itself trying to get free... but now the adrenaline was wearing off and she realized that that didn't make much sense.

With one careful gloved hand, she pulled back the fur around its neck and revealed a long, straight cut across the main artery of its neck.

She curled her lip in disgust and looked around, seeing no one in the alley except her. She disposed of the rat, wiped the blood from her windshield, then started on the road towards home.

CHAPTER 08

Victor and Tash sat across from each other in a cafe in the heart of Duch, Rhode Island, as was their custom. They did not often treat their travels like vacations – they were more often than not thought of as missions – but they took the time at each new stop on the map to find the best cafe they could and frequent it. Small pleasures, Victor had said once when they were both much younger, was made up of expensive coffee and cheap hotel rooms. In Duch they patronized both.

Victor's phone was on the table in front of him, the cheap sort of flip-back model he always used. It looked small in his hands when he picked it up to check the time, squeezing the volume rocker on its edge. The misconception faded when he put it back down, creating the strange optical illusion that implied the phone was altering its size whenever he picked it up.

Tash watched him do this with a wry smile on her face over and over again, but said nothing of it. She held her coffee cup – which was so large and round that when she'd seen it she'd been shocked it didn't also have nipples

– with both hands and sipped gingerly from its edge. The coffee was flavoured with clove and salt and stung at her nose when she sipped it, but left an aftertaste so delightful that she always went back for another.

The sun beat down on Victor's shoulders and neck, making him squirm as he eyed his own, untouched coffee: its mug was much smaller, its contents devoid of any spicing or flavouring. It was so packed with caffeine though that he could feel his teeth rattle with it even just sitting on the table in front of him. He checked the phone again, squeezing the phone's sides without actually picking it up.

"He'll call," Tash said finally, the repetitive action repeating just one too many times for her to ignore. "Stop worrying."

He frowned, though it was hidden by the unshaven scruffs of his beard. "Things are different since San Diego. He doesn't have the same support network."

"I know. He'll be fine though."

His frown worsened at her optimism and he checked the phone again. The minute digital had not changed and that made her point for her better than she could have, so he moved it slightly away from himself on the table and picked up his coffee, his eyes flirting around their surroundings and street level.

Duch was a quiet place. It was the sort of place that city-dwelling yuppies moved to when they settled down and had children and decided that their street wasn't safe enough to raise a child on anymore. It was small but gentrified, each new year's worth of residents bringing with them a demand for things they'd had in their city home and forcing those things further and further out into the suburbs. What do you mean it doesn't have a McDonalds? It has to have a McDonalds. No Starbucks? Surely that was a mistake. It looked idyllic, the sort of neighborhood that Walt Disney would have designed: pastel houses and people on bikes that didn't seem like they had somewhere to be. It was the sort of calm that made Victor nervous: easy to smear on as a veneer, but difficult to penetrate into the flesh of a township. He watched each roaming cyclist and pedestrian couple in matching jumpers with a weather eye, his teeth rattling from the drink.

Tash frowned at him and shook his head. "You meet the parents, try not to be this paranoid."

He turned back to her, surprised, and lay down his cup again. "Pardon?"

"Duch is a simple place. It's known for textiles. That's what the industry here is at the moment... textiles. The father, he... he'll have worked in textiles for most of his life. It's repetitive work."

Victor caught the pauses in her voice and tilted his head slightly, keeping his eyes on her in examination. He did not interrupt.

"Before that he worked in silver, just like his father. More than likely. Shaping it and crafting it into fine jewelry. If you've never made something for minimum wage that some bougee bastard then paid out through the nose for, then you don't quite understand the sort of frustration that can come from that; you can end up walking straight into a situation where he clams up and you can't get any cooperation from him."

"Are you... stressed? About how I'm going to act?"

Victor asked, putting extra emphasis on the word stress.

She lowered her bitter tea from her mouth. "Don't try to examine my intentions."

He frowned, deep enough that she could see even beneath the hay scruff of his mustache, and raised his arms in defeat.

"I'm just saying, drop this tension you're holding in your shoulders before you go in."

"I know how to deal with a victim family."

She laughed openly at that. It came so suddenly she didn't have time to stifle it. "No, you don't. You never have. I have seen you give sympathy visits, it's... no, you don't."

"Please don't act like I can't empathize with a man who has lost his daughter."

Tash opened her mouth to respond, then closed it again, tight shut.

"That's your part of this, anyway," he said, his voice softening again. He took a sip of his hot drink and turned to look over his shoulder at the rest of the street again. "You're the one who's good with people, and I'm..."

She raised both her eyebrows, waiting for him to say something she'd find objectionable.

"I'm the one who's good at *reading* people."

She relented, bobbing her head. That much, actually, was true. She could read a situation as well as most, but she lacked the same prescience about motivation and intentionality that came naturally to him. His ability to do the math, as he so often said. "I'm not going in with you to talk to the parents," she clarified.

"...Pardon?" he said again.

"I want to stay hands off on this, in case you need a pitch hitter at the last minute. It's just us, so if you need that... if you need that objective person who you can just relay the facts to and get help through it, that's me." She paused. "That's why I needed a partner on this to begin with."

He tilted his head at her again, caught himself, then frowned. Before he could voice his objection, his phone went off, scattering the thought to the wind. He picked it up and put it to his ear in one smooth motion. "Three daffodils live in Waverly place, but thirty more live in Roxford with shells," he said it so quickly that the words slurred together.

"Five more in the morning than the afternoon, at tea," Simon croaked back. "We need a new return phrase, by the way. Your lovely protégée used it to score some fake IDs." There was frustration in his tone, despite the time that had passed since his call with Abby. The use of the return-phrase had brought back the memory strong.

"I'm sorry?"

"Yeah, that's a start," Simon growled. "A case of Brandy wouldn't go astray, either." His accent was clear and pronounced in a way Victor wasn't used to, and he realized that he'd caught the man in one of his rare spaces between jobs, and was taking away precious moments of that time. He did not ask more questions about Abby and Alice, instead filing that away for future use. "But you asked. I can't find any link to either of the two major players linking to the Houle family. Or to Duch. Or to Rhode Island, for that matter." He paused. "I might have to move there, come to think on it."

"Two?"

"Pardon?"

"You said two. Either of the two major players."

"Yeah, it's time we stopped treating them like they're three separate things. It's as official as they're ever going to make it."

Victor mouthed a strong curse word, enough of the sound of it escaping his lips that even Simon got the gist of it.

"But, to answer your question... there's no reason to suspect either of the companies has something going on in Rhode Island. Whatever's happening there, it's not them. It's something more... normal."

"Jona was here. It wasn't normal."

There was a pregnant pause on the other end of the line, the silence in Simon's throat audible. "I'm saying, you can check into it without worrying that if you go into a basement, you'd find some kind of lab underneath the suburb or something."

Victor nodded, not realizing that Simon could not see the motion, and Tash smiled at it. "Ten Four," he said, the clipped tone of military pronunciation returning to his accent as seamlessly as Simon's accent had.

He put down the phone, let his massive hand linger over it for a long moment, then sighed and picked up his coffee cup again. Tash did the same.

CHAPTER 09

Abby sat in the back of the lecture auditorium, one of almost a thousand students that were seated in the affixed seating. The chairs were made of thin pressboard and the backs weren't the right size or shape for even one of the chiliad of students presented. They were the type that were all bolted together on a track that ran along the elevated edge of her row, each with its own miniature desk on a hinge that could be pulled up at any time.

Abby's desk was out, a spiral-bound notebook taking up the majority of it. Peeking out from beyond its edges were the corners of a desk scarred by graffiti: blue pen etchings of characters, hands, and feet. Words in bubble letters that had had context in their original setting, like 'Ethnocentrism' or 'Kilometers.' There were slurs that had been crossed out, and proclamations of affection. There were hearts with initials in them, some of which remained and some of which had been violently crossed out, the pen digging down past the wood panel veneer and into the pressboard below.

Desks in school were like playgrounds for tattoo artists, Abby thought, the artistry catching the corner of her eyes even as she wrote. Any classroom could be a classroom for tattooing, as long as there was a desk and a supply of pens.

She was at the back of the hall in the seat closest to the hall that ran up the centre of the theatre, nearest the exit behind her. Still, she remained attentive, keeping eye contact with either Professor Dan Peck or with her notebook at all times, standing out from other students who checked phones or chatted amongst themselves between salient points. She thought he noticed – even in a class of a thousand, she thought she caught him making eye contact with her more than once. People were drawn to eye contact: if you're the only person making eye contact with someone giving a speech, they start specifying directly to you. Positive reinforcement; carrot and stick.

There was a page from an ancient text projected on the screen behind him, the text in Old English (what parts of it were decipherable) and the spacing too close together. Kerning was also a problem. There were drawings along the sides of the manuscript.

Abby scribbled down the words she didn't recognize and made a star next to them to make sure she looked up the professor's notes online.

"So you see here, in the marginalia," Peck said, moving his laser pointer to encircle a drawing that went up the side of the screen. "These images would often pertain to the text, and other times less so. Sometimes they would look like a straight-up fever dream." He motioned to a section of the page that appeared to be a creature the size of a mid-sized dog with black fur and red eyes and fangs, and large ears that shot straight up and back at an un-natural angle. "Often artists were asked to draw animals that they had never seen and had no reference to, working off only vague descriptions or the works of other artists... who also had never seen the creature." The class laughed. "Anyone know what this beast is?" The class was silent.

Abby knew but did not wish to speak up.

"It's a rabbit." More laughter. "So, this is where a lot of mythological creatures come from: people see a thing that was meant to be a rabbit and they say: well that's clearly not a rabbit, something else must have existed. Maybe it's an ancient alien. Maybe it came from the gods... it can't just be that shitty art is shitty." He changed the slide to a side-by-side comparison of a photo of Robert Downey Junior next to a bad tattoo of Robert Downey Junior, wherein he looked more like Kevin Smith. The class laughed again, and he dismissed them, letting them know what to read for next class.

"Abby Hall?" Peck called out, and Abby stopped collecting her notes and looked up. Peck was definitely making eye contact with her now. He motioned her down towards the front of the class. She swallowed, then started down against the flow of students. Several students looked at her as she went, each wondering who she was but only a few thinking they knew the answer.

She stepped down to the third step away from Peck and stopped, clasping one wrist in the gentle grasp of the other hand's palm. With she on the third step and he at the lowest they were on equal footing despite her short stature, able to make and maintain eye contact without either looking up at or down at the other.

Peck was gathering some of the papers on his podium together, forming them into one stack and tapping them uniform. There were two sheets that were longer than the rest and continued to mess up the symmetry of it, and since his mind wasn't completely on it, he just kept tapping them flush. He was a tall man with large glasses and full head of hair, and looked more like a lawyer than a history professor. If Abby hadn't remained on the third step, she'd have only come up to shoulder height on the man. He looked up over his glasses at her. "Was it a good class, Miss Hall?"

She turned back to the projection on the wall, the strange, monstrous filigree that she now saw was meant to be a rabbit, but looked more like a cross between a jackalope and a chimera. "It was, I think. Yeah."

He put his papers aside onto his desk, picked up his class register from it, and laid it on the podium in front of himself as if preparing a speech. "You are the new person in the History Department, are you not?"

She stiffened a little. "I work in Administration, yes."

"Yes," he nodded, smacking his lips together and still scanning down through his class list. He must have looked it from top to bottom at least five times by now. "Yes, I got your name from Melanie. They've put you in charge of increasing enrollment? Contract work?"

"Yes." She felt herself feeling the need to shuffle her feet as if under examination, but as yet there didn't seem to be any malice to his words – so far they were just leading questions. She felt like there was some undercurrent to the questions and hadn't figured out what it was yet, and found herself turning back to look at the empty auditorium to make sure that the last student to leave had left the door open. They had.

"Yes," he repeated, then finally looked up from the register and smiled at her. "Every staff member at this University is entitled to health, dental, a free parking space, an appropriate measure of office space and... the ability to register to one class for free, each semester. To continue education."

She let out a breath she hadn't realized she'd been holding, her smile relaxing and her shoulders lowering. "Yes, I... yes. That's true."

"And you have been seated in the back of my classroom every class, since the week you showed up. I see you taking notes, I see you asking questions, I see you taking notes on the questions you ask, and the questions other people ask. I see you on test day, looking over the test but not filling any of it in. I see you everywhere." He held up the class list. "Except on this register."

"I'm auditing."

"Hm. But I bet that if I sat you down and gave you every test so far the semester, I'd have to redraw my grading curves. I bet – I bet you'd ace all of them."

She felt heat rise to her cheeks a little, but nodded.

He looked back down at the register, clacking his tongue against the roof of his mouth and tapping his foot to the same beat.

She looked back at the door that led out to the main hall. "I've got a lot on my plate. I wouldn't want to start something and not be able to finish it."

"That's fair. That's... I suppose that is fair. I mean, you've been to every class since you arrived, not sure why your work would suddenly start interfering—"

"I didn't say it was work."

"No, I guess you didn't." He paused, still looking down at the class list. He glanced up at her from it only briefly, trying to gauge her level of nervousness. He was applying pressure but was well aware that pressure to succeed could be misinterpreted as other forms of pressure, and was trying his best not to seem as though he were swaying into those areas – avoiding eye contact, keeping socially distant – anything to avoid the wrong intention being communicated. The open-door policy existed for a reason, and when his eyes fluttered up from the page again it was to check to be sure the door was still propped open. It was. "Well since I'm being an ogre," he grinned, chancing eye contact with her.

She smiled at his self-deprecation, some of the tension leaving her, and the situation.

"What if I cut a deal where I let you unregister from the course if things got busy. Without academic penalty, I mean. Technically anyone can unregister at any time. Technically."

She raised her hands to either side and bobbed them back and forth as though they were scales and that she were using them to make her decision. "Is that really fair to everyone else?"

He smirked. When he spoke again the coaxing was gone from his voice and he spoke only in declarative statements, signaling the end of the debate. "I'd like you in this class. I think you'd do well. Actually, I think you're already doing well. I think you'd test well." He paused a beat. "But the choice is yours."

She squinted, her lower lip finding its way between her teeth. She looked back at the doors to the hall and sighed, then smiled.

Abby stepped into the main office of the History department and walked over to her desk, flopping her notebook down onto it. The department office was one room with no separate space between those who manned it and the students that came in seeking help. There were two desks when one entered – the one to the front of the door was Abby's, and the one to the right of the door was Meredith's. There was a closed door to the left of the entrance, that was the office of the department head, and the area between the two desks emptied into the rest of the office: a small couch, a coffee maker, some filing cabinets, two large printers, and a stationary desktop computer that looked as though it was at least a decade out of date. When students laughed about that piece of technology, Meredith always joked that: "It was the History department, what do you expect? New relics?" She said this so consistently and in such consistent cadence that Abby had started lip-synching to the comment in her second week, and was now to the point that they both said it, in unison.

Both Meredith and Abby's desks had laptops in them. The University used to provide desktops and actually build them into the desks, but at some point some number-cruncher had worked out the cost of hiring contractors to take apart and reassemble the desks every time an upgrade or repair was needed, and that it would be cheaper to simply buy each staffer that needed a laptop a laptop once every two years, wiping the old ones and selling to in-need students at a discounted price, so that was what they now did. The only reason the battered old desktop was even still there was so that if the Wi-Fi ever went down there was something hardwired in to print forms from.

Meredith was leaned back on her chair, it on its two back legs and she with her knees propped up against the lip of her desk. She had been filing her nails when Abby had walked in but had stopped when she'd entered the room, her eyes tracking her all the way to her desk. "You're late."

"I got held up at Peck's class."

"You're not even really *in* Peck's class."

"That is actually why I'm late."

Meredith bobbed her eyebrows, then refocused back onto her manicure.

Abby moved around to be behind her desk and sat in it. It was uncluttered, the way she liked it. There were no pictures of family or friends, no toys to show off her personality, no books that she'd read. On some level, that was because she'd only been 'Abby Hall' for a relatively short amount of time – not long enough to be nostalgic for old friends and to have pictures – but on another, it was her sensibility. No clutter. There had been enough clutter in her life and in her space for her liking. Now her desk was smooth and clean, with nothing on it except her laptop, a pen and fresh legal pad, and two plastic mailboxes: one for incoming mail, and one for outgoing mail.

The incoming box was stacked full. Peck's class, though she was allowed it and enjoyed it, was scheduled at the peak of the mail period for the day. She always came back from the class confronted with a teetering pile of post to sort through. Currently there were four regular envelopes stacked atop one large manila one – the sort that usually contained legal documents – which was so wide and bulky that it blocked the view of anything that might have been below it.

Abby huffed, tucked her notebook into her desk, then reached for the first envelope atop the pile and slid it open. It was a recommendation request from an alumnus, she recognized the sort of form format the letter used. She got out a highlighter and began marking the salient parts to add into the Department Head's agenda.

"He's not a bad prof, you know," Meredith said after a long pause of not saying anything. She looked at her watch, put her file away, then started sorting through the department's exam schedule.

Abby looked up from her work, filing the letter in the processed bin once it was on the schedule. She reached for the second envelope, which she knew from the logo on it was a bank statement. She slid it open without looking, keeping her gaze on Meredith. "I know. He really knows his stuff. Especially about Old English texts. Last week he showed us this stuff on watermarks, and it's just wild."

"No, I mean: he's a *good* prof."

Abby winced, glanced at the post and discarded it, then reached for the third letter in the pile.

"There are no complaints about him. He's never been accused of having his door shut, if you get my meaning. And not like, no substantiated accusations, either. Like legit, no accusations."

Abby nodded and hummed, glancing over that third letter, which was a formal request from a student to have the marks of a bad semester deferred. Abby added that to the department head's schedule as well. She paused, reaching for the fourth envelope, her gaze lingering on Meredith beyond it. "Are there... professors in the department where that's not the case?"

Meredith's eyebrows bobbed and she nodded in slow, big motions. "Ayuh. Don't... don't be caught in Ryerson's office with the door closed. Hell, don't even be caught in Ryerson's class." She paused. "While you're at it, steer clear of Smith. Larry Smith, not David Smith. David Smith's alright, far as I know."

Abby opened the letter but barely glanced at it before setting it aside. It was a request to major in the department. "Why... why are they still here then?"

Meredith rolled her eyes. "They didn't start acting out until they got tenure. You know how hard it is to get rid of someone with tenure? We'd basically have to pay them their full salary and just not schedule them for any class work. We'd have you pay their ass to stay home, that's how hard it is to get rid of someone with tenure."

Abby frowned. She laid the letter to her right and reached for the large manila folder, flipping it over. It was blank, with not to or return address on either side of it. Her brow furrowed at it. "Did you see who dropped this off?"

Meredith shrugged. "It was a student."

Abby frowned, got her letter opener, and pierced the side of the package, eviscerating it. She reached in, birthing its contents out into the world, a small stack of glossy photographs, each the same dimensions as the envelope had been.

The top one was a photograph of *her*.

It was large and glossy with a white border around it. It was in black and white, but the contrast was crisp and clear and perfect. It showed Abby with a stern look on her face, about to get into the El Dorado. The wind had her hair even though it had been tied back, coaxing individual strands of it loose and taking them in the wind. She was looking at something in the middle-distance beyond the right side of the frame, and as soon as Abby saw the picture, she knew that she was looking at a student precariously raising a team flag on a ladder. She knew it because the picture had been taken yesterday.

All of the moisture left her tongue and throat. The colour drained from her face until she looked just as pale as she did in the photograph.

She flipped that photo to the bottom of the pile, replacing it with the one that had been second from the top. This one was again of her, in the University mess hall. She was in line with Meredith and they both had trays in hand and were laughing. She herself was laughing so hard that her neck had pushed back and given her neck a double chin. There was a student next to them rolling their eyes. On any other day, the picture might have been comical, but today it set a pit into the centre of her heart.

She flipped back again. This one was grainy, and it hadn't been taken with the same camera or the same hand. It was an edit of one of the photos taken at the arrest of Carla Melquist. Her face was looked strange in the grainy duo-tone photo because it was made from a colour photo and zoomed in. There had been two colours on her face, the red and blue of the police lights, but in the photo they were just variants of grey that made her look sickly. She was watching something with a stern face, and in the present, Abby knew she was watching Chad confront Victor.

The fourth photo was of she and Chad, outside the burned remains of Gavin's house in Atlanta, Georgia. His hand was on her shoulder. Her hair was caught in the breeze just as it had been in the first. Once again it had been zoomed in and cropped from an existing picture.

She was flipping faster now, sitting up straight. Meredith had stopped what she'd been doing and looked at her, but said nothing.

The fifth was of her crying. She never cried, not anymore. She knew when and where it had been taken from simply by the track marks down her face alone: it was the murder of Jasper Hemingway, her first serious partner. The police were there on the scene and their apartment was in burned shambles, and she in its centre, refusing to move as though she were a part of the tableau. The chaos of the room radiated out from her centre. It was the first time she'd seen that particular photograph of the scene, and looking at it made her eyes well with tears. She fought them back, but the image in the room: Jasper's table, his bookshelf, his records... they were all imbued with him, so much that she might as well have been looking at his picture.

She flipped to the last photo. This one was recent again, though deceptively so. It was a collage, and it was in colour. On a desk were three items, the shot taken from above. The items were laid out like a grid, photos within photos, and recognized each of them in turn.

One was a replication of her badge from the University, that had been printed out on paper. It showed her assumed name, Abby Hall.

The second was her *actual* student ID badge from the Port Haven Institute. She recognized the frayed edges of its lanyard, and the teeth marks near its clasp.

The last item on the desk was a copy of the Arizona Daily Sun, dated the day before.

Abby swallowed.

"What is it?" Meredith asked, in a tone she'd never used on Abby before. "What's in the envelope?"

Abby steeled her gaze and controlled herself, clenching her jaw until the growing sting of salt water in her eyes abated. When she had control of herself, she turned to Meredith and smiled, big and bright, showing off the lower rung of her gumline. "It's nothing."

She almost believed herself.

CHAPTER 10

Victor stood on the balcony that surrounded the Duch Vance Motel, staring out at the Rhode Island night sky. It was cloudy, but he could still see the dark velvet of the milky way and the stars that shone from them between the wispy patches of gray fluff.

He had a drink in his hand, a weakly made scotch and soda he'd combined with contents from the mini bar into a tumbler with a thick, heavy base. The rest of the motel was quiet already at this time of night, including the room he shared with Tash. She was asleep now in the bed closest the window, the blankets draped over her frame in a way he'd seen many, many times before. She bunched them at her middle, like a belt. Even when she didn't start that way, she always ended that way.

He didn't move when he slept. It had taken years of training, but he found he could sleep in just about any position: sitting up, *standing* up (if leaning), and on any terrain. Once awakened, he awoke to full alertness, never groggy or foggy. This had also taken time to train in, but not years. That skill he'd learned fairly quickly after arriving in-country.

All of that was assuming he slept.

The air was damper than he was used to, and even at night his shirt clung to him. The long hairs of his whiskers tasted of the scotch and filtered the east-coast air he was breathing, giving it all that same tangy, molasses scent.

His phone rang, sending a volley of chirps and chimes out into the atmosphere. He fished it out of his jeans pocket quickly, pressing the button on its side that would quiet the ringing, aware of the people potentially in the rooms all around him, and of Tash. He turned and looked at her through the window to their room as he brought the phone to his ear and answered. "Victor."

"It's Abby," came her voice from the other end of the line. There was a muffled sound of fabric moving near the mic, as though she had been still pulling on a sweatshirt when the call went live. In fact, she had been pulling a broom closet door closed, and was now huddled into a cramped space between mops leaning out of buckets half-filled with filthy water and a large cabinet of cleaner.

"I know who it is," he replied flatly. He downed the remainder of his drink.

"I need help with something. Something's wrong."

"I'm shocked." He paused, steeled himself, then nodded. "Okay, what's up?"

She lingered on the other end of the line for a long moment, her words caught in the back of her throat.

He took the phone away from his face and looked at it to make sure the line was still connected. "Hello?"

"Are you... is everything okay?"

"It's fine," he said, trying to keep his voice even but

coming off flippant. "Really, it's fine. Just... I don't appreciate you using Simon for his photoshop skills."

"Pardon?"

"That is a resource I have for emergencies... exclusively for emergencies. All the messes we've been in, have you ever seen him alongside us? No? Because that should give you some idea of how big I need an emergency to be before I'd call him in."

She paused on the other end of the line again, the roar of the hall outside suddenly deafened to her.

"Sorry," he said, sighing after a long pause. "It's late where I am, and it's going to be a day tomorrow. What's up?"

Abby lingered, the words on the back of her throat. She swallowed. "The El Dorado won't start. I need the name of the mechanic in town you go to."

Victor's eyebrows raised. "Milligan's, on the south side. Ask for Cody, tell him I sent you. He's got some of my parts in storage." He paused, tisked, then cursed slightly under his breath. "It's probably the damn transmission."

She nodded. "Don't worry about it. I'll get it taken care of," she said, forcing a smile onto her face. Smiling was the key to lying over the phone, Victor had told her once. You could hear a smile. "Thanks."

She disconnected the line. He took the phone away from his ear and stared at it for a long moment, his thumb lingering near the redial button.

He slid it back into his pocket, then retreated back into the room to refill his glass.

Abby stared at her phone screen in her hand, the dried, smelly mops of the custodian's closet too close to her head for comfort but also as far away from her as they could possibly have been, given the geography of the room.

Even though she was the one that had disconnected the call, she still looked at the reflective, oleophobic pane as though she'd been the one who was just hung up on.

She bit her lip. The photos she'd been sent were on the shelf next to her – she dared not leave them on or in her desk at the office – still tucked into the manila envelope they'd come in. Photos never seemed to go into such envelopes with the same ease in which they had arrived in them and were now sticking their edges out of the confines of the package, teasing her. Refusing to be orderly and concealed.

She kept the folder in her peripheral vision, as though concerned that it would do something if not watched at all times. She brought her hand to her mouth and bit off the bit of nail she'd been fussing with while talking with Victor, her thumb having loosened an errant piece.

She sighed, swallowed, then pressed on her phone again. Hesitating, she dialed.

On the third ring, Simon picked up. "You have got to be kidding me."

"I don't have the new call phrase, I'm sorry," she said quickly, as though getting the words out faster would prevent him from hanging up on her.

"Oh, funny you should say that, that is the new call phrase."

"Really?"

"No." She could feel his glare, the sarcasm dripping from his voice. He let out a long sigh.

Abby could hear someone talking in the background, a female voice that was coming in from another room. When it finished there was a muffled sound, as though Simon had held the phone's microphone up to his chest or covered it with his finger. There was a muffled deep voice sound of him replying, a pause, and then more from him.

After that he returned. "Why are you calling?"

"I've been made. The secret identity you made for me isn't so secret."

He stifled a curse. "What do you mean you've been made? Be specific. Like some student recognized you, or —"

"I got photos in the mail, photos of me. Some of them are from this week! The rest are police report photos, news clippings and stuff. And my old Port Haven ID card."

"Fuck me," Simon said, his voice haggard. "What have you done since starting? Retrace everything. Have you reached out to anyone as Abby Fisher when you're supposed to be Abby Hall? Bought something with a credit card? Talked to someone and let it slip?"

"No. I've paid attention."

"Had someone over to Payson, then? Talked about something specific from your past with a workmate? Anything that might let something slip."

"No, nothing like that."

He cursed again. "Well, if that's true than there's a bug in my system somewhere, and if that's the case we are all fucked. So figure it out, mull it over. Whatever you need to do."

"I am. I will."

"Do you understand how fucked we'd be? Because I feel like you don't get it. Fucked fucked."

"I get it."

He sighed. "Pore over the pictures, get me anything you can on them. I'll get you a secure phone. In the meantime, try and figure out if Alice has been hit, too. Have you guys been in contact out in the world?"

"No."

"So if you're the only one hit, we know where the hole is," he said, his tone almost accusatory, but not quite. The other voice in the room chimed in again, this time chiding. He sighed. "Don't... don't be too forthright. She hasn't been doing this as long as you, and she doesn't have Port Haven training. We don't want to scare her into making a move that would expose her too, if she isn't already."

"Roger," she nodded.

"Ten-Four," he corrected, putting stress on the words.

She hung up the phone and again brought her nail to her mouth, anxious at the idea of having to lie to Alice. She picked up the envelope with the photos and left the closet.

CHAPTER 11

Victor stood in the Houle house archway, his back turned to the front door and looking in at Michelle and Pedro Houle sitting in their living room. They were not sitting together, Victor noticed, the way couples typically did when there was company over.

There were two couches with a garish green-and-red patterned design that would have been expensive thirty years prior but that you now couldn't give away sitting on either side of a coffee table in the centre of the room, and they sat on either side of it. If Victor had wanted to come in and sit, he would have had to pick one parent to pair with over the other.

It was a subtle bit of division he took note of. Not something apparent or something they were likely even aware of, but it was there, and he wondered how long it had been there. Had the division been present before Lauryn had gone missing? Or was it something that had occurred hence, the slow dissolving of a good thing in the constant present of a bad thing's acid? He didn't know, but he made the mental note to take mental notes on it.

The house was large but oddly designed, the sort of house that showed its age and its character in its basic structure. The ceilings on the first floor were too high, with light fixtures that could never be easily accessed and moldings that attracted dust but could never be properly dusted, while the upstairs ceilings looked too low. A cursory glance up the stairs when he'd come up had told him he would have to lower his head to go from room to room if – and when – he was allowed up there. It looked like a normal house design that had been skewed in Photoshop: the lower half stretched up at the expense of squatting the upper. But he knew that the house long predated Photoshop, by at least one hundred years. That was the real culprit to houses like these: houses started without blueprints, built in segments over time, and with measurements done with a weather-eye instead of a ruler.

Victor looked around at the moldings and framed pictures around the burgundy walls. They were all of Lauryn, of course. They didn't all feature her alone, but they all featured her at various ages. Young Lauryn with grandparents. A large shot of extended family, Lauryn among them. Lauryn with a younger Michelle and Pedro. Lauryn alone at graduations, one for every school year it seemed. Victor took all of that in from the archway, his arms crossed in front of his ample chest, holding the coffee cup he'd been given underneath the elbow of his left arm.

"So, she was a smart kid, from everything I'm hearing," Victor said, finishing his eyeing of the room and circling back down to the two of them. The mother nodded, the father did not. The lack of motion did not seem to be in disagreement, but in not wanting to answer at all. Victor's head tilted a little at the father and a smile piqued over his lip, but he moved on. "Tell me about that. About how smart she was."

"Well," Michelle started.

Pedro raised his hand. He sat up straighter than usual. "You say you're here because you're an... occult expert?"

"Cult," Victor corrected, without any tone or inclination to his voice at all. "Not the occult."

"What's the difference?"

Victor raised his eyebrows and bobbed his head from side to side. "How real you think the magic is, I guess."

Pedro warbled his mouth around his teeth, clearly unsatisfied by the response.

"I'm here because a colleague of mine thought I could help find your daughter," he said, working hard to keep his voice even.

At the word *find*, Michelle's eyes watered, and he noticed.

"But if you don't want me here, I don't have to be here."

"She was smart with everything," Michelle blurted, as though wanting to get it out before Victor turned to leave – which he had had no intention of doing. "Chemistry, Physics, Biology, Math... she was good at it all, top of her class."

He nodded. She was proud, and he could see that she was proud. Her anxious excitement to answer the question had evaporated almost immediately and had been replaced with that sort of humble-bragging tone that only a parent talking about their child could have. There had been something else in the voice besides a lack of humility though, a sense of surprise, perhaps, even after all this time.

"Comes from a long line of scholars, I assume?" he asked.

"No, honestly. No. She was the first person in our family to get into college. She was accepted to Brown, you know." She motioned back onto the wall behind here, where an acceptance letter had been framed in the same fashion that a degree normally would have been.

Victor looked at it, then nodded his head towards it. "May I?"

She nodded. Pedro sat back on his chair and folded his arms, his legs spread wide.

Victor watched him for a moment as he stepped by, squinting, then made his way to a spot on the floor directly in front of the acceptance letter. It was positioned exactly at his eye level, and he stared at it for a long moment. There was nothing unique about it – it was a form letter from a department that likely had sent out hundreds that day – yet he read every word.

"Take it you've never seen one of those before?" Pedro said. He clasped his fingers together and propped them up on his knee. Hs voice had an acidity to it that Victor recognized.

"Not from Brown, no," Victor answered evenly. "And if you're inferring I wasn't much of a scholar myself, you'd be right."

"But you still think you can come in here, where so many others have tried, and just make this work? Some people been looking for Lauryn for close on three years, and you think you can just come in and be the big shot, smarter than everyone else?" Michelle tried to tap his knee to stop him, but they were so far away she could barely brush him with the tips of her fingers. Pedro motioned to her. "And upset my wife; every time someone thinks they got the answers, they get her hopes up and upset her more and more."

"Stop it, Pedro," she hissed.

"Someone's got to do it," Victor said, again in an even tone, stepping over to the bookshelf. He wasn't looking at Pedro when he talked to him to see that his face had started to turn red.

"What do you mean 'someone's got to'? Like you're the one to come in and tell us what we done wrong?"

"I didn't mean that," Victor said. He ran his finger along the edge of several books and different stages along the shelf, turning his finger around to look at it after each one. "I didn't mean I'm special. What I mean is: sometimes it takes fresh eyes. Someone who can see things the first people looking into it couldn't, someone who can looks at the same things and see something new. Statistically at this point, as good as the local PD were, it's not going to be them. I wasn't saying 'someone's got to' as in 'they did a bad job,' I was saying 'someone's got to' as in 'at this point any help is going to have to come from an unexpected place, and I'm as good as any.'"

"We're sorry," Michelle said, leaning forward enough to have cupped her husband's knee. Pedro still leaned back. Victor turned briefly to look at it, the story of the division in their marriage laid bare all at once.

"I'm not offended."

She spoke for them both, and Pedro leaned away, his lips clamped shut angrily. "We're don't mean to be rude." She squeezed his knee. "He doesn't... he doesn't like..."

"I don't like G-Men," Pedro spat, finishing the sentence Michelle was having trouble articulating in a way that wouldn't offend, not caring if he did.

Victor turned back quickly at that, his long hair whipping around. He caught it by its split tips and held it up. "I look like a G-Man to you?"

"Yeah, actually," Pedro said, lowering his eyes at him. "Quite a bit. You can let your hair grow out, but that posture says everything. I ain't never seen it on a man that wasn't Gee."

Victor pursed his lips and attempted to un-square his shoulders, but found it was actually difficult. He sighed and turned back to the bookshelf, motioning towards the whole of it. "All the books to the right of this one, they were Lauryn's... right?"

Pedro turned to look over his chair at where Victor was motioning, saw the text Victor was looking at, and nodded in synchronicity with his wife. "How'd you know that?"

"Dust, mostly," he said, holding up the pad of the finger he'd brushed the spines with. "No offense. But also, subject matter. Scholarly types think lower middle-classers don't read but they do, they just might only ever read one thing. Clive Cussler and Steve King put out so many books in their heydays that you could read a book a month for the rest of your life and never touch another author." He pointed to a long row of Cusslers that were smooth and undusted, then moved the finger to Pedro.

"Cusslers."

Pedro nodded.

Victor then moved the finger back to a long collection of Agatha Christie's, then turned and aimed it at Michelle. "Christie."

She nodded.

He motioned to the rest of the shelf. It was made up of all different authors and genres. Romance. Western. Text-books with the spines well creased. Science-fiction. Fantasy. Classics. Modern lit fiction. "Not one author repeats over here. Not one. She had varied interests and wanted varied points of view, but once she found out what each author was about, she moved on."

Pedro nodded. The hint of a smile started across his lips. "We used to give her money for the book fairs at school." He paused. "It was never enough."

"I bet."

"She used to come upset," Michelle smiled, tearful again. "About all the books she had to leave there. She'd talk about it like she was leaving friends there."

At the word friend, Victor's head immediately snapped up to the collage of pictures above the shelf, all of which had Lauryn in them in some capacity and with some other person. "Tell me about friends," he said under his breath. He narrowed in on one in a black frame, a picture of Lauryn in a blue graduation gown flanked by two girls dressed the same. Both were laughing and seemed like they were about to lunge at the camera, while Lauryn stood straight and smiled, the pointer finger of her right hand caught in the grip of her left near her middle. "Tell me about these two."

"That's Nevaeh and Kate," Michelle said, craning her head a little to follow Victor's eyeline. "They were friends all up through high school."

"Best friends?"

"Lauryn didn't have best friends. Not the same way I did, anyway. She wasn't one of those kids who deluded herself into thinking her friends in high school were going to be her friends forever. She understood that things like that came in episodes, that friendship was episodic."

Victor pressed his lips into a thin line, nodding. "Are they still in town?"

"Kate still lives in town, she commutes to Brown. Nevaeh went out of state. I think she's married now; she came out a year or so after she left."

Victor let his eyes travel from Nevaeh to Kate and finally to Lauryn again, examining their body language and their expressions. He tried to remember that such things could be faked on celluloid, that there were pictures taken of he himself where he looked happy but wasn't. Still, there was personality to the picture – it was why Michelle had chosen to hang it over a dozen others like it to begin with that had likely been more posed and professional.

He let his eyes wander away from the frame, scanning over a half dozen others in concentric circles, expanding out from the epicentre of the graduation photo. He passed by candid photobooths that had been blown up to fit an entire frame and shots with grainy pixilation that had been printed off from social media posts she'd been tagged in.

He stopped at a photo that looked both professional and candid at the same time, with contrasting depths of field that focused in on Lauryn. She was leaning against the erect hood of a car with hands tucked into overhauls that were covered in grease and soot, some of which had been smeared under her cheeks as well in that way where one was never sure if it was accidental contact or a conscious fashion choice. She had a baseball cap on backwards, her hair pushing out from either side of it in uniform drapes. There were men all around her, but none were looking at her, nor was she looking at the camera. The shot did not appear posed.

"She worked down at Breen's Repair, sometimes," Pedro said. There was a hint of pride in his voice. "She started out asking if she could volunteer, be a gofer and that. Wanted the experience, wanted to learn mechanics. Eventually they hired her on. Just to help, mind. She'd have had to go to school to get a lot more money at it, but... they saw she was good." He paused, his gaze lingering with Victor's on the shot. "The picture was from the local paper. It wasn't about Lauryn or anything, they were doing charity work fixing up a classic car for a show. But it was a good picture."

"It's a very good picture," Victor nodded, moving on to look at more. "I have an old El Dorado I'd have liked her to have looked at, I think."

"Oh?" Pedro said, his eyebrows raising. "What year?"

"All of them, at this point, it's so frankenstiened to-gether."

Pedro nodded. He had the look of someone who had almost been about to smile, but then reality had set back in and removed the urge. Victor imagined that it had been so long since the man had had a true, honest smile that by now the sensation itself would produce an emotional response. Possibly a negative one.

He scanned through several years worth of school photos, finally landing on a group shot of Lauryn and a half dozen other students in a chemistry lab. There was a teacher posed to their right looking the way teachers did when posing in pictures with students: hand by the side, plastered on grin, dead eyes. Several students were holding a plaque-mounted award and Lauryn was gesturing to it excitedly in the shot.

Victor looked back from the picture back to the dust-laden side of the bookshelf, then stepped back a pace so that both were in view. "She was *really* smart."

"Ayuh," Pedro nodded. "Chemistry, Physics, Mechanics, Engineering, Biology... she was good at it all, top percentiles. Before she... before it happened, every big department at Brown wanted her."

Victor watched Pedro out of the corner of his eye. There was no longer any hint of a smile attempting to peek across his lips, only the slack, null expression of despair and disillusionment. His gaze went past Pedro to Michelle, and for once the both of them were in synch.

"I'm gonna need a few of those books, if that's alright." Victor paused, noting their apprehension. "They'll be returned." He paused, brought his hands together, then turned away from the photo wall and the shelf and toward them. "May I see the bedroom, now?"

Victor opened the door to Lauryn Houle's bedroom.
He let out a breath that shook his cheeks, his air com-

ing up from his diaphragm faster than he'd ever felt it, and without his request. He brought his hand up to his chest and squeezed, feeling the tension there as anxiety – seemingly from nowhere – reached a fever pitch.

It was long and thin with a low ceiling, like the rest of the house: a victim of its time. To the immediate left of the door was the head of the bed, leaving no room for a nightstand or anything like it. Instead, the stand was at the foot of the bed, and he pictured her reading at night, nearing sleep, then getting up to lay her book down at the foot of her bed, waking herself again. There was a desk lamp with an adjustable neck glued to the wall, the head of it aimed down at the pillow. Its cord dangled from its base, long since disconnected.

The room smelled hollow and unused. It was somehow not antiseptic but also not dusty and abandoned, but somewhere in the harsh realm in-between where nothing felt right. There was dust though, despite it not smelling like it, but as there had been dust on the bookshelf downstairs.

He breathed hard, air coming in short, hyperventilating hisses.

There was a small, thin desk lined with models on the right side of the door, opposite the bed, and Victor placed the cleft of his rear against it and sucked in his gut to shuffle in. He had to duck slightly to enter, the low ceiling consistent and oppressive, combining with the cramped horizontal space to make him feel like a sardine in a can.

At the far side of the desk was Lauryn's closet, one of those sorts made up of venetian panels that had been the rage in the nineties and were a favorite of horror movies that wanted their protagonist to be able to hide in the closet but still be able to see the monster.

Victor maneuvered his way to the end table and squat down to peer into it. There were more books in the small shelf that was its base. *Travelling Tuscany* was one, its odd design making it push out of line with the spines of the others. The spine on it was well worn. There were other travel books there was well: to Egypt, to Canada, to Eastern Europe. All of them with weathered, well-worn spines.

There was a model of Big Ben on the nightstand, the sort that was bought in a box with all of the pieces on punch-out cards and put together over a long rainy weekend with glue and patience. He turned back to her desk, where there were more of them. There was a model of a pyramid and another of the Treasury at Petra, and several more. There were two models of Wonder Woman, models where all of the body parts came as separate pieces like a dismembered corpse and had to be glued back together and painted. One had a lasso on her hip that was made of real gold-infused string.

He winced, opening the top desk drawer. Balls of wool puffed out at him immediately, the drawer had been packed tight with them in a variety of colours, along with needles and guides. There were hooks and thread for crocheting and knitting and cross stitching, all pushed into the same space. Victor let out a breath through his nose, then closed the drawer with some effort.

The second drawer was packed with colouring books and lead pencils. Not children's colouring books – although there were several – but the adult ones, sold as relaxation aids. He picked up one that was devoted to elephants and flipped through it, seeing that Lauryn had coloured them in the pinks and soft teals, reminiscent of the painted elephants of India. Some were accurate, and some had been altered to more western colour schemes.

He laid it down and picked up another, which bragged of 'easy to tear out' pages even though a quick scan of its foredge revealed that no pages had been. He browsed through it. It was full of tranquil-looking scenes paired with phrases that were slightly rude, like 'Today is Going to be Fucking Awesome' and 'Fuck Anxiety, But Pour Me More Coffee.' He smiled at them. 'Today is Going to be Fucking Awesome' was painted with greens and soft reds, as though the text were a rose opening its petals for the first time. She had an eye for colour.

He sighed and put the book away again, then stood, extending as high as he could.

Feeling tension in his chest, he stepped over to the closet and opened it. It was empty, clothes that had started to go mouldy having been sent off the goodwill. He tried to step inside, found that it was too small, then stood in its door and looked out at the rest of the room.

He couldn't see the monster, but it was there. He could feel it.

CHAPTER 12

Abby laid the manila folder down on the desk in Victor's study with a firm, stagnated flop, kicking the door shut with her heel. Finally cut off from the world in a way she hadn't felt until now, she let her hands travel up and into her hair, clutch it by the roots, and scream.

It wasn't a scream of terror or even one of anger. It wasn't overly shrill like they always were in horror movies, nor was it the low growl of monsters in horror movies. It was primal, yet somehow devoid of emotion or hysterics. She screamed the way some screamed into a pillow, just without the muffling factor of the pillow.

When it was all out, she staggered on her feet, the blood having rushed to her head, then steadied herself and stepped to the desk and pulled out the chair.

She sat, closed her eyes, then let out a long breath with her hands by her sides. She alternated tapping her thumb against her ring and pointer finger until she felt some of the heat drain from her cheeks. She'd never been taught this, she'd merely tried it once assuming it would work and it had... which to her was all the more proof that the affect was largely placebo, though she tried not to examine that too closely. Examining a placebo effect that was positive to you was a good way to break its hold and end up with no positive effect whatsoever.

She reached for the top desk drawer with her eyes still closed as though she had done it a thousand times before, finding the handle and pulling it open. She opened her eyes and pulled out a magnifying glass and a long, sharp pair of sheers.

Taking the pictures from the envelope once more, she spread them out across the desk. She spread them out wide until they were each as far apart from one another as they could be on the desk. There were six of them, in two rows of three. She looked from one to the other, considering each in turn, until she no longer felt her blood boil to her head upon the sight of them.

When she was calm again, she reached for the picture of her IDs and flipped it over. It was the most different from the rest, and she scanned its poorly trimmed edges. She picked up the magnifying glass and started over its back like a grid, finding nothing but the clean, glossy white of untouched photo paper. She turned it back to the image side and did the same, scanning each section methodically, every square inch mapped on a grid in her mind to be checked and rechecked.

The pixels were huge and bled into each other upon closer inspection. It hadn't just been taken with a bad digital camera, it had been taken and then cropped and then screenshotted on a device like a whole, compounding issues upon more issues. The edges of her Port Haven ID feathered out into the desk surrounding it, and her face had that kind of gaussian blur that only ever showed up on bad home-printed photographs and Instagram models.

She put the magnifier down, flapped the photo between her fingers, then laid it to one side, apart from the others. She picked up a second – the one with she and Meredith in the mess hall – and examined it as well. There were no distorted pixels or feathered edges in this shot; everything was clean and vibrant like a frozen moment in time.

She scanned the picture methodically, looking for a reflective surface of any sort that might have caught the photographer, but knew in her heart of hearts that it was futile. The picture, though crisp, was zoomed in. The photographer would have been too far away for any meaningful data to have been captured. She slipped the page over and did the same as she'd done to the last picture, scanning line by line. This time there was something, the vague outline of words when held up to the light at just the right angle. There were several of them, diagonal and on a one-inch pattern in either direction from each other in stylized lettering.

It was a watermark.

She remembered Professor Peck talking about watermarks in class several weeks ago. It was something that had originally only existed in text and was achieved by changing the thickness of the paper, changing the way it interacted with the light. The thinner, stamped page would appear lighter than the page around it and stand out when held up to the source. It was done while the paper was still wet, he'd said when asked, and thus referred to as a watermark.

This one was chemical, she knew. It was a print mark from the photo lab that had done the printing. It said 'Payson Canvas,' with the name Payson being stylized to go up to a mountain peak in its centre and then back down again, and the word Canvas was straight along its base.

She'd seen the studio before, wedged between a coffee shop and a discount department store near the heart of town.

Abby flipped the remaining four photos over. It was on each of them. Holding it up to the light, she thought she could have even arrange them in the order they'd been cut from the master sheet of photo paper, if she'd been so inclined.

She sighed. All but the printout of the IDs was done at the same location, locally. Whoever had done it had likely been worried that the IDs would arouse suspicion. It had her name and picture on it, someone could have easily used it to find her if they'd seen the pictures and were worried. The photo with the IDs had been done at a quick stop photo-print station of the sort big box stores had. It might have also been a home printer, but she thought that if they'd had that tech at home, they'd have printed them all there. They were travelling light.

"But they're here," she said aloud, moving her mouth around her teeth as it went suddenly dry. "That's the other reason to get it printed here... to let me know that wherever they came from, now they're *here*."

She turned her attention suddenly to the manila envelope that the pictures had come in, as though it had materialized suddenly in her peripheral vision. She stacked the pictures together and laid them aside, then brought the envelope under the light and examined it.

There was no handwriting on the front or back, which made sense. The only thing that would have been necessary would have been her name, and that would have given away the game – either they'd have put down Abby Fisher and their blackmail would have been useless, or they'd have put down Abby Hall and played into it to no effect.

She peered inside the envelope, holding its innards up to the light. She snatched up her sheers and made a long, purposeful cut down through the centre of the back, eviscerating it like a corpse upon autopsy.

The insides were dry and crisp, like paper that had never seen weather. It folded neatly to either side and remained there without needing to be creased, as though it had been taken from its vacuum-sealed packaging just earlier that day. It even smelled new, the way delivered packages rarely did, mired by all of the scents and circumstance of delivery.

It was clean, save for one ragged red tear that went along the bottom edge like a wound.

Abby reached back into the drawer and retrieved Victor's tweezers without taking her eyes off of it. She plucked at it and it moved, raising it high and to the light. It was a single, long, red hair.

"Hello, whoever you are," she said softly to herself.

"Who are you talking to?" Alice said from the doorway.

Abby turned quickly, forced a smile, then turned back and pressed the hair between the cover and first page of a book on Victor's desk for safe keeping. "Ah... nothing," she said, her voice gaining the same customer-service tone she used on students at the school. "Nobody. I didn't hear you come in; how was work?"

"Good," Alice nodded, stepping in and looking around the side of the door. She looked as though she'd never been in there before, as though she'd forgotten that this part of the house existed. "What're you doing in Victor's office?"

"Ah... school project. Examining old texts. Needed some of his tools." She picked up the magnifying glass as if to illustrate.

Alice nodded, stepping in but relaxing her stance.

Abby collected both the glass and the pictures in one smooth motion, laying them into the open top drawer and then closing it.

"You finally registered for Peck's class, then? Like, *registered* registered?"

She nodded. "Yes, they... yes. He wants me to take an exam to cover what I've missed so far."

"You'll ace it."

"That's what he said." She paused. "And yeah, I will."

Alice stepped over to the bookshelf, running her hands over the shelves in reach. She looked past it at first, to the wall of their pictures and Victor's strange code behind them. "This room is so weird without him in it." She waited a beat. "Does a room still belong to a person if they're not there to claim it?"

Abby watched her move but didn't respond. She didn't know how to.

Alice finally let her hand rest upon the solid wood base on his eyelevel shelf. She waited there for a moment, as if merely touching it had had an effect on her, then opened its broken latch. Victor's gun rested there in a pool of red fibers, its magazine in a slot that had been made for it next to it. "What about this? Is this his, too? What makes something belong to someone else?"

Abby squinted, tilting her head compassionately. "Is everything okay?"

"Hm? Yes. Fine," Alice said, her head snapping away from the weapon and the hand that was holding its case open falling to her side.

"You were late coming home the other night," Abby said, her tone even. "How are things... going? At work?"

"Good," Alice replied, after a pregnant pause. "Yeah, everything's good. They asked me to go out after work to some karaoke thing. It was fun."

Abby raised an eyebrow. "Did you sing?"

"I did, yeah."

"I would have liked to have seen that."

"Well, you missed your shot, because that is never happening again," she laughed, sitting down on the edge of Victor's cot.

The moment of levity faded slowly from the room, dissipating with nothing else to fill it until there was just a feeling of vacuum where it once had been. They both felt it, their eyes falling away from each other – Alice's left to the door, Abby's left to the envelope on the desk, and the book she'd wedged the hair into behind it. She cleared her throat. "Have there been any problems at work?"

Alice winced, then forced a smile. "Problems?"

"You know. Issues. Someone being a jerk, or someone being too nosey. Just, you know. Any problems. Any issues."

"You'd be shocked how little problems there are in a workplace once you take the men out of it," Alice laughed, deflecting the question. She didn't meet Abby's eye as she laughed, yet somehow still made it feel genuine.

Abby straightened a little, paused in thought, then nodded. She turned back to the desk for a moment, picked up the dissected envelope she'd left there, then helped it into the drawer with the photographs. She did this without circumstance, bringing no alert to the motion, then paused again and turned back to Alice. "Do you... *like* working with all women?"

Alice raised an eyebrow slowly, and smirked.

"Sorry, that was... sorry. I don't know what I meant by that," she laughed. It was an honest laugh that filled the room, forcing the tension out as both were unable to occupy the same space at the same time. "Did you... want to watch something? It's been a day."

Alice smiled at her, nodded, then stood up. Halfway to the door she turned back. "What about you? Everything okay at the University?"

Abby paused, found the desk drawer in her peripheral vision, then made one big nod. "Yes. Yes, of course." She smiled in a way she never had with Alice before.

CHAPTER 13

"Thanks for doing this," Alice said, stepping down the last of the darkened stairs of the Howse building and out into its foyer. The sun was setting outside, and it looked like it might actually drizzle, so she flipped up the hood of her coat, hiding her face.

"Hey, no problem. If you feel like it's needed, it's needed," Deidre responded, without sarcasm or sympathy. When most people spoke, there was what they said and then what they were *saying*, but Alice had yet to see that side of Deidre, at least to her knowledge. What she said was what she said. "We used to have a buddy system, but we got slack with it and before you know it, it's been cancelled without you having cancelled it." She paused at the bottom of the stairs, as if her own outer monologue had surprised her, then nodded decisively. "I'll draft a memo; we'll bring it back."

Alice nodded, waiting for her on the curb. She eyed two people as they passed but smiled politely to them. They didn't respond, not out of rudeness but obliviousness, but she kept her eyes on them still as they stepped away. Deidre joined her and they both started down toward the mouth of the alley that would take them around to the lot behind.

"So, did someone... attack you the other night? Or say something to you?" Deidre asked, tentatively. Abby turned to her as they walked, surprised. There were words behind these words, subtext for the first time in their working relationship: *were you hurt?*

"No, not at all. Nothing happened."

"Oh, whew," Deidre smiled, letting out a laugh that was more like a sigh. "If something had happened to you after I dragged you out, I'd have been devastated. But you should tell me if it did, don't let that stop you."

"It wouldn't, nothing happened."

"Okay. Good." She smiled.

Alice turned back to the sidewalk in front of them, smirked without humor as she mulled their exchange over, then turned back. "Why would you think something had happened to me just because I wanted to be walked to my car?"

Deidre pursed her lips. "You're strong. Strong women don't usually ask for help unless some asshole has made them feel weak."

"I'm strong?"

"Yeah," Deidre laughed, this time with great humour. "Yeah, you're... strong. You're buff. Confident."

Alice's brow wrinkled as she digested this point of view. She did not argue it, but also could not yet get herself to agree with it. It was the character she was playing that Deidre was seeing, she decided, not her.

The walls surrounding them felt like they were closing

in in the dimming light of day, the way old houses did, the headlamps of vehicles staring at them as they stepped by to Alice's car.

"It looks like we're good," Deidre said matter-of-fact-ly, her tone returning to one without subtext. Her hands were on her hips, like a 'father knows best' or 'Superman' -type character. "Just drive me back to the—" She stopped, seeing it.

There was an albino dead rat trapped beneath Alice's driver side wiper, just like there had been the other night.

Alice sighed, then started to step towards the back of the car to get her rubber gloves.

"What the fuck?" Deidre said, stepping closer to see if the rat was real and then stepping back two paces quickly when she saw that it was. "What the fuck?!"

It was the first and second time that Alice had heard Deidre curse. Alice looked up at her from over the lip of her trunk and saw that her hands were shaking. "It's okay," she said, looking around. "Whoever left it, they're gone." She stepped to the rat and peeled back the wiper blade, hating the sound it made.

The wound that had killed the rat was grislier this time; a long sharp blade – an ice pick, Alice thought – had been driven up through the soft flesh under the creature's chin and exited up through its eye socket, mangling its tiny face in the process. She picked it up carefully and started towards the trash bin with it.

"That is not okay," Deidre said, gasping. "That is not okay at all. That is... that is terroristic."

Alice raised an eyebrow, snapping off her gloves and

looking from the rat in the can to Deidre and then back again, as if trying to see what she was seeing. There was a growing pit in the centre of her stomach, though. "I don't... maybe?"

"That's a *threat*, Alice. That's not okay." She swallowed, looking around. "Walking buddies are definitely mandatory. And there's no security cameras out here... why aren't there security cameras? Dumb." She cursed herself. "We'll have them in by close tomorrow, I don't care who we have to call. They'll be in." Deidre nodded at Alice as though she were the one that needed reassurance, when really she was reassuring herself.

"Get in, I'll drive you back to the office," Alice said. Her tone was calm and flat, and it was only in contrast to Deidre's shaking, quavering voice that she even thought to ask herself *why* her own was so calm and flat.

CHAPTER 14

Victor lay on his bed in the motel room with his boots still on and a smattering of books beside him, shifting with every move he made. The books beside him had started in a pile, but one too many motions of the mattress had made them topple and fall, scattering down the length of the bed with one overlapping the other like sandwiches on a banquet display.

Tash was reading through local newspapers she'd gotten from the library, lying on her bed with her back against the headboard much like he did, but in her bare feet. She tilted down the corner of the newspaper to peer over it and the small pile of dried dust and gravel that was collecting beneath his boots at the foot of the bed. "That's going to drive you insane when you try and sleep tonight."

He turned and raised a wry eyebrow at her from across the expanse of the table that separated them, a scant smirk barely visible through his scruff.

She elevated her shoulders only slightly in response, tilting her head in a 'wait and see' sort of motion, turning back to her paper.

"How's the local news panning out?" Victor asked. He struck his pointer finger in the book he was flipping through – the travel book about Tuscany with a bright orange cover – and then closed it with his digit acting as the bookmark as he talked.

"Better than could be expected. It's a local paper that exists apart from the AP network, so, you know, there's some doozies in here. I'm skimming the Letters to the Editor section because I don't want to spend the rest of my night Googling things I already know aren't true just to make myself feel better."

"I don't understand how you can let things like that bother you."

"It's *reality*," Tash stressed. "I don't understand how you can not let it bother you."

He frowned. "The G-Man in me I guess," he said glumly. "Always was able to keep two truths in my head at once."

She bent down the paper again and looked at him, but he didn't meet her eye or say anything. "Anyway, without national news from the AP, the paper still has to fill the page count for advertisers, so they do it the way they used to back in the day before faxes – police reports."

"'Back in the day before faxes,' jeez we sound old."

"We are old, deal with it." She paused. "'Police responded to three separate domestic disturbance calls, one of which ended in arrest. Police responded to a call of disorderly conduct at Louise Square, three teens were brought home but no citations were issued. Police responded to a reported theft—"

"I get it," Victor said, cutting her off without malice.

"Tracking incidents that way looking for patterns could take a while. Like a long while."

"She's been missing for years," Tash said, stressing the word years until it sounded more like ears, the twang of Atlanta's influence on her accent coming through. "Everything easy has been tried."

He looked as though he were going to counter that statement, then did not. He relented and opened his travel book again.

"How's the Read-A-Thon coming?"

"Like a tour through my on-tour days, actually," he joked, holding up the Tuscany book. "Remember this?"

She smirked. "Unfortunately." She paused, doing a double take. There was a photo of the Piazzale Michelangiolo on one of the pages he had opened, misspelled to Michelangelo. There was a circle around that main photo of it in red sharpie. She indicated it by swirling her finger in the air. "What's that?"

"I think she's circling places she wants to see," Victor said, leaning over and tossing the Tuscany book down to the bottom of the pile. He picked up another travel book, this one for Germany, and riffled through it, stopping at several places to indicate other natural wonders or tourist attractions that were circled. "Like a kid circling things in the toy catalogue they want before Christmas."

Tash stood a little straighter, seeming more intrigued than she had a moment ago. "Did she get to any of them?"

"None overseas, it looks like," he said, putting down the Germany book and picking up a thinner volume revolving around Atlantic City. He opened it and flipped several pages in, where the Hard Rock Cafe was circled in red but had a green checkmark in the top right corner of the circle.

"Not exactly the Piazzale Michelangiolo."

"No, it isn't. But she was young."

"The curse of the young is that they don't know how young they are."

He nodded. "Maybe she got out," he said, under his breath. "Maybe she's out there traveling South Korea all this time and wasn't even around the Internet to know that the whole world is looking for her."

"You don't believe that," Tash said, in a matter-of-fact tone.

"I do not."

"For one thing, she checks off the places she's gone. Why wouldn't she have taken the books with her."

"And for the other," he sighed. "There's the feeling in that house."

She laid down her paper, folding it in one fluid motion and setting it aside onto the untouched side of her bed. "Bad?"

"The tension there is... it's unimaginable. You can feel it the second you enter that house. The parents, they're about to snap. They're apart, in every conceivable way. And he's snapping and she's trying to chill him out, and he resents that she's telling him how to react to this and she resents that he's pulling away when she's just trying to help, and... and it's all downhill." He paused. "Her room is the worst though, the second I walked in I could just *feel* the pain and the tension and the fear... It started to get to me, honest."

"They're missing their child," she paused. "You should know the feelings that engenders."

His head snapped forward to look at her as though she had just barked his name in anger instead of spoken calmly and benignly. He looked as though he were about to speak with a tongue tipped with venom, but restrained himself at the last moment with a deep, practiced breath. He nodded. "There's something I'm missing," he said after a moment of reconstitution. "Something small, but... big at the same time. I know that it's missing, I just don't know *what* it is that's missing, you know?" He turned back to look at her, his expression more normal.

She nodded, swallowing. She was not meeting his eye, her gaze falling over the line of books laid out like a platter.

"Are you okay?" Victor asked, his eyebrows moving together and his tone changing.

She turned back to face him and nodded unconvincingly.

"You're anxious."

She frowned. "I'm worried I've gotten you into something you're not going to like in the end."

"That's never stopped us before."

She smirked. He got up from his bed and made his way to the mini fridge to grab a soda for each.

CHAPTER 15

Breen's Repair was the sort of one-floor bungalow repair shop that every town had, with a front that was made up of three large garage doors and one small entrance next to a storefront window, and a sign above it with the word 'Breen's' in red cursive font and the word 'Repair' in thinned Impact font. Every patch of paint on it was chipped and weathered, to the point that Victor didn't think it would look right if it wasn't. Like perhaps there was an unknown process to making your paint appear bubbled and stripped ahead of its time, making it look more authentic and seasoned.

There was no one in the office portion, they could see that from the street. Rather than step inside and ring the bell and wait, Victor and Tash stepped up and into the open garage doors and into the workspace of the men who worked there. The mechanics were oblivious to them at first and they looked at each other before heading over to a long workbench strewn with greasy tools.

Victor had seen mechanic shops that were pristine and well lit. When he had been young that had been the norm, then some Hollywood executive that had never been in a real garage had popularized the idea of the grease monkey, and eventually reality had begun to imitate art. He remembered stepping into garages as clean and white as tech companies tried to be now, slick with nary a spot or a stain anywhere.

"Hey, you can't be back here," someone said, finally looking up from their work.

Victor stared at the man from between curtains of blond as the rest of them stopped their work and looked up. When the noise and grind of machinery had stopped, he tilted his head up, sticking out his chin as though about to say something momentous.

"We're here looking for Lauryn Houle," Tash said, stepping forward and speaking loud enough that she could be heard.

Victor scanned the mechanics when she said the girl's name, making eye contact with each one of them in turn.

"Is there anyone still here who knew her?" Tash continued.

Of the four men present, three raised their hands.

"Anyone here feel like they knew her well enough to answer a few questions?"

One man lowered his hand.

Victor stepped away from the bench to be shoulder-to-shoulder with Tash, looked at the two men with their arms still in the air, then cocked his head at the younger of the two. He was against the far wall and had black scruff along the ridge of his jaw coming down from a red cap. His eyes were big and blue, and he looked over at the both of them with his hand obediently in the air, waiting for one of them to tell him why.

"That one," Victor said, his voice laced with gravel.

The boy in the red cap was named Marcus, and even though he was clearly at least twenty-five, Victor had trouble thinking of him as more than just a boy. It was something about the way his sideburns splayed out over his jaw, even though the rest of his face was so cleanly shaven Victor was sure that he simply couldn't grow hair.

"Lauryn was awesome," Marcus said, even as he moved tools aside on his workbench to give himself room to lean. "She was smart, real smart, but didn't act it, you know? She never came in here with her shit and tried to make me feel worse for not knowing it. She came here to learn, and she learned quick." He paused, wiping his hands with a cloth he'd produced from his pocket and looking down. "She was awesome."

Tash turned and looked at Victor, who was silent and still for a long moment, then nodded.

"Tell me a story about her," she said, her voice honey. "That usually helps."

Marcus shot her a quizzical look, then shrugged and looked away, thinking. He turned back quickly, smiling at the memory. "She came to us still in high school. I'm not much older, I'd only just started. But she came to us and asked for a job and we weren't hiring so they said no, so she offered to work on commission and the boss, he says no. We need all the few commissions we get for the guys who work here." Marcus motioned around to the crew. The action looked foreign on him, and both Tash and Victor understood that he was imitating the gestures that the pit boss had given Lauryn. "So, she asks if she can intern. I don't even think Carl had *heard* the word intern before, didn't know what it meant. People don't usually intern at mechanics."

Tash nodded. She glanced at Victor, who was watching Marcus intently with his hands on his beard, but said nothing.

"He was real hesitant, too. I think he thought something was fishy; can you blame him?"

"Not really," Tash said with apprehension.

"I'm on the same page, don't get me wrong," Marcus said, holding up his hands as though it made a shield. "I'm not saying it's weird to have a girl around the shop, I'm not one of that generation. I'm just saying... anyone comes looking for a job so hard that they mind up offering to do it for free, you gotta wonder what their motivation is."

"Understandable," Victor said, barely moving his lips.

"So he says to her, he asked if she has a crush on one of the guys here, because he doesn't want a Me Too situation going on." Marcus paused. "I don't think he really knew what that meant, I think he'd just heard it on the news a lot. Anyway, she said she just wanted to learn about cars and mechanics and that they wouldn't teach it in school and so, here she was. She was just here to learn."

"Sounds nice," Tash encouraged.

"It was, but we didn't know that then. We were thinking we'd have some idiot underfoot, asking about everything. Thinking it would hold up work because we'd have to stop and explain what we were doing, rather than just do it. When I say we, I mean that was the attitude going in from the team."

"But you knew better?" Victor asked, picking up on something from his tone.

Marcus nodded. "Like I said, she was a few years behind me in school, but I remembered her. Always smart, with everything." He paused. "So, Carl takes her on, and not long after this client comes in that's been in a dozen or more times this month, and he's rip-roaring. His car is still making this nasty, gross sound intermittently and we can't figure out what it is. He keeps bringing it back and we keep thinking we got it and charging him labour, and he keeps getting madder and madder because it ain't fixed. Now that's a problem, because now he thinks we're scamming him and he doesn't want to pay anymore, but he wants it fixed. It's a problem because you can see his point of view, we want to fix it for him." He motioned to them both.

Victor and Tash nodded.

"But we haven't been able to fix it yet when we were *paid*. If we agree to do it pro bono because of everything he's already paid, now many man hours is that going to take up? So Carl, he calls us all into the office to talk it over, and he leaves Lauryn out on the floor. Forgets about her, she's still new at this point. And when we get back out, she's found the problem and knows how to fix it."

Victor raised an eyebrow, almost smirking. His gaze shifted to Tash.

"She just figured it out? No training?" Tash asked. She didn't seem surprised, but impressed.

"Fresh eyes, man. Sometimes all it takes is fresh eyes. Everyone else, they went in with their own ideas and experiences and biases." He paused, clucking his tongue against his cheek. "We only think of learning as learning knowledge, but we learn biases, too. Sometimes I think we get one bias for every one piece of knowledge, like a yin and yang." For a moment he sounded less like a grease monkey and more like a hippie who had just stepped away from a concert hall. "She went in with fresh eyes and looked at each part and just found the problem. AC was loose, of all things." He paused, looked down, then met their eyes again. "After that she was just part of the team. I don't think it was a week later Carl found the budget to hire her on, just a few days after school and some weekends and stuff. She had a lot going on."

Victor nodded. "Anyone give her a hard time?" he asked, casting a weather eye over the rest of the shop and noting the other workers that were there.

Marcus stopped fidgeting. His fidgeting hadn't been pronounced enough to be noticeable until he'd stopped it, but now stood out like a sore thumb. "Hard time?"

"Come on. Young girl, male dominated profession. Someone must have got it in their heads that she was there to be eye candy for them."

Marcus furrowed his brow as though the thought had never occurred to him, but was still thinking about it. After a moment, his eyes lit with recognition. "Jim asked her out, when she'd been here a few weeks." He motioned to Jim, who was on the other side of the work area.

Jim bristled at being motioned to, then relaxed and nodded. He looked slightly older than Marcus, maybe by a year. He was old enough that if he'd been successful in his gambit to date Lauryn her parents might have taken issue with it, but young enough that society at large wouldn't have.

"Did he give her any trouble?" Victor said, his accent coming out like molasses in a way it didn't typically. "Come at her too hard? That kind of thing?"

Again, Marcus knit his eyebrows together. "He asked her out for a soda and she said she wasn't dating right now, so he apologized and they both had a good laugh. Then he invited us all out for soda so she wouldn't feel weird. Four of us went, it was fine." He made a face at Victor as though they were on two different worlds about the subject. "I asked her a while later if she was okay working here, if anyone had made her feel bad or anything, and she said she was fine."

Victor considered asking why Marcus thought she'd have been honest with him with that answer, but decided against it.

"Do you have any idea about her plans for after school?" Tash said, stepping in and letting her calm voice smooth over the roughness that Victor's had left behind like a hot knife.

"She talked about keeping this up," he said, picking up a large wrench from the bench behind him and starting to fuss with it. His fidgeting was back.

"She wanted to stay at a small town chop shop?" Victor snapped sarcastically.

"No," Marcus laughed. "Mechanics. Engineering. She said she'd wanted to go in for mechanical engineering or something the like. Said she'd wanted a job here to see if she had a knack for it." He looked away then, the way someone did when their words got away from them and brought them into a sad avenue they hadn't been expecting. "She did."

Victor frowned, so much so that it creased the lines of his face on either side of his mustache's handlebars, turning them into deep trenches. He turned without another word to Marcus and walked out of the garage.

Tash started after him, then stopped, laying a hand on Marcus' arm gingerly. "Thank you for taking the time. You helped."

Marcus nodded, and watched as she jogged to catch up with Victor, shaking his head.

"You could be nicer, you know," Tash said, finally reaching Victor as they hit the main drag. "This is a small town. If word gets around that you're an asshole, we won't be able to get anything from anyone." She caught her breath. "It's not like we have the ability to get warrants or compel testimony."

"He's not going to complain," Victor scoffed. "He's way too timid. OCD and never had a thought about a girl in his life, he was so shocked when I asked if someone had tried to give her the business. He might have Aspergers."

"He might just be *nice*."

Victor shot her a look. He frowned, looked both ways and waited for a car to pass, then crossed the street.

"Do you think he knows anything? That anyone in there caused her trouble?"

"I think assigning him knowledge would be a mistake."

"*Victor.*"

He sighed, coming up short just side of the sidewalk and turning to talk to her without fear that they would be run over. It was a small town. He looked away, looked at the sky, then finally frowned and brought his gaze back down to meet her. "No. I think he honestly thinks what he's saying his true. He didn't fidget because he was uncomfortable, he fidgeted when he wasn't, when we brought him into new areas. Same thing with looking away, it wasn't lying, it was general discomfort." He paused, shaking his head. "Boy's never had his hand between—"

"Your crassness isn't needed at this juncture."

He paused, then nodded.

Her shoulders relaxed when she saw his do the same. "Not everyone has something to hide."

He spun on her, meeting her gaze and sending his hair whipping around. "That's nice at tea. When there's a missing person, that's a problem."

CHAPTER 16

"Lauryn was smart, yes. Very smart," Professor Brae said, touching his hand to his too-tight watch strap.

He was obese. Not fat, not big-boned, not slightly larger than normal and you called him obese because you're an awful person who lives to hurt others, and not slightly higher than normal on the BMI scale to others: obese. His head was thick and square with it, his mouth too low across his face and his eyes too large behind coke-bottle glasses. His hair was wispy and so blond it was almost invisible, brought around his skull in a Trumpian weave. His skin was red from the strain of pumping his blood and pocked with blisters.

He sat in the lawn chair across from Victor with a glass of lemonade at his side. They were sitting on his front stoop: Brae had insisted that his home was too badly kept to see people in, but had still wanted to talk with them. Tash stood leaning in the doorjamb behind Victor and glanced over her shoulder into the kitchen and could confirm it to be true.

Victor shifted. The wooden lawn chair he was in was

built for someone Brae's size. He felt like a child in it, with too much space on either side of him before the armrests appeared. He subconsciously kept trying to place his elbows on either rest and steeple his hands in front of him, but every time he tried his arms connected with nothing and fell into the gap at his sides. "Go on," he said, when it became clear that Brae wasn't going to continue of his own accord.

"She has brilliant. There's not a lot more to say about it. She took to the periodic table the way most kids take to their ABCs. She'd just come in and *know*, you know?"

Victor narrowed his eyes thoughtfully, but nodded and feigned a smile.

"The year she—" he paused, stopping himself, the word catching in his throat as though it had caught him off guard and he now might choke on it. "The last year she was in school, we went to the nationals in the CADUMs... the Chemistry Academia Demonstrative—"

"I know what it stands for," Victor said. Tash gave him a look that said she didn't believe he did, which he didn't see.

Brae nodded. "The last year she went with us, she knew everything. Every question that came to her, she just knew it. She didn't have to use a timeout or an extension or a pass, none of it. You asked her a questions and BAM—" he snapped his fingers, but they were too large and the skin too loose to make the sound and were instead a pantomime of the gesture "—she knew it."

"No small wonder she was getting into Brown, then."

"That was me," Brae stepped, straightening his shirt and fussing with the metal strap of his watch again. It was far too tight on him and dug into the flesh of his wrist. The holes it gouged were dry, as if the blood in his veins wasn't able to get the extra energy needed to reach the surface of his flesh.

"You know someone at Brown?" Tash said, raising an eyebrow. "Pulled some strings to get her in?"

Brae shifted uncomfortably, more redness finding its way under his collar. "I wrote a wonderful recommendation letter. Glowing. She sent it in with her application. I'm sure the people there read it and saw she'd be excellent for their chemistry program."

"Was she signed up for chemistry?" Victor asked. He leaned forward slightly. "I'd heard she was going in for something different."

Brae shuffled and made a chuffed, huffing sound. "I suppose that was Sanders over in the Biology department that told you that, hn? Or the Physics teacher? They were both trying to get her to go in for those, I hear Sanders even made her go in and talk to the head of the biology department there. Vultures." He chuffed. "She was a smart girl, all around. She was smart with all subjects so they all wanted her. She was smart with music, too, but nobody was fighting for her to be a musician. She was interested in the *chemistry*, not all that other noise. She tutored younger students in chemistry. She was in my chemistry club."

"She wasn't in clubs for any of the other subjects, then?" Victor asked.

Brae stopped at that, chuffing again. "She may have been, but that looks good on a résumé. She was a chemist though; she was going to be a chemist. Top of my class, she was going places."

Victor turned over his chair and looked at Tash, who nodded.

"I'm starting to get a hint as to why this girl left," Victor said, sitting back on his side of the booth in the cafe.

Tash looked up from her ice cream in mid-bite, taken off guard by the grievance. "... Are you back to thinking she left of her own accord?"

He frowned and sighed, in the way men did when they hadn't thought through the implications of what they were saying and caught themselves in a Freudian Slip. He turned and looked at the lazy, small town traffic milling its way about the window. "Seems like everyone wanted her for something."

She nodded reluctantly.

He narrowed his eyes, watching one specific child as he strutted up the street towards a confectionary store. His chest was out, his head was high, and he wore a white shirt striped with light purple that looked as though it were new. "People always think you're wasting a gift," he said to the window, his tone faint and almost whispered. "If you're the type that's good at something – real good – people think you're wasting your talent if you just sit inside and play video games. But what if you *want* to just sit inside and play video games? It's your talent, isn't it your choice whether or not to use it?"

"She didn't seem like the gamer type."

"No, she didn't."

"But if she had been, I bet she'd have been fucking aces at them."

He turned back to her and frowned. "I was good at one thing when I was a kid. Just the one. And they put me to work at it." He paused. "Took me years to figure out that that wasn't what I wanted to be. A lot of years of following orders, and a lot of help."

She smiled a little, out the corner of her mouth.

"This girl has a *lot* of talents."

"Do you think she had some kind of inherent ability?"

"No, I think she was fucking smart. And I think when people say 'you're letting yourself down' for not using your talents, what they mean is you're letting them down. They know they're not as good as you, and they want to live through you. Brae could be a high school chemistry teacher, and that's it. He liked chemistry more than he liked anything else in the whole world, but that was still the highest he could climb with it." He sipped his coffee. "You look at someone like that, someone who could cure cancer if she set her mind to it, and you put all your misspent aspirations onto her. Then suddenly you can't fathom her pursuing anything except *your* dream. Multiply that by a dozen or more talents, and you get a bunch of pissed off, disappointed people. *Annoyed* people. 'Why did I sink so much of my time into helping you if you're just going to do something else' people."

Tash tilted her head. "So, you're back on something external coming at her?"

"I don't know what I'm on," he said, frustrated.

"Straight," Tash said suddenly and under her breath, looking over his shoulder. He straightened instantly and put on a customer service smile.

"Sorry I'm late, the commute was murder," said a young woman as she stepped up beside their table and extended a hand first to Victor, then to Tash. "I'm Kate Ashlyn." They each shook it in turn, and Tash moved over to the far end of the booth, giving her room to sit and place her bag down.

"Thank you for meeting us," Victor said, twirling a single finger in the air to alert that more coffee was needed.

"All respect, I've had a long day and a long drive, and I'm going to need something stronger than that if we're going to be talking about Lauryn."

Victor raised his eyebrows but nodded without judgment. When the serving staff came over, he asked for a refill on his coffee and told Kate that whatever she wanted was on his tab. She ordered an import beer and specified it be in a stein. It was delivered and Tash asked her about her day, and she talked about her classes. She was a student at Brown and commuted back and forth, daily, a choice which had seemed wise at the time but now she would have traded the extra expense of campus living for the hours of the day she was missing out on a hundred times over.

"I need that ninety minutes – both ways – so much that I started listening to my textbooks on audio book. Can you image that? Popping in audio books of a textbook and letting it play on your commute, because there won't be enough time to read them otherwise. Bullshit."

"What are you taking?" Tash asked, leaning on her own arm and smiling with genuine interest.

"Pre-Law."

"I didn't do it," Victor said, raising both his hands mockingly.

Tash turned and smiled at him. It was a Dad Joke, and he rarely told them. For a moment it was as if he'd forgotten himself, and she hated to bring it back to business.

"Not the first time I've heard that one," Kate smirked.

He worked his lips back and forth as though his mouth were dry, but was actually working the smile off of his face. "Speaking of Brown and course loads, we've gotten some... conflicting information on what Lauryn was going to be taking. Hoping you could help us with that."

Lauryn laughed, but it was tinged with sadness. "They're still on that, huh? She's been gone years, and every single mentor of hers out there is still chaffed at how she was going to be *their* big success. Another reason I should have left this town and moved onto campus, I tell you."

"Did you feel bad about being left behind at first?" Tash asked cautiously. "Nevaeh moving away and getting married, Lauryn moving away to Brown?"

"Oh, no," Kate laughed again. "Lauryn wasn't going to go to Brown. She got the letter, sure. But she let the admission date slip right by."

Victor and Tash threw each other a look.

"Why's that?" Victor asked, his tone now serious. "She decide to stay here?"

"*Decide*? Lauryn? No." She curled her lip a little but played it off as a laugh, then took a sip from her stein. "Lauryn could never decide anything. She was the way she come out of the box, minute one. The way she was was just the way she was." She paused, considered her glass and the bitterness in her own voice, then cocked her head and decided she was fine with the both of them. She took another drink, swallowing the last of it.

Victor motioned to it and she nodded. He motioned for another drink. She looked over at Tash.

Tash nodded, reached into her bag, and produced the dark orange *Travelling Tuscany* book. "What about these? She was going to travel, right? Circled places she wanted to go?"

Kate jolted forward, her lower face in a laugh. Had she had any drink in her mouth at that point she would have spit it out. It wasn't a bitter laugh or a mocking one, but a nostalgic laugh. Judging by her age and her reaction, Victor thought, possibly, her first. "Oh my God, I'd forgotten about these. These are a trip!" she said, taking the book gingerly by its edges. "Her travel books!"

"So, she did want to go?" Victor asked.

"Oh yeah, she wanted to go. *Wanting* to go was a part of her default setting. It was how she came out of the box." She ran her hands over each of the letters of the title furtively, no longer able to make eye contact with Victor and Tash. Every time she tried, her head swiveled back down to the book.

"You can keep that, if you'd like."

Tash shot him a surprised, alarmed look, reminding him with her wide eyes that the books were, firstly, evidence, and, secondly, not his to give.

"It's fine," he said. "I'll tell the parents. They'll be fine with it." He said it in a way that did not reveal to Tash if he actually would or not, or if he were just saying he would to remove her objection. "So why does everyone else think she's going to Brown? Or going in for automotive repair? Or any one of thirty other things?"

Kate pursed her lips. Her next drink was delivered, and she took a sip of it eagerly, but drank less this time than she had during her first sip of her first drink, slowing down. "Lauryn was a Rorschach test. People saw in her what they wanted."

Tash tilted her head, reached back into her bag to produce her notebook, then opened it and started to scribble a jot-note for herself without turning her gaze away from Kate.

"She was this blank slate – good at a lot of things, but not actually *interested* in them. With big things – art, science, stuff you could build a big career at – people tell themselves you have to love it to be good at it. It's not always the case. You think about it in terms of a job lower on the social ladder, it becomes real clear."

Victor nodded slowly, not in agreement but following her train of thought. "You can be a good cashier, that doesn't mean you're interested in it."

"Exactly," Kate said, clicking her tongue as she shot a finger-gun in his direction. "I try and keep that in mind even now, actually. In law we make that same assumption. 'Kelly did this job for three years, we can assume she liked it;' no, we can't Bob. Not unless we're in some kind of non-capitalist society all at once and nobody needs to pay rent anymore and everyone does *only* what they like best, and only for that reason." She had parlayed into lecture for a moment, and her tone had shifted. It was as though she were quoting from her own research paper. She brought two fingers to her mouth suddenly, buttoning it. "Sorry."

"Don't be sorry," Tash smiled. "Sounds interesting."

Kate turned to look at Tash, gaze fluttering quickly from her hand on the table to her face, then smiled naturally.

Victor watched this and tilted his head at it, then smirked. "Go on."

"Right. Sorry." Kate took another sip. "Lauryn was this blank slate. This cipher. She never showed much emotion, she never showed preference. So people inferred their own preferences onto her. Like a human Kuleshov test."

Victor raised an eyebrow.

"Sorry, I took film studies as an elective. I saw this back then and it instantly made me think of her, it just fits with her, perfectly." She put her hands out in front of her, thumbs connecting, to make a screen. The more alcohol she got in her the more she talked with her hands, they both noticed, or perhaps she was simply loosening up in general. "There was this guy, Kuleshov, in the early days of film, and he had this theory, that two shots together meant more than one in isolation." She brought the 'frame' up to frame her face. "So, he took this ten second shot of himself looking at the camera. Straight at the camera, no expression, not giving anything." She let the smile drain from her face until her expression was blank, illustrating the effect.

"You could act," Tash mused.

"Thanks. Anyway, he takes that footage, and he pairs it with three things: first kids playing, then a kid in a coffin, then young girls walking. Same shot of him, every time remember. Three things happened." She held up her fingers, pressing down so hard that they bent back as she ticked off the results. "First, people assumed that whatever the second shot was was what he was looking at. He wasn't really looking at any of it, he was looking at the camera. It was stock footage. Second, they inferred things on the clip of him based on the second clip. Third, they inferred even more when they put all six clips together."

Victor squinted. "I'm lost, sorry. Go back to the second thing?"

Kate nodded, bringing the frame up to her face again. "First shot, guy looks at camera."

He nodded.

"Second shot, kids playing. You assume, what a nice man, looking after his kids playing."

He nodded.

"Back to the shot of looking at the camera, next shot: dead kid. You assume, on look at the sad man, his kid must have died."

Victor's eyes lit up with understanding and he nodded more enthusiastically, but let her finish.

"Back to the face for a shot, last shot: girls from behind, focus of their lower halves. Ew, what a pervert. And remember: his reaction shot was the same footage, repeated three times. The viewer infers three separate emotional states from the same clip, based on the which one it was paired with."

"And when you put them all together it changes them again," Victor said, his tone one of reverence for this new idea he'd been given. "Suddenly he's a guy who was watching kids and hunting them, and at the end he's watching young women, maybe his next victims."

"Bam," Kate said flatly, pointing to him again. "You get it. That's what they'd do to her. She was good at everything, but she didn't show preference. So everyone inferred that preference onto her. They brought their own baggage to her blank slate. She's good at everything but I like physics best and she shows no preference, so I'm going to assume she likes physics best, too."

"Sounds exhausting," Tash said, her voice glum.

"It wasn't, when we were young," Kate smiled. She touched the letters of the travel book again. "When you're young nobody expects you to pick a direction. It's fine to have a million different interests when you're a kid... but then they want you to whittle it down and make a choice. You can be interested in a dozen things, but you've got to focus on one. Got to pick a Major, assign one of your interests chief. You get a Minor too, a second in command. But you have to choose." She drank. "That choice, that finally being forced to narrow it down – stop being a Rorschach and actually say what she was... that was stressing her. That stress was so hard on her she was barely the same person the last few weeks before..." she paused. "*Before*."

Victor nodding, thinking back to the picture of Lauryn, Kate, and Nevaeh in their graduation gowns. Kate and Nevaeh were leaned forward and silly, while Lauryn had stood ramrod straight, her hands clasped together apprehensively. Yet her mother has described it as *them* having fun. Lauryn had Kuleshov'd them: giving nothing, and her emotional state being inferred by the others in the frame with her.

"What did *you* infer her interest in?" he asked, suddenly and with the barest hint of sharpness on his tongue.

Kate stopped mid-drink, stiffening. Tash's head snapped at him, caught off guard as well.

Kate lowered her glass, looking away for a moment. She had the look of someone whose own logic had been used against them in a way they'd never considered, and it was shattering. "Maybe a lot," she said finally, her voice drained and hollow. Her hand felt the letters again. "You're right, she couldn't commit to anything. Not where to vacation or—" she paused.

Victor tilted his head at her. Tash reached out and touched her hand empathetically, and Victor saw it and tried not to curl his lip at it. "Or?" he asked. Tash shot him a look that said *stop pushing*.

"I guess I have a lot more in common with this travel book than I thought."

CHAPTER 17

Payson Canvas was a small, thin slot with a large window wedged between a local chain coffee place and a discount clothing store. There was also a dentist's office, Abby had realized once she'd seen it in person. Both Payson Canvas and the dentist's office took up so little real estate on the front end of the building that their width barely exceeded the width of their signage above the door. Abby stepped in expecting an equally small space, but it went up far and all the way back, stretching far beyond the area accessible to customers. People were working in open view, stretching out sheets of canvas and mounting them. None of them looked up when Abby entered, and she understood immediately that they weren't the people to help her.

There was a desk against the wall to the right of the entrance, with a woman in her early thirties behind it at a computer. She was dancing with her shoulders only, jutting them back and forth as she did her work. Her mouth was curled into a small bow making 'doo doo doo doo' sounds that, to Abby's ear, wasn't an existing song or even

a coherent melody, but merely her need to fill her immediate area with music. She wore massive, round glasses
with thin frames and had pink hair that was so light it was
almost white. It was back in a bun now, but some rebel-
lious wisps had escaped and were moving with her to the
beat she created, their single strands illustrating what the
whole wanted to do.

Abby liked her, instantly.

She stepped up to the desk and was greeting with a
warm smile. "Hi," she said, but the last remnants of the
music in her made it come out to the same tune she was
making up and sound like 'hIiIi.' In that brief moment,
she looked like a stage member of Jem and the Holograms
come to life. She continued to dance with her shoulders
even as she turned to Abby, but scaled it back to just the
bare minimum of movement needed to keep the beat.

"Hi," Abby said, returning the smile but not the music.
She laid a new manila envelope on the desk between them
and then leaned back to see the name placard in front of
the person. "Kat."

"That's me."

"You do photo printing here, right? I have the right
place?"

"I don't do it," Kat said, jutting both pointer fingers
towards her central plexus. "Gretchen does that. She's
the hardest worker here." She transitioned her hands into
pointing with thumbs, gesturing back over her shoulder
at a printer that was even now spitting out photographs
at an alarming rate. It produced them one at a time onto
a tiny elevator that brought them up to a conveyor belt,
brought them along one at a time while giving them a

moment to dry, them deposited them in piles with the others. A mechanical arm then wrapped a plastic sheath around them, separating them into print jobs. To Abby it all seemed ludicrously unnecessary, a Rube Goldberg machine for printing and collating photographs.

"Okay, but you're—"

" Gretchen's boss, yes. Absolutely." She brought her thumbs around seamlessly into a thumbs up.

"Okay, I need your help with something," Abby said, pinching the end of the envelope with one hand and sliding the pictures out of it with the other. "I need to know about the person who printed these." She slid the photos across Kat's desk at her. Only five of the photos were in the stack, she had left the sixth – the one of her IDs that she suspected was from a more publicly accessible printer – at the house.

Kat looked at the top photo, which Abby had strategically rearranged to be the one of herself crying in Jasper Hemmingway's destroyed apartment. The colour – and her endlessly cheery expression – drained from her face. Suddenly her smile receded into splotch of formless red in the bottom of her face, despite how she tried to keep it customer-service on. She didn't have a fake mode, Abby decided. When she was 'on,' it was because she was really on. "I can't give out any client details."

Abby forced herself into a thin smile and nodded, glancing around the small corner that was Kat's desk. There were photos framed in the same shade of pink as her hair, most of them containing Kat herself and a man about her age. They were yin and yangs, except for the smiles. His smile matched her own, big, bright, and honest. There was a shot of him on one knee next to a water-fall, she with a shocked expression on her face. "You seem happy," she said, looking from picture to picture.

"I am," Kat said, exhaling a breath she'd been hold-ing.

"Were you always?"

Those thin, plunked eyebrows curled up at their crease. No answer was needed.

"I didn't think so. It's hard to find someone who is... isn't it?" She swallowed, pushing the photos forward and swallowing hard. "I had a hard time, once. The sort of hard time a lot of people have. I thought for a long time that it was me." She spread out the photos. She was there crying, she was there in front of police, twice. "I changed little things about myself, but it started to dawn on me that I'd need a *big* change. A scary big change." She swallowed, choosing her words carefully. She did not want to lie to sell the story, but also did not want to be too forthright with the truth. An insane ex was something most people could identify with, her exact situation: less so. "I changed my name. I got a new job. I've moved away from family and friends... and yet I went into my work the other day and this was waiting for me." She flipped the photos to the one of her in front of the University, standing beside the El Dorado.

Kat swallowed.

"I get your policy, I do. But the person who did this—"

"Fuck our policy," Kat snapped, meeting Abby's eye with a determined, actualized look. The curse was sur-prising given her nature, but also seemed at home in her mouth. She said it often, Abby decided. It did not have the hesitation stutters of one who typically avoided such things.

Abby breathed a sigh of relief.

"It wasn't a guy that came in, it was a girl. A woman. Taller than you, but not by much. Long red hair, thick. Looked like natural red that was made even more red with a dye job, but maybe not. I could just be jealous, because it was super red. Red red."

Abby nodded.

"Her ears poked out, even though her hair should have covered them. Not a lot, just a little."

"What do you mean?"

"I mean," she reached down and produced a sparkly pink bag and laid it onto the chair. She reached down into it and pulled out a pair of pointed ears that matched her skin tone. She held them up to either side of her face as if to illustrate. She looked like something out a Star Trek, briefly, while she held them. "Like this"

Abby nodded, and did not comment on the fact that Kat had had those at the ready, always prepared with elf ears the way some girls were always prepared with condoms. "Anything else?"

Kat thought for a moment, her tongue pressed firmly into her cheek. "Yeah..." she said finally. Her pause wasn't hesitation, it was thinking about how to phrase it, and Abby did not interrupt it for fear of her losing that train of thought. "She had a walk."

"A walk?"

"Yeah. A walk. Like the way military jag-offs walk. Not *all* the military, just the jag-offs... does that make any sense?"

Abby nodded. The description made sense, just not what it meant to her.

Abby stepped away from Payson Canvas with a grin on her face, having come away with more than what she'd gone in with. The photos and the envelope they'd come in were wedged under her arm in a gaggle, one not tucked within the other as she had thanked Kat and gathered them up.

Tall. Red hair. Atypical ears. And a pseudo-military gait. It wasn't a lot to go on, but it was something. She—

She stopped dead in her tracks four feet from the El Dorado.

There was a dead rat on her windshield, caught beneath the wiper. Its head was craned back to face her in a way that was awkward and obscene, its mouth wide in an unending snarl. There was blood on it, and all up along her windshield.

Abby turned and looked around the busy parking lot.

Nothing looked out of place.

CHAPTER 18

Abby pulled into her house with blood still dried across her windshield, as though this were the end of her desire to flee the scene of a hit and run. She came to a screeching halt on the gravel driveway, stopping up short so loudly that it drew Alice's attention in the kitchen.

Alice looked out the large front window of the kitchen and saw Abby, sitting in the car with the motor still running, her forehead pressed firmly against the steering wheel. There was glare from the afternoon sun on the shield, making the thin streak of red that stretched from the lower right to the upper left look black. "Damn," she said, slapping the window jam and heading out to meet Abby.

Abby got out of the car and slammed the door to the El Dorado just as Alice was making her way barefoot across the lawn towards her. It didn't make the sort of punchy, definitive sound that she'd wanted, so she opened it and re-slammed with more elbow grease on it. Her teeth were gritted past the point when it was safe to have done so, barred and aligned against one another. She was red in the face.

Alice looked from the red streak across the windshield, then to Abby. "What happened?"

"Someone left a goddamn *rat* on my windshield. A big, fucking, albino *rat*." Abby opened the door and slammed it again, her cheeks puffed with unspent energy and broken blood vessels. She gave up after that hit, bringing both her hands down on the hood and curling her fingers.

Alice stopped stepping forward at the mention of the rat, frozen in her tracks.

Abby noticed, her breathing slowing as she narrowed her eyes. "You don't seem as surprised as you should."

She paused for a long moment. "... it's not... I mean..."

Abby straightened and came around to the other side of the car and leaned against its door, nothing between them now. "I got sent pictures, too. Little snaps of myself at the University, and here. Like whoever's doing it is saying 'I know who you are.' Crazy, right?"

Alice winced. "I've gotten rats."

"Pardon? Plural?"

"Twice, yeah. Both left on my windshield while I was in Demeter." She stepped down to be on Abby's level, then went to the back of the car and got spray and a squeegee, as if on autopilot. She brought them to the front of the car and started spraying.

Abby kept her back to her at first, then turned to watch. She watched as Alice sprayed a liberal coating of the agent all across the windshield, then started to strip it – and the blood it had loosed from the glass – with every stroke of the thin squeegee. It made a long, drawn-out squeaking sound that grated on Abby until, on the third stroke, she whipped out her hand and snatched it away from Alice.

Alice looked surprised by the sudden, swift snap, but it loosened back into her resigned state quickly.

"Why didn't you tell me?"

"Why didn't *you* tell *me*?"

"No, not the same. Simon was worried that only I'd been hit, so he convinced me to keep mum in case you found out and freaked out and outted yourself."

"Well, that's bullshit, because I *was* hit, and I didn't freak out, and I know that because nobody knew I had been hit, even the person I'm living with."

"No, for real," Abby said, slicing her flattened hand through the air as though cutting through the bullshit in it. "Why didn't you tell me?"

Alice worked her mouth around her face for a moment, facing that question fully for the first time herself and not liking the taste of the answer in her mouth even before she said it. "I thought... I didn't think it was because they were calling me out on the identity change."

Abby squinted sarcastically.

She paused. "I thought it was someone at my job. I thought someone was saying, 'You don't belong here.' Because sometimes, all this time later... I still feel like I don't. I'm the outsider. I'm the one who doesn't get the references, doesn't laugh at the right time, doesn't use the right phrase in the right way. I'm the one who doesn't know the songs at karaoke. So, I thought... I thought this was someone or all of them saying: you don't belong." She paused. "And I didn't say anything, because I thought they were right."

Abby's face was at war with itself for a moment, trying

to stay upset and failing. Finally she relented and dropped the squeegee, stepping around the El Dorado and embracing Alice in a hug.

Alice's arms stayed outstretched for a moment, as if unsure even in that moment what to do. Her shoulders loosened, and the stiff appendages seemed to melt until they were around Abby's back. They squeezed each other, tightly, for a long moment.

"So, what do we do now?" Alice asked, breaking off the embrace and pushing her hair out of her face.

"What we're best at," Abby said, her voice her own for the first time in what felt like forever.

CHAPTER 19

Abby, Alice, and Meredith stood near the entrance to the University cafeteria, acting like bottlenecks. Every student had to step past them to enter or leave, and after a moment of their occupation of the space the students had seemed to automatically adjust: entering students brushed past them on their right, exiting on their lefts. They weren't obstructing traffic; the hall was huge. Barriers that would have made it seem less so were translucent, as was the far wall. There were times when she ate here that Abby thought, if the light had been quite right and there hadn't been any people in the way, she'd have been able to see for miles. To the curvature of the Earth.

"That's him," Meredith said, cocking her chin towards a young man sitting with a friend at a table in the middle of the room. He was just on the other side of one of the frosted glass walls, facing them. His friend's back was to it. They were laughing.

The young man Meredith had gestured to was gangly and lanky, a person still escaping the awkward end of teenage years when they grew up faster than they grew out. He looked like he was in someone else's clothes and skin, a red plaid shirt hanging off his shoulders and revealing a local band shirt beneath. Half of his hair was dyed bleach blond and the other half jet black right down the middle, though he unconsciously adjusted his part throughout the day so that the part of his hair no longer matched the gap between colours, and the effect was unnerving. His eyebrows were thick and dark brown, and one was pierced with heavy rings to balance the lip on the opposite side that was the same. They looked like they had been there for some time and had altered the shape of his lip as a result, curling it down until it mimicked Sly Stallone.

"You sure?" Abby said, keeping her eye on him. She had been subtle about it at first, but as the moment of action came closer and closer, she found herself openly staring at him.

"Yeah. Yes, absolutely. Michael, I think his name is."

Abby nodded, simultaneously in thanks to Meredith and as a trigger to action for Alice. They both broke off from Meredith at the same time, taking different paths to the same destination like tributaries. Abby broke off to the left and headed around the glass barrier, and Alice to the right. They did this without telling one another it was what they were going to do. They just worked together: two parts of a whole.

Michael looked up from his conversation with his friend and saw Abby coming around the corner towards him, and the easy smile he'd been wearing fell from his lips. He said something quickly to his friend then started to rise and gather his things, turning to walk in the opposite direction of Abby.

He bumped into Alice, knocking chests with her as he rose.

"Maybe sit back down," Alice said, pushing her purple hair back behind her ear. She turned to the friend, a young man with shaggy hair who was staring at her now with wide eyes. "Maybe take a walk."

The friend stiffened but didn't immediately move.

"It's okay," Michael frowned, even as Abby completed her descent onto him.

Abby flapped the manila envelope down onto the table in front of him. "Look familiar?"

Michael stared at it and swallowed, never knowing that the envelope was not, in fact, the same one that he had used to drop the photos off. He didn't have to speak; she could see it in his eyes that he knew.

"Tell me what you know," she said, her tone deep and authoritative in a way that Alice had rarely heard before.

"I don't know anything," Michael said, pushing the envelope away with the tips of his fingers. "I don't even know what was in that, I swear."

Abby and Alice looked at each other. Alice nodded, then sat down next to Michael. "Well, you know what a threat is, right? How about a terroristic threat? Because someone got you to deliver a threat to my friend here, and you know something. Even if you don't think you don't, you do."

Michael looked from Alice to Abby and then back again, the panic growing on his face as he did. "I didn't... I don't..."

"Red head, my height," Abby said, sitting down across

from Alice and bringing him to eye level. Her words were clipped and short. "Ears that come out a little, to a point. Military, maybe." She paused. "Add to that list of traits."

Michael's eyes went wide for a moment, and then his brow furrowed. He turned to Alice again, as if his instinct telling him that if he was to reason with someone, it was going to be her. "The chick?" he asked finally, incredulous.

Abby and Alice looked at each other.

"She wasn't there?" Alice asked, her voice slightly smoother than Abby's.

Michael turned abruptly. "Don't 'good cop, bad cop' me."

"Fine. Are you telling me she wasn't there?" Alice asked again, letting the bite that had always been behind her words out.

He recoiled, regretting calling her on it. "She was there, but that was it. She was just... there. She walked in with him, stood aside when he talked to me, then left again." He paused. "I wouldn't have even thought about her if you hadn't said."

Abby looked at him for a long moment. She didn't tell him to keep going, she just stared at him until he did.

"He was tall. Taller than me. One of those big, broad-shouldered beefcakes. He was wearing plain clothes, but you could tell he was military or something like that. My dad was military." He paused, the mention of his father sticking in his mouth like a frog. He turned away, processed whatever he was feeling, then looked back and resumed without being asked to. "He wore normal stuff that didn't look normal. Like that meme, like he was stepping up and saying, 'Hello Fellow Youths.'"

Abby nodded.

"But like... it wasn't like that at the same time? Like the mask was a mask, too. Like he didn't mind that everyone there knew it was a con. Almost like he was saying, 'go ahead, call me on it' with his tucked in denim shirt and shit." Michael pursed his lips. "He even still had the army boots on, I think."

"What'd he say?" Alice pressed, trying to keep him on track. Abby looked at her.

"He came up to me and he asked me if I wanted to make two thousand dollars. I laughed and I told him yes, but I thought it was a scam. It was right in front of everyone, so it had to be a scam. Only other explanation would be if he was looking to buy my ass or something, and he wasn't going to pull that in front of a hundred freshmen, either. So it must have been a joke, but it wasn't. He hands me the envelope." He touched it, not knowing it was not the same one. "And he told me all I had to do was drop it off. The red head, she'd walked up with him and when he'd come to talk to me, she'd stayed against the wall with her arms crossed. Right behind him." He swallowed. "Almost like a puppeteer, now that I think on it."

"And you took the money?"

"It was *two grand*," Michael stressed. "I've got loans."

"Didn't occur to you to wonder why he wasn't delivering it? Or her?"

"It was two grand."

Alice looked as though she were going to continue pressing him, but Abby raised a hand and stopped her. "What'd he look like?"

Michael shrugged. "Military. Black hair, broad. You know the type. Cookie-cutter military."

Abby nodded, then cocked her head up by way of dismissing him. He swallowed and got up, gathering his things quickly and leaving.

When he was out of earshot, Abby leaned forward on the table between them, frustrated.

"That's not a lot to go on," Alice frowned.

"More than you think."

Abby connected a blue wire to the metal base of the windshield wiper of Alice's car and felt the air charge as she did so, her hair standing on edge. "That should do it," she said, softly, stepping back and slamming the hood.

They had spent the day rigging their home and the grounds surrounding them for security, prepping the way that only people who had seen great strife could. They installed cameras at every entrance and thoroughfare and around the yard, all connected wirelessly to Abby's laptop. They set up door jams behind every door that they could swing out and lock in place if they needed it, barring it against an intruder. They found Theo's old swords and practiced with them in the backyard, until Alice was almost as competent with them as Abby had been when she'd first started out.

They checked Victor's gun and made sure that it was loaded.

Alice pressed the button on her fob to lock the car, then raised the small stick she was holding and dropped it onto the windshield wiper. It surged to life, jolting with electricity. She pressed the fob again and it stopped. Gingerly, she reached out and took the stick away again. She patted the wiper apprehensively, expecting it to be hot but it wasn't.

"They want to leave us any more surprises this way, they'll have a few of their own," Abby smirked, poking her first against the meat of Alice's arm.

They checked all of the hotels and motels that were open for the season in Payson. When none of those panned out, they started checking outside Payson, between Payson and Flagstaff.

The Motel 83 was a long, one floor building that snaked this way and that, forming an S along the grounds behind the main office, which was separate. The connective tissue between the three main long sections of the building were just metal awning, but the affect was still there. All the rooms were on the ground level, and they all had a doorway on either side of the rooms: one that led out to the parking lot, and another that connected to a long shared highway filled with vending machines and ice makers.

Each of the rooms were dark, with no overhead lighting: only bedside lamps, and any light that came in from the bathroom. The paint was grey, the floor a deep, earthy brown. They knew because they'd stayed in them before.

As they walked up to the main building, Abby eyed the room she'd shared with Chad when the team had stayed at the motel. It was unlit and dark, and she could imagine he was there, somewhere, within those shadows.

The main office of the Motel 83 was a deep mauve, all of it. The roll-out carpet that protected the floor from whatever transients tracked in was mauve, the walls were mauve save for a gold patterned trim that went all the way around it at waist-height, and the ceiling was mauve. Stepping into it was like stepping from one reality into another. It reminded Abby of the Red Room from Twin Peaks, and brought with that same anxious feeling of sur-reality.

There was a large man with jelly bracelets hanging loosely from each of his wrists behind the counter. He was smoking a menthol cigarette from a theatre-length black holder. It expelled more smoke than he inhaled, sending it wafting toward the ceiling in swirling ovals. His name plate introduced him as 'Shirley – Manager.'

Shirley smiled, showing off huge, crooked chicklet teeth that still somehow managed to have the appearance of a gap between each one, the sort of corn kernel effect that many, many years of smoking can bring. The smile was tiny but clearly all he had, the muscles of his mouth not strong enough to push his large, shaking cheeks up any further. "How are you two?" he said, in a way that implied insinuation. Smoke fell from his mouth in the per-fect circles.

"We're looking for some people that might be staying here. Or might have stayed here," Abby said, in a tone that had been honed through saying it multiple times, both in person and on the phone.

Shirley looked at her, the directness of it surprising him. There were three wedding bands hanging from a chain around his neck. The chain disappeared into the folds of loose skin. They were dull for the most part, made grey with sweat and the grime of dead flesh. All were men's bands, and all were of different sizes. His eyes were sunken and bloodshot and went from shocked to sinister in a far too quick a transition. "No one like that here."

"There'd be at at least two of them," Alice piped up, stepping out from around Abby. "One's a woman, taller than my friend here. Red hair. Very red, from what we're told. Ears slightly pointed – not a lot, just like, a little."

"No one like that here," Shirley repeated, in the exact same tone and with the exact same head motions as the first time.

Abby nodded, and they both turned and stepped back out towards the door.

"We don't want no G-Men around here," he called after them.

They stopped in their tracks, Alice's hand on the door to go back into the real world. They turned slowly back around to face Shirley.

"G-Men are bad for business. Tell them to fuck off."

"But they were here? They tried to get a place?" Abby stressed.

"She came. They were trying to get here. There wasn't two of them though, there was four. Four rooms they wanted, three together and one off by its lonesome."

Abby paused, working her mouth around a tense jaw. She looked at Alice, nodded, then turned back to Shirley and thanked him.

Her jaw did not loosen the entire drive back to Payson.

CHAPTER 20

Victor stood in the door to Lauryn's bedroom, following the tilt of its long, low ceiling with his eye.

There was a feeling in the house he had never quite experienced before: fear on an almost molecular level. It got on him and in him, clinging to the hair on his arms and collecting there until it made a home, like a tumor. It was present even when the parents weren't there, circling in the air and making chests tight and heads shrink.

He breathed hard, air coming in short, hyperventilating hisses. Despite his attempts to calm himself, those bad feelings kept coming. He pictured them, thick like gelatin in the air. Red like blood spilled in zero gravity, left to shimmer about and glom on to anyone it came across. He could picture it sucked into his nostrils upon one of his deep breaths, slipping in and around his olfactory senses without taste or smell. But he could feel the effects of it: that squeeze in the chest, that inability to breathe.

This house, this town, this family. They were suffocating.

He tried to image what it would be like to have lived

here, and at first couldn't. Slowly, a memory of a place perhaps equally as confining came to him. The anxiety and fear in the air had a mirror in him, though it was a twisted and distorted funhouse reflection.

There was a small thin desk lined with models on the right side of the door. Victor entered the room pressed against it, squeezing in with the cleft of his rear pressed against the board. He had to duck slightly to enter, the low ceiling consistent and oppressive, combining with the cramped horizontal space to make him feel even worse. Claustrophobia atop anxiety.

He stood amongst the models of monuments she had never been to and stared across them, his gaze finding each and every one, feeling the anxiety in the room build to a crescendo as he did.

Victor stepped down the Houle stairs breathing out a long, deep breath. The lower he got the less tight his chest felt; by the time he'd left he felt like the ragged red fear filling the room had also filled his lungs, leaving the barest sliver of space at the top with which to draw air into. He expelled it more and more the further he descended the stairs, and by the time he reached the bottom he almost felt like he could receive a full breath.

Pedro stared at him from the bottom of the stairs, but waited until they were at eyelevel to speak. "Have you had any luck?"

The anguish on Victor's face was plain. "Luck isn't in my skill set." He turned away from Pedro and looked to curse at himself.

"Have you found anything out?"

"I don't think she would have left," Victor said, low and under his breath. He turned around the corner from the stairs and peered into the kitchen, but did not enter and did not articulate why. "But I cannot for the life of me figure out why she would have been taken."

Pedro pursed his lips, nodding.

"Was she *really* going to go to Brown? I know she was accepted... but was she *going*?"

Pedro opened his mouth, then stopped and closed it, a sullen look passing over him.

Victor tilted his head, watching him. "The next time something like that comes up, you put your own ego aside and you be straight with me. Swallow it however you need to. I'll get you water if I must."

He nodded.

Victor ran his fingers along each other for a long moment, staring into the air. He turned back toward the top floor of the house. The air of it was almost thick with humidity and tension. "I think you and your wife might need a night away from this," he said, as though it were fact.

CHAPTER 21

Abby stepped into the main office of the History department and stopped short in the null space between Meredith's desk and her own. Meredith was behind her desk but not working or fidgeting, her hands clasped before her and waiting. The department head was across from her, leaning against the doorframe to her office, the air between them thick with tension.

"A delivery boy brought it," Meredith said, her voice hollow and almost defeated. "I questioned him. He didn't know anything, about anything."

Abby nodded.

"I didn't open it."

On her desk in front of her was a long, white box. It was less than a foot high and in depth but a full three feet long. It was pristine and smooth, the gloss coating over it reflecting fingerprints and grit but finding neither. It looked as though it barely even touched the desk, as if refused contact with anything physically hers. A break in the reality of the school.

She stepped over to her desk but did not go around

to sit in it. Her fingers twitched above the box for a moment as the box loomed, discreet and unassuming and yet sinister at the same time. It stared back at her blank faced, revealing nothing. She swallowed, then pulled back the cover of the box to the screech of the tight fit.

Meredith stood up onto her toes, leaning over without getting up from her desk to see what was inside.

It was a bouquet of roses, easily twenty-five of them. They nestled into wrapping paper the same shade of white as the box, and looked like a corpse in a coffin despite their vibrant, bright red. Their petals still had drops of dew on them they were so fresh, the stems long and terminating in clear plastic that trapped water.

There was an envelope affixed to the front of them, facing her.

"Oh. That's... fine. Right?" Meredith asked, her tone hopeful but hesitant.

Abby pursed her lips. She picked up the envelope and placed it gingerly to one side, then took the roses out of their paper cradle.

"Careful. The thorns," Jennifer, the department head, said.

Abby turned and looked at her, then nodded.

Out of the box it was plain: there were twenty-four roses, each lush and red and supple... except two. Two in the very centre were dead and blackened, their petals flaking off like dried skin with every motion of the bouquet. Their flakes shimmered out into the rest of the bunch and onto the floor at her feet like confetti.

"Death twins," Abby frowned under her breath.

"What does that mean?" Meredith asked.

"Nothing. Just a nickname someone gave me and my sister." She put the flowers back down and picked up the envelope again, opening it. There was no card inside, just one piece of laminated paper that she recognized right away: it was her photo ID from when she'd worked at Shane International. Her younger, washed-out, faded face stared back at her through the gap of time. Somehow she looked older there than she felt she did now, a consequence of the way she'd lived then.

On the ID, someone had underlined her real name, Fisher, with red sharpie. She turned it over. The words 'I Know' were scrawled onto the back of it in the same shade, a red so bright that it put even the freshest of the roses to shame.

"What was in it?" Jennifer asked.

"It's private."

Jennifer stepped forward, examining the bouquet even as Abby slid the ID back into the envelope and the envelope into her pocket. "This is a threat," she said, in a tone that implied she'd never experienced anything of the like before.

Abby nodded.

"This is a sly, *terroristic* threat."

"I wouldn't go quite that far," Abby said in a neutral tone, not meaning what she was saying.

"I would," Meredith offered.

Abby was about to turn and respond, when the box started to ring, startling all three of them. Jennifer jumped back a full foot. "Fuck," Abby cursed, pushing her hands into the paper that lined the box and returning with an old-fashioned flip phone. She looked at the number on the screen, was unsurprised when it was blocked, then opened it and brought it to her ear anyway. "Hello?"

There was silence on the other end of the line for a long, tense moment.

Abby resisted the urge to say 'hello' again, her lips pursing and curling. There was a sound on the line like cracking paper that was almost a death rattle, that sound of a microphone stuttering, but little else. She couldn't tell if it was interference or foley or vocalization, but it was unnerving. She kept her pulse steady, not letting it waver her.

"You're not normal," the voice on the other side of the line said, finally. It was distorted by mechanics and bile, but still unmistakably feminine. "You're not normal and you shouldn't go around like you are."

Abby set her jaw. "You're the redhead, I take it?"

The crackle on the other end of the line increased, as Abby wasn't sure if it was the static of switching the phone from ear to ear or a gross, perverse laugh. In either case, it sent ripples of gooseflesh down her spine.

"You're a lab rat," the voice came again, in the same tone as it had the first time. The words were rehearsed, and Abby's responses were not changing them, merely the time it took the speaker to compose herself between lines. "There's a reason they don't let lab rats leave the lab. Why they don't send them back out into the world... they'll fuck up the normal rats. You can't just be out there in the world. Can't have it."

"You're from Shane, I take it?"

"Fuck you," the speaker snapped, and it was the first time her tone had deviated from the range it had allowed itself into. She took a moment to compose herself, then continued. "You're going to be called again, soon. Today. When you're called, answer."

"I'm a busy person."

The call disconnected.

"Fuck," she cursed, checking the screen to see that the line was dead and confirming that it was.

"What'd they say?" Jennifer asked, stepping back forward for the first time since she'd jumped back at the ring. After a moment of tight-jawed silence, she pressed again. "Abby?"

"I need the rest of the day."

∞

Abby stood in the closet, looking around anxiously even though there was nothing there to see. She held her phone against her ear and listened to the agonizing sound of its ringing. Her foot tapped as if she needed to urinate, but didn't. Or at least she thought she didn't.

On the ninth ring, the call connected.

"I don't have much," Simon said without greeting, his first words almost cut off by the call connecting. "There's been a little buzz in some of my circles, but not enough for me to update you on."

"There's a team of them. Four or five jarheads and one woman. And it seems like she's the one in charge," Abby spat, afraid Simon might hang up.

There was a pregnant pause on the other end of the line where all she could hear was his breathing. Then: "Go on."

"The woman's tall but not too tall, about my height.

Red hair. Really, really red, from what I'm told. So red that some people think it came out of a bottle, but others not so much. The people she runs with, they're either military or ex-military and they don't mind showing it. They've been putting the barest effort into hiding it, they want you to know. Almost like a fuck you, daring you to call them on it. And the girl, she called. She sent me a cell, told me to expect another call."

"What?"

"I'm sending you a picture of the sim and serial data now, but I don't think we'll get anything from it."

"Me either, but can't hurt to check."

"But when she called, she'd sent my Shane ID, and I asked her if she was with Shane... and she cracked, Simon. She was neutral, calm the whole time... but when I asked if she was with Shane, she snapped at me like I'd called her a slur or something."

Simon was quiet on the other end of the line for a long moment, save for the sound of his tongue against his dry lips.

"Simon?"

"...Anyone say anything about her ears?"

Abby straightened, standing suddenly upright as though a shock had gone through her. "Yeah, she's... yeah. People that saw her said they're pointed at the tips. Not a lot, mind. Not like something out of high fantasy or anything... but a little." She swallowed.

The other end of the line was silent. Then there was a sigh, followed by more contemplative silence.

"... do you know her?"

"By reputation."

Those two words sent new gooseflesh shimmering over the surface of Abby's arms. They were said with a weight and gravitas that Abby had never heard from Simon, even when he was trying to imbue his words with those qualities. She waited for him to continue.

"She works for a Circe squad."

"Circe?"

"A rival to Shane and other companies. What Shane does through drug trials they do through espionage, and they're good at it. And none of them are better than her. With what I do, I've come across her work a few times." He paused. "Once I was sent in to north China to try and dig deep into a facility there. It was going to be deep cover, months of it. When I got there she had gotten there first, and the whole thing was just ashes. She raised it to the ground."

The colour left Abby's cheeks.

"She works with them but not for them. She's not in charge of that squad but they call on her when they need her, and when they need her, they listen to her or she won't come again. That's the type of... the type of presence she commands."

"What's her name?"

"I rather not—"

"*Simon*. What is her name?"

He paused. "Aisli. I don't know the last name. It's spelled weird though, when I've seen it. A-I-S-L-I."

Abby nodded, making a mental note of it. "What does she want with us?"

"I have no earthy idea, but I know you have to *get Victor*. This is bad, and it isn't going to get better."

Abby agreed, then hung up the phone and pressed it tight to her lips. She scrunched down into a ball in the janitor's closet of the History department and composed herself before leaving. It took several minutes.

Abby sat on the couch in the living room, leaning forward until her rear barely touched the edge of the cushion. Her arms perched against her knees as though they were divers, ready to plunge off the caps at a moment's notice into the waters below.

Alice looked at her from the archway into the main hall. She was leaned against it with one foot kicked up, several strands of her purple hair in her mouth being chewed nervously.

Abby watched the analog clock on the wall as it ticked through each second in its circumference, pecking away at time itself. It was 8:00 in the evening.

The black Motorola stared at them from the table in front of Abby, its screen unlit and mocking them.

"She could just be fucking with us." Alice said. There was a grim reality in her voice. "They've been pushing fear and anxiety, and if this isn't—"

The phone rang, cutting Alice off, and Abby had snatched it up and flipped it open before the first ring was even complete. "Hello?"

"There's a quarry on the edge of town. Meet me there this time, tomorrow."

"So you and your little hit squad can take me out? Or leave Alice alone so that you can—"

"It'll just be me," Aisli said, calmly cutting her off.

"And from what I hear, the girl's hard to kill. But bring her along, if you need to feel safe." She said the last words with bite to them, knowing that there was no amount of precaution that would facilitate that feeling.

"Why are you doing this?"

There was silence on the other end of the line for a long moment, then the call disconnected.

"What'd she say?" Alice said, stepping forward into the room.

Abby turned and looked at her, her nostrils flared angrily. "Get me Victor's gun."

CHAPTER 22

Victor and Tash sat across from each other, each of them on a different garish green-and-red patterned couch, the coffee table between them and both their teas on it, billowing steam up into the evening air. They hadn't known what sort of tea the Houle's would have had on hand and didn't want to impose on them so they'd bought their own before arriving – hers was a herbal blend meant to build antioxidants made of apple and cinnamon, his was toffee flavoured like a dessert, made from chunks of caramel, cocoa beans, and cornflower blossoms.

Despite how inviting and sugary Victor's had the promise of tasting, it remained on the table even as Tash picked up hers anew and took a third sip, lowering it past the half-filled mark. "How are you feeling?" she asked, peering over the top of the cheap mug at him.

She could taste the plastic coating on it, and swore to herself that if this night stay became more than a night's stay, she would venture to a local thrift store to find some china to bring in as well.

Victor had gotten Lauryn Houle's parents a night at

the Duch Vance Motel, in the room opposite the one they still rented but did not currently occupy, and had asked if they could stay the night to fully investigate. Pedro had told him yes and had given Victor the key to his liquor cabinet. It sat on the table between them now like a weapon of last resort, a gun placed in the centre of the room between two combatants with both glaring at each other, trying to see who would move first.

"It's tense in here," Victor said, bringing his massive hand to his solar plexus and shifting his breast muscles around it, as though he could adjust the tight skin like a shirt. He winced and looked around the room, at the pictures of Lauryn on the walls behind him. He sat where Pedro had sat the first time they'd met, stretching and craning his neck to see all around but never once considering the option of rising.

"You knew it was tense here. You commented on it after our first night."

"Yeah, but... I think I'd assumed that was the parents, you know? That I was feeling something they were putting out there. Years of the stress of having a missing child poisoning them against each other but making them need each other more and more at the same time...that kind of sick dance that people play, ripping each other's lives apart."

"But you're saying it's not that, now."

"No... Yes. I don't know." His frown deepened and he reached for his tea finally. It was colder than he would have preferred it and blamed the Houle's kettle, not the time he'd taken to drink it. "I can't do the math on this one. Tense parents equals tension in the house, I get that part of the equation. But remove the parents and still get the same tense house?" He sipped again. "You shouldn't be able to remove something from an equation and have its sum have the same value."

"You can if the element wasn't worth anything to begin with."

Victor laid down his cup and gave her a droll, even look from across the table. "I'm using the math as a metaphor, don't take it literally."

"So am I," she assured.

He paused, leaned forward with a sigh, then let his head crane around the room again. Pictures of Lauryn went all the way to the ceiling, as if Michelle had tried to fill as much of the wall with her as possible to make up for her absence in the home.

"What did Jona want here?" he asked to himself, staring at a high up photo of Lauryn and Kate on a Ferris wheel.

Tash put down her cup. "Let's talk it out."

Victor sighed. He brought his hands up into his hair and ran his fingers through it, scratching and scraping at his scalp. "He came after she was missing." He paused. "You're examined his travel history before, was he ever here before? Before she went missing?"

"Not that I can see."

He nodded, finding a spot on the floor and fixating on it unconsciously as the gears on his mind worked.

She sipped her tea and watched him. She watched him as though she could see giant cogs behind him moving one by one, him turning a small crank which attached to a small cog that was attached to progressively larger ones until eventually the largest moved and shifted, shaking the foundations of the home with its weight. She loved watching him think, it was one of her rare joys, and yet she did it now with a mix of joy and apprehension.

"It could have been Gavin," Victor said, his voice dried by the name. "The timing matches. Gavin could have seduced her away and Jona could have come to clean up the mess, sorted the parents away so that they looked left and not right."

"Does she seem like the type who'd get taken in by someone like Jona?"

"Kelly was taken in by Gavin," he countered. "What're you saying about her?"

"Kelly was a child who has grown a lot. And even she, when she saw how bad it was, had the mental fortitude to get out of her own free will. Lauryn was an adult, or very nearly, and had been accepted to Brown."

He nodded his acceptance of her point.

"Also, you'd already ruled out a cult just based on her personality profile, so don't try and back over yourself."

He raised his hands. "I'm just thinking outside the box." He laid his head in his hands, then turned it towards the stairs that led up to her bedroom. His hands went to his chest and pressed against it, as if just looking up towards it made it tighter. "She could have done anything, but everyone thought she was doing their thing. Everyone impressed their opinion on what she should be onto her." He stood, making his way to the photo of Lauryn, Kate, and Nevaeh. He plucked it off of its nail carefully, bringing it back and holding it in front of his chest for Tash to see. "It looks like she's having fun, but she's reserved. Anxious. You feel like she's having fun because the other two are having fun, but look." He covered Kate and Nevaeh with his massive fingers. Suddenly Lauryn looked alone, and anxious, the finger of one hand held by the grasp of the other, possibly even biting the inside of her cheek.

Tash nodded.

"Come or go? Work or school? Gay or straight?" She couldn't make those kind of choices.

"Thankfully some of those choices aren't that binary. From personal experience." She raised an eyebrow at him.

"Yes, fine. But let's not make it about us. Reality aside, this is how she felt. It's how a lot of young people feel. Those choices loom and are hard."

"No, let's make it about us. I disagree." She leaned in, taking the picture as though she were taking a shield and laying it face up on the table between them. "Because she couldn't make a choice, and for some of those things that's an option. You *can* not make the choice between gay and straight, and deny the opinions of others putting those labels on you... but you can't do that with the others, can you?"

"You could do neither work nor school. Take a gap year, put off the choice."

"Hence the travel books," she chimed, raising a finger into the air. "But don't treat that like it's avoiding a choice. That's just *adding a third option* to the choice, innit?" Her twang came out for just a moment then, and he heard the influence Atlanta had been having on her speech. "That's the thing with feeling like you can't make a choice: every option your brain comes up with to escape the problem just manifests as *another choice*."

"She could have just..." he trailed off, looking back up the stairs towards her bedroom again. He had a spark in his eyes for a second, as if he had something and then lost it.

"She could have just stayed?"

He nodded.

"Said bugger to all of it and just stayed where she was? No school, no work, no travel?"

"But that's still a choice."

She nodded. "And it's a bad choice. You can plant your feet in the ground like a tree and refuse to let anything change, but often that just means letting everything around you change. That means doing nothing as people leave your life." She tapped on the image of Nevaeh in her graduation gown. "Because there's only one state you can be in where nothing truly changes."

He started to nod slowly, his face slackening, then he blinked hard. He squinted, then his head snapped back to lock eyes with her. "What are you talking about?"

Tash took a sip of her tea. "The girl, obviously. What else would I be talking about? We're trying to figure out what happened to the girl."

"It sounded for a second like you were trying to make this about me. Your voice did that thing it does when you're teaching one of your brats."

Her face lost all hint of amusement at that term. She put her cup back down and glowered at him. "If you see yourself in this situation, Victor, then perhaps it would be better for you to examine that feeling on your own time. Engage in some self reflection on your actions of late."

He puffed out air through his nostrils, dismissively. "I'm not one of your students."

"You were my *first* student," she corrected, finally breaking. "And yet sometimes I think you'll be the last to graduate. If you ever do. And you can question my methods all you like... but look at the state of my team, and look at the state of yours, and I think you'll find the results speak for themselves."

Colour rose to his cheeks, then flushed from it again, and he stood and turned his back to her. For reasons he couldn't understand, the dead robin he'd found in his gutters returned to him, and he found himself wondering if it had died waiting for its chicks to return to the nest. The tension in his chest tightened.

"The authors," he said, finally. "She wasn't more well-read than her parents – well, she *was* – but wasn't why she read so many different authors, was it? She couldn't make the choice. She'd bounce from one writer to another, one book to another, and not be able to settle into one, consistent narrative. About characters, about herself..."

"About *yourself*," she pressed, making no effort to hide her facade now.

He turned to glare at her, then back towards her room. "She couldn't have left, even if she'd wanted to. That would have been a choice. And she couldn't have stayed, even if she'd wanted to... that would have been a choice. And nobody could have seduced her away from that choice – not Gavin nor Jona nor that grease monkey back at the shop – that would have been a choice. And she couldn't make choices. So why was he here, then?"

"Why indeed?"

"There's no answers left," he sighed.

She swallowed, clearing her throat. "When you eliminate the impossible, whatever remains, no matter how unlikely, *must* be the truth."

He turned to look at her again, then back and made

his way towards the stairs. This time she got up and followed him, catching up to him at the top of the stairs. He stood in Lauryn's doorway, staring past its frame into her empty room as though it were a photograph.

"What're you waiting for?" she asked, touching his shoulder.

"I feel tight. Like my heart's racing."

"You're fine."

There was dust everywhere in the room. He could see even from here where he'd stepped before and what he'd touched before from the absence of the dust: the impressions of his large, sausage fingers on the 3D models and puzzles around the room. There was a small thin desk lined with the models to the right side of the door, and when Victor stepped forward, he placed his rear against it and sucked in his gut to shuffle in.

Tash smirked, shaking her head at him balefully. "You can't even see it."

He turned back to her. "See what?"

She stepped forward towards him, sliding to one side and brushing up against the desk as she entered, just as he had. There was less of her than there was of him, so she didn't have to tuck in at all to get through.

He watched her, squinting, only seeing an action he'd performed a half dozen times now that he was watching someone else do it. He stepped back out into the hallway, this time sliding out against the bed opposite the desk. He turned back, only aware of what he'd done after he'd done it. He locked eyes with Tash across the frame of the door, then cast his eyes down to the gap in the dust between them. "No."

CHAPTER 23

Victor stood between the entrance to Lauryn's Houle's bedroom and her parents, who stood at the top of the stairs staring at him. Pedro already seemed visibly frustrated by having been led there, and the anxiety of the house was stronger here, getting to them all.

"Your daughter didn't want to go to Brown, did she?" Victor said, flatly and evenly.

Michelle turned to him sharply, as though his words were a knife in her gut. Her tear ducts filled and began to overflow, but when Pedro tried to comfort her, she pulled away. After a moment she closed her eyes and nodded in response.

Victor nodded in time with her. "I mean she may have, but no more than she'd wanted to do anything else. Travel. Work. Anything. Nothing."

She nodded.

"Why are you saying this?" Pedro asked, angered by the pain the questions were causing his wife and his inability to do something about it.

Victor pursed his lips until they were a thin line dividing his facial hair. He reached into his pocket. "We'll get there. I promise. But first, real quick, this man was here, right?" He produced a wallet-sized headshot of Jona that looked as though it had been clipped from a newspaper and then printed on photo paper.

Pedro nodded. "Yes. Yes, he came to try and help find Lauryn."

"And he said he didn't, right?"

Pedro squinted at the wording of that, but nodded. "Yes. Correct."

"But he didn't step in this room, did he?" he asked, pointing a finger in towards Lauryn's room as through it were a revolver he'd shot from the hip.

"No. He said he couldn't. Couldn't bear it."

Victor put the photo back where he'd gotten it, retrieving a second in the same fluid motion. He held up a picture of Tash that looked like a driver's license image. "What about her?"

Pedro nodded again. "Natasha. Yes. She was here with Jona."

Victor's gaze went blank for a moment, his jaw setting. He nodded curtly, then put her picture away, too.

"Why?"

"No reason. It'd just have been harder to have asked once this was over." He motioned for Pedro and Michelle to enter the room. They stepped forward, each of them turning to one side and brushing past the desk before straightening back up again once inside. "Damn."

"What?" Michelle asked, looking around the room.

He sighed. "There are people with... abilities. Stuff that normal people can't do. Sometimes it's subtle. I know a guy: he has incredible luck. Like, impossibly good luck. Sometimes it's less subtle. Shooting sparks, things like that."

Pedro scoffed, and looked as though he might turn to leave.

Victor raised his hands in defense. "It's not important. It'll just make the answer easier to swallow. Just keep it in your mind, whether you believe me or not." He paused, waiting for a rebuke. There was none. "Your daughter was brilliant. She had all the options and opportunities available to her... but she couldn't choose, could she? As in, was almost incapable of making a firm choice. Of picking a path."

Michelle looked as though she might well up again but didn't and nodded. She had the look of someone who was being confronted with a truth she'd hid from herself for a long time.

"She didn't know if she wanted to go to Brown or to travel. Or to stay here and work. Or do none of it. If she did go to Brown, what would she take? Chemistry? Mechanical Engineering? Physics? Biology? Something else entirely?" He paused. "If she got in, would she commute or stay at home? I know *you* had a preference, but please ask yourself... did *she* ever present one?"

Pedro looked as though he were going to open his mouth to answer, then didn't. Couldn't.

"I didn't think so. Which was fine when she was still in high school... but as graduation approached, she'd have to make a choice."

"She didn't have to—"

"Ah," Victor held up a finger. "But making a choice,

in this situation, is making a choice, isn't it? Standing still and letting the world move on without her, that's a choice, too. If she didn't choose, time would have made the choice for her. So I think... I think that's what she did. Though I think she didn't try to."

Pedro squinted, stepping away from Michelle and marching forward as though he wanted to get up in his face, but stopped a good two feet away from him, divided by the doorframe. "What're you're saying is absurd."

"Why aren't you up in my face?" Victor asked.

Pedro stopped, unsure of what he meant. "What do you mean?"

"I mean, why'd you stop there instead of coming forward?"

"I stopped where I wanted to stop."

Victor smiled without humour and nodded. "It's the same with the guy I know with the luck powers... things just go his way. People just go his way. And if you ask them why they did something a certain way, they'll just shrug and say it was what they'd wanted to do anyway. And there's no way around that logic."

"This is a waste of our time," Pedro hissed, then turned back to Michelle. "This is a waste of our time!"

"She couldn't make the choice of what to do, but she couldn't make the choice to stay either. She couldn't do anything, and she was way too smart to have someone come in and make the choice for her. She'd never be taken. So if she couldn't leave and she wouldn't be taken... when you eliminate the impossible, whatever is left must be true." He stepped forward the last inch he could towards Pedro before coming up short, the full foot and a half between their noses.

"She's still here?" Michelle gasped, looking around as though she expected her daughter to suddenly appear.

Victor nodded. "She couldn't make the choice, her anxiety wouldn't let her. So when she reached the point that time would have made the choice for her... her ability activated, and made it so that she didn't have to."

Pedro stepped back away from the door, looking around like his wife. He hadn't believed at first, but more and more he looked anyway. "Where is she?"

Victor squat down. "Dust tells us a lot of things. Her room is very dusty."

"I just don't—" Michelle started, as though defensive.

"I'm not judging. It happens with every parent who loses a child... believe me. But this..." he motioned in a circle in front of him. "This doesn't happen."

They both stepped forward to see what he was motioning toward. On the carpet in front of Victor was a perfect circle where there was no dust. It went from the tips of Victor's shoes to the prints of where Pedro had stood, moments before, unable to have come any closer.

"What is this?" he gasped.

Victor stood and stepped back a pace, gesturing Pedro forward with all his fingers. "Come at me."

Pedro frowned, marched forward, then stepped to the side and slid by the desk before righting himself and pushing forward again. He stopped after he'd done it, wide eyed, and turned back to look at the gap in the dust he'd avoided as though he'd expected something to be there. Instead, his gaze went straight through it and to the shocked expression on his wife's face. He stepped back through it toward her, pivoted to wedge around the gap in the dust, then spun around again once he was in the room.

"It's why Jona couldn't go in," Victor drawled. "He's too big." He swallowed. "She's just there. Frozen. Out of time. She was making her choice, coming down the stairs to tell you what it was – whatever it was, on whatever subject – and the anxiety was too much and she froze herself in a bubble. Froze herself in time, where she'd never have to change. Froze herself out of time, because time... was the real enemy. And we just... can't perceive it. It's a break in reality, so we walk past it and we don't even consider that we're doing it."

"So she's okay?" Michelle said, her voice breaking through the tears that streamed down her face, smiling wide and bright.

Victor frowned, staring at her pityingly until her smile faded. "You can't... run from change," he said, finally. He said it as though the words were difficult to get out. "You can lock a butterfly in a jar and seal it to keep it beautiful, but..."

"It'll run out of air," Pedro finished, his voice a gasping whisper.

Victor nodded. "It will run out of air. Time marches on. Change is inevitable. If you can't adapt... you suffocate."

Michelle broke again, falling to the floor of her daughter's room.

"Are you sure?" Pedro said, pleading with his tone.

"That anxiety she was feeling, it's been trapped too. It's been bleeding out ever since, filling the house with it.

There's a part of you – evolutionarily – that understands human emotion. That part is beyond reason and it's your reason centres that she's hiding herself from. That instinctual part of you, it sees her. It senses that anxiety and it's rubbed off on you. It's why things have been so tense."

"But how are you sure? That she's gone?"

Victor pursed his lips. "Dust tells us a lot," he repeated, motioning to the dust in the room again. "A good chunk of dust is dried skin."

Pedro broke, collapsing down next to his wife.

Victor stepped forward. "I'm sorry. I needed you to be ready for when it happened." He stood at the edge of the dustless circle.

They stared at him for a long moment, realization coming to them at different times, then nodded.

When he saw it on both of them, he placed both hands in front on himself palm up, as though he were holding a pizza box. Keeping them apart, he tilted them to the side and then pressed them forward into the gap between the circle and the door frame.

With great effort that showed on his face, he scooped his arms through the air above the circle, pushed them towards the other side of the frame.

His left hand caught under Lauryn's legs and his right cradled her neck, and suddenly she appeared in his arms. He stepped forward as he scooped, clutching her tight to his chest and bringing her forward onto her bed.

Pedro and Michelle broke down in tears, unable to come forward to her for a full minute.

She was blue, her lips swollen, and her eyes bulged, as though she'd been exposed to the vacuum of space. Her cheeks were distended and wore burst blood vessels so copious they looked like red spiderwebs. Her hair was brittle and dry and flaked off even under the gentle motion of Victor's touch.

There was a piece of paper clutched in her hand and Victor pried it loose. She held it so firmly that it ripped when he withdrew it. He flattened it and looked over it.

"What does it say?" Michelle asked, stepping forward and touching her daughter's hand for the first time in years and breaking again.

"Nothing," Victor said, folding the page and putting it in his pocket with the photos he'd shown them. "It doesn't say anything."

He stayed with them until they called the police to report the body, coaching them on what to say as best he could.

CHAPTER 24

The Quarry was a deep scar in the skin of Payson a quarter mile across and another quarter mile deep, its rims so high at its bottom that it blotted out any light from the sun and moon except at their highest points of travel. Its edges were smooth stairs that went down at a consistent, sloping angle. Even in the dim light of the night Alice could see that they were rich with veins of white marble.

The both of them walked along the centre of the Quarry's bottom, bisecting its lower edge. The ground beneath them was damp and had the consistency of a sponge, squishing beneath their sneakers and threatening to take them with the slightest misstep. This continued until they reached its centre: a large, man-made pond that had come when the diggers met the water basin.

Abby and Alice both stopped and stared into it. It was so blue it seemed to glow, the white of the marble within it making it shimmer in the moonlight. There was dust and silt floating in it, yet between those specks the water was clear all the way down. It seemed to go down forever, far further than a pond of its circumference would in nature. It was a hole in the world.

Abby looked all around at the vast empty of the Quarry, surrounding them like a giant's staircase. There should have been guards, she knew enough to know that. Even if only for insurance reasons, there should have been at least one guard trotting around, asking them what they were doing there and threatening them with a bright flashlight.

"Hello?" Alice called loudly, hearing the echo come back through the multiple layers of stone. She waited for an answer, but ended up just waiting for the sound waves of her holler to peter out. It took seven rounds, by her count, before it became inaudible.

"There's no one here," Abby frowned, scanning the edges of the cave system at the Quarry's bottom. "They're wasting our time. Getting us to dance like monkeys."

"Do you think they're at the house, or...?"

"*Maybe*," Abby stressed. "Let's get back and we'll—" Across the gully, an excavator started up, its headlights blaring into them and the roar of its diesel engine blaring into the echo chamber around them, the sound reverberating back again and again until it became deafening.

The both of them raised their eyebrows, blinded by the light from the machine but looking towards it anyway. Abby motioned right and Alice started around the water that way, Abby going left. They kept their eyes on one another, creeping along the water's edge with care until they were on the other side of the light and converged on the excavator.

There was no one there.

Alice turned her attention to the Quarry wall behind

it as her eyes adjusted to the dark, trying to find any hint of movement, while Abby climbed the machine's rickety steps and shut it off. There were two envelopes on the excavator's cushioned seat, each one marked with their names. The ink on each letter A was so fresh that it bled still, secreting out and taking more and more of the manila fibers.

Abby collected them both and stepped down out of the machine just as Alice stepped back up alongside her.

"There's no sign," Alice said, breathless. She scrunched her face at the envelope with her name on it that Abby was holding out to her, then opened it and pulled out its contents.

Abby read hers and then read it again. Then she read it a third time, more carefully. "They want me to join Circe," she said finally, her voice hushed. "That's what this has been about. Why they didn't just come at us... they want us in." She looked up from the paper to Alice.

Alice's cheeks were as white as the sheet in front of her.

"What does yours say?" Abby asked, her tone changing to a more hushed one.

"The same," Alice nodded, but slid the page back into the envelope without showing it. "Come on, let's get out of here."

CHAPTER 25

Abby sat behind her desk and pried open more mail from alumni and peers for Jennifer. She had to look at each piece between three and five times to get its meaning and understand the salient points that needed to be passed on. It was hard to focus. Her brain kept moving in and away from the task at hand, some strand of data irrelevant to her day job taking hold and dragging her back to unreality.

Meredith watched her glumly, as distracted by Abby's preoccupation and tension as Abby was by the events of late. They hadn't asked what was going on, but the question was still hanging in the air between them nonetheless, and she could hear their whispers when they spoke alone in Jennifer's office. She couldn't hear what was said, only the fact of the whispering, but even that was enough to set her hackles on edge. There had been no whispering in this office before this week – only varying degrees of animation and excitement.

Whispers were the way of Abby's old life – of calls to unlisted numbers and secret schools and knowledge that only a few knew – and it had infested her new life like a cancer.

She highlighted three lines on the page she was working on, then set it aside for Jennifer to read before reaching into the inbox for another letter. She stopped in mid-motion as she did, only then noticing the woman that was standing in the centre of the office, smiling at her expectantly.

She was wearing a uniform, of the sort you'd wear at a school where they made you dress according to gender. Green and black plaid shirt that went down just past the knees. White stockings that rose to meet them. Button-up shirt with a school crest hidden by a letter sweater that was draped around her shoulders, and a smile. They didn't tell you that a smile was a part of the uniform, but it was. It was the one part of the uniform they'd remind you of constantly if you were missing it: smile. Smile more.

She had two binders in front of her, held by both hands. Despite the perfection of it, she looked wrong: less like a uniformed schoolgirl and more like the uniformed school girls seen in adult films – someone who got the details right but missed the point, until the whole was not *quite* right and gained an air of the uncanny. The hair was a part of it: the bottle look contrasting harshly with the rest of the school-girl attire. It was so red that it couldn't be natural.

She smiled down at Abby with that full row of perfectly white teeth, head tilted slightly in expectation.

Abby stared at her for a long moment, her hand still frozen mid-reach for the inbox. "Can I help you with something?"

"I'm your two o'clock," she said, punctuating hard syllables with a bob of her head. "I'm here to interview about the History department, see if it's right for me."

"I don't have a—" Abby started, moving items away from her desk calendar as she spoke. When she cleared back the present date a chicken-scratch notation made a liar out of her, circled twice in red. She paused, nodded to compose herself, then extended a hand out. "Glad you could make it...?"

"Gail."

"Gail," Abby finished, her cheeks beaming in that way only customer service people did – a pantomime of a smile. She motioned for Gail to bring a chair from the wall over, and she did.

They sat across from each other as Gail settled, Abby sitting up straight and focused, trying not to let her mind wander. Gail unzipped her notebook from its casing and flipped it to a blank page. Her hair fell into her face as she leaned forward performing these tasks, but she didn't push it back. When she was ready she looked back up and met Abby's eye.

"What do you need to know?" Abby asked, her hands clasped before her and her every word annunciated properly.

Gail paused, a slow smirk creeping over her lips. It was an honest smirk, not the Barbie's Dream House smile that she'd worn as a part of her uniform at first. She let it linger in silence for a full ten seconds before she broke it. "What made you pick History?"

Abby stiffened. "Pardon?"

"History. The History Department. What made you go into it, as opposed to... literally anything else?"

"I like History. I like the... certainty of it. The present always seems malleable, and the future seems impossible to predict... it seems like every time I turn around there's a new discovery in medicine or more data to take into account in finance or *something*. But we can always agree on what happened, at least. What happened, happened. What we extrapolate from that is open to debate, but what happened, happened."

Gail nodded. "That's an interesting perspective, coming from one of history's winners."

Abby squinted.

"History is made up of dominant narratives. It's made by the *winners*. You can squabble over how true that is in this instance or that instance in recent history, but if you really want to break it down... history is made by the men. It's *his* story."

Abby nodded, following the argument. She'd heard it before, even in History Department lectures. "What's this interview about again?"

"Choices."

"Hn. Well. I can't speak for what this History Department – or any, throughout the history of History Departments – has done to push along those narratives, but I can tell you that the classes I've been in are righting the ship. There's less talk of 'this historical document says this happened so it happened' and more talk of 'who wrote this document? Why? Who were they writing for it to be consumed by? Why?' Things like that. There are still certain benchmarks that remain steadfast: dates, names. We don't argue that the document *exists* – but yes, you're right. It's not as cut and dried as I made it sound at first. There's always context."

"That's the big lie," Gail said, jabbing a finger towards Abby. "That's the *insidious* lie, the one that gets people like you brainwashed into working against your own self interests. You think you can come up from this system – benefit from it – and still come out the other side clean. That you can use it for good. That you don't have to burn it all down: slow, incremental change is enough." She scoffed, turning to look around. "Who do you think built this school? What kind of narrative do you think they pushed out in the world for decades before they decided to tack on an acknowledgement that, hey, other people existed once, too?" She leaned forward, her hair bobbing toward Abby from the inertia of it. "You can't fight a beast from inside its belly. The only thing to do is burn it down. Burn down every trace of it and start over again." Gail shuffled, the emblem crest on her shirt turning to display more towards the person across from her.

Abby's eyes darted toward it, but she forced them back up to meet Gail's eye. "Some mixed metaphors, there."

"No, it wasn't. Only one of those was a metaphor."

"Mm. I don't see it that way, obviously. Or else I wouldn't be here. I think that the nature of a thing is always in flux...a knife is just a tool and is used for good, until it's used for violence. Is it imbued with that violence, then? Can it never return to its previous state? Become an artifact? Become a tool again?"

"The original state – the original intent – of what you're defending was violence. Violence against counter narratives," Gail said, poking her finger forward with every syllable.

"Right, so you're saying the original use can't be changed. So the knife can *never* be seen as an instrument of violence... even as it's sliding between your ribs? Or are you saying that only *negative* change is possible? That good things can become imbued with bad intent and become bad, but never shed it? And never can a bad thing be imbued with good intent? Because it that's the case, it's not long before *everything* on the planet's been tainted. Then what do we have?"

"Kindling," Gail snapped. She smiled at the end of it though, ruefully.

Abby cocked her head towards Gail's notepad. Her hand was resting on it as though it were ready to write, but there was no pen in it. "You haven't been taking notes."

"Should I have been?" She grinned. She snapped the binder shut and wedged it into the space between her waist and the arm of the chair. "That was good though. Did they teach you debate here, or at that fancy indoctrination camp out in Los Angeles?"

Abby sat up straight. Her eyes went back to the emblem on Gail's breast suddenly, instinctively. It was the crest for the Port Haven Institute. Her cheeks went white.

"At least they teach real shit at this school. Not fencing or targeting or Krav Maga or whatever." Gail pushed the too-red hair of hers back behind her ears, revealing them to be slightly pointed at their tips. Nothing strange. Nothing that would cause you to stop and stare in the street or even to notice, but enough. She smiled, but there was no joy behind it. It was a crocodile smile.

"What is this?" Abby asked, her voice a hushed whisper. Her gaze darted first away from 'Gail' to where Meredith sat, filing requests from students with earbuds in, unaware of the exchange happening just a few feet to her left. Abby's gaze swung back then, darting to the letter opener that lay six inches past the edge of her hand.

"This?" 'Gail' asked, her voice unnaturally pleasant as she opened her arms, revealing the crest of Port Haven – and the entire uniform – in full. "This is my cosplay. I'm you, can't you tell? Gail? Abigail? Abby? No? Too subtle? I'm Abigail, and I went to a nice finishing school run by monsters, and they taught me history and art, and also how to aim a blade right for a good vein. But don't worry, it's all good. They told me so, and I got an A in that class."

Abby's eyes darting toward the letter opener at the mention of the word 'blade' again.

"Don't," she said, pursing her lips and shaking her head. "Just don't. It'll end... very badly."

Abby swallowed. "You're Aisli."

"Yes. Well. Gail wasn't much of a pseudonym. Do you know what it means, by the way? I looked it up while I was getting this together."

"It means 'My Father's Joy,'" Abby answered, her mouth dry. In the back of her mind, she could almost hear her fencing lessons replaying in her head as though they were being spoken to her now. Could imagine the marks all along Aisli's frame as clearly as they'd been on the test dummy she'd used to learn where to jab. Where the arteries were. "In Hebrew."

"All the old world names are Hebrew, aren't they?"

Aisli hummed. Her posture had changed slowly, shedding the character of Gail. She let the sweater she'd worn around her go and looked around the office, taking it all in. "Names can say a lot though. Look at you: the Joy of your Father. Keeping doing what they started, doing things the way he taught you, and then telling yourself you're doing good. You're the girl-boss now, in charge, and you tell yourself that's progress even though you're just continuing on what he wanted, brainwashed. And he gets to see his system live on while getting to pat himself on the back because now it's helmed by someone who looks a little different. How woke he must be."

"It's not like that," Abby said, through gritted teeth. "*Nothing* is like that."

Aisli laughed. "'My Father's Joy'... how many young girls do you figure screamed that into the night before someone decided it sounded nice together? Battered and bruised, walking home to their mothers: what happened to you? My Father's Joy! My Father's Joy! Abigail! Abigail!"

"I think it's using Father in the divine sense."

"We can go down that road if you'd like to, but something tells me we'd be here all evening."

Abby swallowed, her hand still lingering near her blade but having made no effort to inch closer to it. She was constantly aware of it though, some analytical corner of the back of her brain constantly calculating and recalculating the tenths of a second it would take to secure it and bring it forward. "What's this about?"

"This is about burning it down. All of it. I was brought up in a lab, just like your little friend at the Insurance place. I was trained by people with agendas, just like you were at that sweet little school in L.A. I'm a lab rat, but I know what I am. Not like you, parading around like you can be normal. Like you're not infecting the world just by being out there, in it. Pretending you're not just another lab rat." She paused, waiting for Abby to respond. When she didn't, Aisli continued. "I escaped. But you, and the other one... do you think they didn't want you out in the world? Spreading their shit around? Meeting people, having babies, keeping their work going? It's all just still *part* of it. You're still playing their game and the only way to win it – to *end* it – is to find every last branch of that tree and lop it off. It's the only way to make a better world."

"What about you?" Abby squinted, cocking her head at her from across the desk. "You're a rat, too. When everyone else is done, do you think you're going to just retire to some island. Have babies? Start the whole cycle over?"

"I said I wanted to make a better world," Aisli spat. "I didn't say there was a place for me in it."

Abby stared at her for a long, solemn moment. Finally, she nodded.

"What?"

"I get it. I didn't think I would... but I get you. I see what you are."

"Oh? And what's that?"

Abby leaned forward, letting her hand fall away from the blade. She knew she wouldn't have to use it. "A *hypocrite.*"

Aisli set her jaw tight, then gave one curt nod. "Shane. Engen. They have to be stopped."

"I don't even know what Engen is. And I'm not with

Shane."

"Engen made me. They made me in an Engen lab and they trained me in an Engen lab and if it wasn't for some Circe people getting me out I'd still be there now. Or I'd be out in the world, doing what they do best. Engen and Shane used to be rivals, but they're getting along now. That's a problem in and of itself. As for Shane... they trained that little monster friend of yours in Black Springs. Brainwashed her. They did the same to you at Port Haven, after they pumped you full of drugs at their main office."

"They didn't—"

"You're their *Abigail*," she stressed, drawing out her name until it was almost a hiss. "You're your Father's Joy. Exactly what they want you to be."

Abby stiffened, and clasped her hands in front of her. "Thank you, for this."

"You thinking about taking the offer?" Aisli smirked, knowing the answer.

"No. No, but I'm pretty sure now I know that there's only one way to deal with you. So that's good. That brings clarity."

"Is that your Father's way, by chance?"

Abby paused. "No. No, he tries pretty hard to preach non-violence."

"Guess it depends on who you think your daddy is," Aisli shrugged, smoothing out the plaid skirt that suddenly looked very odd on her and smiling. "But in my experience... people who spout off that they don't want things to get violent usually have an axe behind their back. That the case with who you're taking after?"

Abby set her jaw as firmly as Aisli's, and said nothing.

"I thought as much." She got up, leaving the sweater and binder behind on the chair, no longer needing those parts of her costume. The folds of her skirt moved and flowed as she arose, and it caught her eye. She looked down and swerved her hips, watching as the skirt continued her motion for her. She smirked, then turned to Abby. "These are cute. Did you have to wear these when you went there?"

Abby shook her head. "They got rid of the uniforms long before my time."

"Hm," she hummed, then watched the fabric flow for just another moment. "Pity." She turned and walked from the room just as she'd come in.

Abby glared after her, a rage in her that she had never wanted to be there while in this place, this life she'd made. But it was here now, and she would use it.

CHAPTER 26

"And you're sure it was her?" Alice asked, running the alarm wire around the base of the door jam.

"I'm sure it was her, and I'm sure she's coming here," Abby said, using her teeth to rip off a long strip of duct tape. She ran it over the wire Alice was pushing down, securing it into place. "If you'd been there, you'd have seen it to. She doesn't just have a problem with us, it's... it's where we come from. It's that we have something to fall back on. It's..." she trailed, her train of thought consuming her.

Alice tilted her head. "It's?"

"She'll come here. She *has* to come here and burn it all down."

Alice nodded, then went upstairs and made sure Victor's gun was ready.

The hotel they were staying in was closed down for the season, its lights off. They planned their attack by candlelight, eating MREs accentuated by stale junk food from the unmaintained vending machines. Davies and Forrest sat on the edge of the bed in the room they were using for prep, a bag of Cheetos between them that they were sharing. Crenshaw stood at ease to the far wall, the wrist of one hand clasped in the grip of the other at the small of his back.

Aisli paced around the room as she readied herself.

"Why are we going to them?" Davies asked, running his hands over his face. "Home team advantage goes to them."

"Home team advantage goes to them no matter where we go things," Crenshaw said, before Aisli had the chance to. "This town's theirs. Whether it's at home or at the insurance place or the University or on the road between: it's theirs. They know it, the landscape, the way out. All of it." He paused. "If we attack at the home, we threaten the home. That affects the way they'll react; it'll throw them off their game."

"We're attacking the home because the home needs to go," Aisli corrected, raising a finger. "They have gained much from the bad systems that made them, and I will not have it. Not anymore. We burn it down. All of it."

Crenshaw stiffened, twisting in the gaze of Aisli's finger, still pointed at him. He nodded.

Alice came down the stairs with Victor's weapon in hand, checking to make sure its barrel was clear once more before lowering it to her hip and keeping it pointed to the ground.

Abby watched her as she made her way to the window and checked out it, hesitantly. The light that came in from the sun when she peeled back the blinds got caught in her hair, reminding Abby that it was purple and not the deep black the shadows in the home had turned it.

"When do you think they'll come?" Aisli asked, checking the tree line around the property once more before letting the blind flap shut.

"I don't know," Abby said, reaching into her duffel bag. "But we'll be ready." She withdrew a double-barreled shotgun in one swift motion, followed by a hacksaw and several boxes of birdshot. She took the gun and the hacksaw to the living room table and set the gun on its edge and started to cut.

Alice followed, her brow furrowed. She raised the handgun, only a little. "You sure you don't want this? It's more your speed. And it was Victor's. You've known him... longer."

Abby turned from her task, already sweating from sawing the barrel down. She looked over her shoulder, staring at the service weapon. As she did, Aisli's words returned to her. *Keeping doing what they started, doing things the way he taught you, and then telling yourself you're doing good.* She panted, staring back over at Alice across the curve of her back. "I want my own," she said, turning back to her work. "I want something new."

∞

Victor pushed his socks into the bottom of his knapsack, forcing them as far down into the body of it as he could. He did it with violence, as though the knapsack had some terrible secret he were trying to get out of it, then stepped back and got his jeans to do the same.

Tash watched him go back and forth to the clothes on the bed, pick them up one item at a time, then bring them across the space between the bed and the desk to deposit them. He made this small trip for each and every article of clothing, never once being alert and present enough to consider moving the bag to the bed to pack. He stomped the two steps between them every time, a tantrum in miniature, his cheeks flushed and red.

She sat in the chair next to the writing desk, her packed bag at her feet.

When all the clothes were in the bag, he stepped back to the bed one last time. There was a single sheet of paper left, one with serrated edges from being pulled from a book with 'easy to tear out' pages. It was a tranquil-looking scene with the phrase 'Today is Going to be Fucking Awesome' painted across it with greens and soft reds, as though the text were a rose opening its petals for the first time. He stared at it for a long moment.

"She had an eye for colour," Tash said. She could not see the page. It was currently a thin slit in reality coming from his hand from her point of view.

He glared over it at her, then turned and brought it to his bag. He folded it once, carefully, then placed it in, wedged between a wall of carefully folded clothes and the wall of the bag.

"I wonder if she made that the day it happened."

"You came here with *Jona*," he said finally, the name shaking its way from his cheeks as though he had to force it out. He said it with his face down at the bag. He was angry, and he was angry at her, but even in that rare moment he could not direct the anger *at* her. His hands clenched the sides of the bag. "Why? I'm trying to understand, I just—"

"I brought him here to learn a lesson," Tash said calmly, standing up and crossing the room to him. She took the curve of his bicep in her hand and used it to turn him toward her. "The same reason I brought you here. I'm not sure if he learned it."

"And what was that? Hn? Some powers suck? Freezing time is bad? Please help me, because I cannot figure the math on this point. What did you have to show him that was worth... all of this?"

"That rigidity is a problem." She annunciated every syllable crisply and cleanly as she spoke.

He stopped, his shoulders falling. He looked like a balloon that the air had been let out of. "What?"

"Any member of your team could have solved that, from the second they walked into that house. Theo would have known what was wrong, he would have seen the thoughts frozen in the air and known what they meant. Abby's power would have been triggered by it, immediately. Chad would have noticed the gap you were walking around long, long before you did. Immediately." She paused for a beat, letting that sink in. "And Maximus would have listened to the parents and the people and understood what they were saying, because he knew what it was to feel alone even in your own home."

The anger had fallen from his face and left it slack. He was staring past her shoulder, focused on nothing as he processed what she was saying.

"Both of you, so rigid in your beliefs that no one can rise to them. No one will be exactly *you*, and so there's fault in everyone. You can't let other voices in because that might change the mission – it might alter the course. So you have to push everyone that's different away, until everyone's gone and then you're—"

"Frozen in time," he finished, his voice breathless.

"Exactly." She crossed her arms, stepping back to her chair and snapping up her bag. "I took him here... to try and make him see beyond the way he was seeing. To see a solution that he couldn't have before. A peaceful one."

Victor licked his suddenly very dry lips.

"I'm a *teacher*," she said, in a tone that let him know it was the final word on the subject. "That's what I do."

Victor took a long breath, then let it out slowly. "Did he learn it?"

"Hm?"

"Jona. Did he... did he learn it? Is there another way this can end?"

She stared at him for a long moment, her mouth a razor's edge. "I honestly don't know."

He nodded, then turned back to his bag. He zipped it shut, the final epitaph of Lauryn Houle disappearing from view. He slung it over his shoulder, then picked up his phone and pressed its side to display the time.

There were thirty-seven missed calls and text notifications from the blocked account Simon used.

"What the hell?" he frowned, pressing to open his voicemail and bringing his phone to his ear.

Tash's eyebrow raised and she started to ask what was wrong, but he held up a finger, trying to hear the rushed message.

When he brought the phone away again, his face was white. "There's a problem in Payson."

CHAPTER 27

Sometimes, randomly, Abby could still hear him singing.

She was filling her hip pack with birdshot rounds, making sure each was accessible and that she was fitting as many in as she could, and that she knew where the rest were.

Alice was watching the perimeter from an upstairs balcony.

Abby was going about her task, and before she knew it, she was humming the tune to Ziggy Stardust's *Starman*. And after a bar or two of that, she found herself transported. He was humming that same song under his breath lightly as he worked, the sizzle of meat frying on the pan keeping time and rhythm. She was no longer sitting with her back to Victor's couch preparing for siege, but was instead curled up on her own couch in her own living room. There was a tabby cat on her chest named Mimi, playing with a feather toy.

Mimi had been another casualty of that night, just one of the long list of things that had blown up in Abby's face.

The cat had not been the worst of them, though.

She stopped filling her pouch and stared off into the space between the hardwood sections, entranced by it for a moment. If she tried – and tried hard – she could slow the memory of that moment down. Jasper fiddling with beef, its smell filling the air. Mimi's paws — too big for the rest of her — batting at her as she tried for the feather. She could slow it down and make that moment last forever.

But it always ended the same way: A knock sounded at the door.

Jasper had turned to her quizzically, raising one of his bushy eyebrows. Nobody had buzzed up to their apartment, and they hadn't been expecting anyone. Abby had shrugged back to him, scratching behind Mimi's ear. She wondered, now, what would have happened if they hadn't answered? If they'd just ignored the random knock and let whoever it had been go.

"Do you want me to check who it is, or should we just leave it?" she called out.

"Let me go get it, hun," Jasper smiled, looking up from his cooking. "There's no need to be making my princess get up." He spoke like that, in exaggerated, goofy platitudes. For no reason at all sometimes he would talk like a character from an old movie, putting on that faux Mid-Atlantic accent that was always fake but seemed even more so on him. He did this often enough that it peppered her memories of him and made them seem uncanny and unreal, as though she were remembering a dramatization of the events on an old film reel.

He wiped his hands off and walked over to the door, peering out through the peephole for a few seconds. After a moment he turned away, confused. "There's no one there," he frowned, his brow furrowed.

There was a load *bang*! and a single shot came through the door, splintering the wood and tearing a maw in Jasper's chest.

"*Jasper!*" Abby had screamed, diving for him and sending Mimi flying.

There was already a pool of blood was forming on the floor where he had fallen. His head urged up and down as he tried to speak, but could not for the amount of blood surging up in his throat.

She spoke to him, but she couldn't remember what she said. Not a word of it.

The door crashed open and she ducked toward the bathroom.

Then she exploded.

It was as if each cell of her body were fighting to go in different directions. The heat was unbearable, every single thing caught fire – and then, suddenly, she was whole again.

She was whole, and everything around her had exploded into flames. Everything she loved.

"Are you done with that?" Alice asked, coming down the stairs. She was holding Victor's gun to her side, at the ready. "I don't see anything, but I heard motors in the distance. I think they drove up to the end of the highway and are hoofing it in, now."

Abby nodded, shaken free from the memory. "That makes sense."

"No, it doesn't," Alice frowned. "Why not drive up? They know they haven't got the element of surprise."

"It's the slow walk up. The knock at the door. It's the 'we're so good we can take our time and announce our presence.' It's what they're use to."

Alice stared at her for a moment, then turned back to the window. "There's movement around the tree line. Might be the wind."

"It isn't," Abby said, pulling the zipper of her pouch nine tenths of the way closed – leaving enough for her fingers to withdraw another round from if need be – then standing and cocking her shotgun.

Alice nodded, and they headed up to the balcony.

CHAPTER 28

The staccato crash of running pierced the hall, annihilating any silence that had previously existed there.

The figures emerged from the smoke, gasping for air and getting nothing but burning, smoldering smoke. They held their sleeves up to their faces and pressed on, plummeting toward the end of the hall.

There were three of them, one man and two girls – one no older than five. Their eyes stung and watered feverishly, sending floods of water down their cheeks and making it impossible to see.

Blonde hair escaping from her braid, the older girl bolted ahead of the others and reached for the doorknob. She let out a shrill shriek and withdrew her hand, now sizzling and covered in pustules of raw skin. The smell of burnt flesh mingled with the odour of chemicals and her eyes began to water even more from pain and the stench.

"Damn it, Lil!" the man hissed, pushing his glasses up before helping her to her feet. "I told you they would burn the labs, too. They don't want it to survive. They never have."

The small girl sobbed, golden tears falling down her flushed cheeks.

"Aisli, stop blubbering and start running!" he ordered, pushing Lillian and Aisli back down the hall and toward a smoky stairwell they'd emerged from. It wasn't long before they were once more gagging on the thick black cloud that made its way throughout the facility and into their lungs. Lillian pulled Aisli behind her, trying to see through tears and smoke, all while fighting the throbbing pain that had become her right hand. Eyes burning and almost blacking out as she attempted to climb the stairs, she neared the point of breaking. "Robert, I can't do this anymore, we need a way out now!" she screamed, pulling as much oxygen in as she could from the smoky interior before starting into a fresh coughing fit.

Robert turned to glare at her over his shoulder for a moment, then pulled them both into his arms and continued up the stairs and into the smoke.

"We can't get out this way," she said, struggling to find the breath for each word. "You're going to get us killed."

The child's eyes widened, and more tears came.

"The only way we can go is up into the smoke," he said, not bothering to stop or even look at her when he spoke. "Down would mean going through sector D, which should be filled with flames. The only way out is up through the smoke, through a window or an exit."

If Lillian still questioned this, she did not say so out loud.

Robert did though, although he tried his best not to show it. He'd seen the effects of fire on human flesh before and did not want to experience that for even an instant; but he'd also seen the bodies of people who'd died from asphyxiation, their lungs drowning when there was no water in sight and burning when there were no flames near. It wasn't much of a choice either way, and certainly not one Robert liked to make. Despite the fact that the man seemed to be indifferent to the suffering of his companions, Robert had worked at this facility since its first walls had been put up. It was his entire life, and now that life was quite literally in danger of being ended. Maybe if things hadn't gone the way they did, maybe if he hadn't been so adamant on completing the project even once they realized it was a failure, the building wouldn't be burning and they could have started over from the beginning.

But it was too late for that now though.

After what seemed like stumbling through poison forever, they reached an unlocked door. Robert noted that Lillian's wheezing had all but stopped and that Aisli had ceased sobbing. Lillian's breath had become harsh and ragged and was becoming fainter by the second. He flung the door open and dashed inside without bothering to check where exactly they were heading. As long as it meant breathable air, he didn't care.

He eased the girls to the floor, then shut the door behind them in a vain attempt to lock the smoke out. As the door latched, they were plunged into darkness. The soft plinking of water on tiles filled his ears, and his smoke-filled nostrils were suddenly alerted to a sickening scent that the recesses of his mind quickly identified.

"Activate lighting system," he whispered, and like magic the room was bathed in an eerie violet glow. He swore softly under his breath as he took in the surroundings.

The mess hall was filled with bodies. Dozens of people lay dead, spread across tables and strewn over counters, some face down in overflowing wash basins. The bulletproof glass that had once stood between the service area and the space for lineups lay shattered on the ground and driven into a teller's body. Blood was spattered onto the white walls of the room like lipstick on a mirror, reflecting the devastation that had taken place. Without realizing, Robert sank to his knees in a pool of half-congealed blood, soaking his already soiled lab coat in a fresh layer of filth. Until now, it hadn't even occurred to him that the violence had struck during the mid-day break.

"Robbie, why aren't we moving?" came a soft whimper from behind him.

Startled back from his reverie, Robert turned to face Aisli. She was clambering to her feet to see around the room better. The child's lilac eyes stood out against her pale skin, startling and foreign looking on an otherwise normal face. That is, if a child with such striking features was normal. Her high cheekbones and wispy body gave her the appearance of a faerie changeling, and her small red lips made her appear Geisha-like. The combination had been blinding to Robert when he had first seen her, and still was.

"We need to get Lil breathing again," he muttered; then speaking up, "Aisli, I need you to help me. Lil's not breathing because of the smoke. I'm going to need you to find me an oxygen canister. There should be one in the emergency stash; you know where it is, in the kitchen."

She nodded and dashed off, darting between bodies as if she were simply walking through a crowded room and not a graveyard.

When she returned, Lillian was barely conscious. She dragged several canisters of oxygen and masks behind her. Wordlessly, she attached a mask to a canister and placed it over Lillian's nose and mouth. Ever so slowly, Lillian's eyes fluttered open as she began to fill her weakened lungs.

Robert watched her until he was sure she would be okay,

then turned to Aisli and attached a mask to her face as well, and then one to his. Within minutes, the trio was set to continue.

Getting up carefully, Lillian picked up Aisli and following Robert to the door, she threw him a wary glance. "Where's the closest exit?" she whispered, her voice hoarse as if she had been screaming. Condensation formed around the plastic lip of her mask with every word she spoke, then faded again before the next. "We have to make it out of here alive, even if it's just for everyone else's sake. No one deserves what's happened here."

Robert's brow furrowed, but Lillian couldn't tell if it was in disapproval or thought.

Slowly forcing out the words as if they were covered in glue, Robert answered her: "There's an exit by the elevator that takes you straight into sector H. It's the least likely to be closed off or guarded." His bloodshot eyes couldn't meet hers as he placed a hand on the door handle and yanked it open. She couldn't know, he wouldn't tell her. Only hours before they had been laughing together as they came out of this same room. Only hours before, the station had been intact, and no one had been killed. Nobody had been hunting them down and he couldn't bear to tell her that the one person outside of the station that they had trusted was the one that had murdered the life they had led here.

They ran back out into the smoke, continuing up the stairwell. The further up the stairs they got, the less smoke they encountered, until finally they reached a door labeled Sector H: Exploration Unit. A thin beam of light peeked out through the dimness of the hall, and Lillian recognized the small beacon to be the light coming from a control panel.

"Robbie, do we have clearance to get in here?" came the soft lilt of Aisli's voice from the dead silence.

He pivoted to see the girl, clutching on to Lillian's shoulder *and looking back at him, pale face covered in a layer of dirt.*

Before he could speak, a loud crash echoed through the facility, the sound of metal grating metal piercing their ears. Quickly, Lillian slid Aisli off her shoulder and with her uninjured hand she punched a twelve-number access code into the lockbox just above the knob.

The door began to open shakily, sticking as the power flickered. The gap was just wide enough that they could squeeze through single file to the other side.

The glass hallway that had once been the window to the hundreds of government researchers housed within the facility was shattered. Test tubes and vials were overturned, workbenches were smashed, and blood was splattered across every visible surface. There was not a single body in sight, but the air smelled of acids and the decomposition of flesh.

Lillian wrenched and fell to her knees. As Robert bent to help her, he noticed Aisli seemed rather unaffected by the whole ordeal. She didn't even exhibit any signs of being in shock, as if the tears she had shed earlier were simply for show. It puzzled him that such a young child, previously unexposed to violence, would not cower in fear at their present situation; however, he hardly had the chance to ponder this observation further as the sound of gunfire rang clear, amplified by the sheer volume of shattered glass. Lillian's head shot up, eyes wide, and in a split second she had managed to place herself in front of Aisli, shielding the girl from any bullets. Cursing to himself, Robert raced toward them, lifting them up and carting them toward the exit.

Before they were even halfway to safety, he felt a bullet splice through his upper thigh. Warm blood flooded down in a torrent as he raced with the girls toward their freedom. He stumbled then, tumbling behind an overturned table that only barely pro-

vided them any cover.

Silent tears marred Lillian's face as she attempted to stifle the blood that was flowing from Robert and leaving him without life. Glasses askew across his nose, he attempted to push them up, but only left a streak of blood on their surface. Managing a weak smile, he caught her eye and spoke his last words. "Get Aisli out, love. I don't want to see you for a while yet on the other side." Eyelids fluttering, his head drooped, and his body went limp, leaving Aisli and Lillian alone against an undetermined number of pursuers.

"Lil, we have to go now. Leave Robbie here, it's what he wanted," Aisli whispered, voice level, as if she were reciting the alphabet.

Lillian looked up into Aisli's eyes and nodded, picking the girl up and peeking around the corner of the table. Bullets still flew in their direction, but as Lillian darted out of the protection of the table, they seemed to dance around the pair.

They were just feet from the exit when the door swung open. "Cease fire, troops!" was the order issued by a stern masculine voice.

Lillian froze, clutching Aisli to her chest, mesmerized by the familiar voice that had once played to happier dialogue. It couldn't be him; he would never harm anyone this way, especially not her or Aisli. Stepping into view, however, was Lillian's worst fear realized.

He was tall and greying, with short wavy hair falling into his sharp blue eyes. They had once smiled at her, wrinkling in a welcoming way that lent the knowledge he had earned in his years. There was no smile present now though, simply a thin line painted across a stubbly face. The long blue-grey coat he had worn every other time she had seen him was replaced with dark green fatigues. Lillian only felt despair as she looked upon the face of her mentor, realizing that he too had been swallowed up by the bureaucracy that they had fought against.

"Lillian, sweetheart," he said, his voice as easy and as soothing as it had ever been. It made her want to throw up. "I really would hate to have to kill you for the experiment, but if you can't hand it over, I'm going to have to. The old man has a taste for traitors being served to him on a silver platter, and I'd rather be able to tell him you cooperated to the fullest. What do you say to that? A life for yours?" He smiled, and it was so like the way he used to smile that she realized it must have been an act all along. He reached his hand toward her, keeping constant and hypnotic contact between their eyes.

"A life for a life, Colonel? Is that what you call killing thousands of people, just so you can terminate an experiment that evolved into more than we could ever dream?" Lillian spat, wrapping her arms around Aisli more snuggly. "There is no way in hell that makes sense."

He laughed at her and took another step forward. "Sweetheart, you're holding onto that abomination as if it actually has some place in this world. Hand it over, and you won't have to die. You can start again, with a new position in a new centre. There's no reason for you to lose your life over a failed project." His words felt cold as they lodged themselves into Lillian's ears, hardening her to his cause.

"You were like a father to me," Lillian whispered shakily. "I thought I knew you, but I see now what you really are. You have no right to call me sweetheart, and Aisli deserves better than for you to call her an abomination. She is living, breathing, thinking, and just as human as I am, and certainly more human than you are!" She was shaking in rage, but Aisli seemed quite

content to remain in her arms, and gave no signs that she was upset by the Colonel's words.

"Lil, could you please put me down for a moment? There's something I'd like to show your friend," Aisli asked calmly, her fist cradling some hidden object.

Lillian and the Colonel stood for a moment, shocked that Aisli had spoken. He glanced at his firing squad, and then at the two girls.

"Troops don't shoot. Lillian, put it down and we won't harm it. You have my word," he barked.

"Like that means anything."

"Please."

Lillian couldn't tell if it was a ploy to get Aisli, or a moment of sheer stupidity on his part, but she could tell that Aisli had something up her sleeve.

Literally.

Hesitating for a moment, she gently placed Aisli on the ground and let the girl waddle over to the Colonel. His curiosity getting the better of him, he bent down as Aisli approached so as that he could be eye-level with the child.

Slowly, she extended her closed fist toward him and then opened it, palm up.

Lillian strained her neck to see, but only caught a glimpse of the Colonel's puzzled reaction before Aisli blew on her palm. The room, and seemingly the whole world, exploded in a blinding light.

Aisli stood crouched in the trees, peering through the branches at the Infinity House. It was large – even larger than she'd expected. Most houses built before 1980 seemed large to her, but this one triply so.

Her men were behind her, waiting.

"Why don't we go?" Crenshaw asked, not pushing but simply asking.

"They know we're here," she replied. "Let's wait for them to show themselves."

After a moment, and as if on cue, Abby stepped out onto the top floor balcony, followed closely by Alice. Abby had a shotgun held up to the sky as though she were posing for an action movie poster. Alice's hands were hidden behind the rail of the balcony, but were together in a way people's hands only ever were when they held a gun. They were both looking in the general direction of where they were hiding, but not directly at them.

Aisli stood. "Come on. Let's go."

They stepped up to, then out of, the trees surrounding the house.

CHAPTER 29

Aisli, Crenshaw, Davies, and Forrest stepped of the trees and immediately began walking toward the house, and toward Alice and Abby atop it. Their eyes were locked on them during their ascent over the grassy knoll that led up to the main property – neither of them checking peripherals or scanning tree lines. Every party was in plain view, and every party knew that every other party was. On either side there was honesty and purpose.

Abby leaned her head back and called out, "You're trespassing" with an extended larynx, when she thought that Aisli was close enough to hear. She said it, somehow, with a gallows humour that almost made Alice break.

Aisli smirked. She and the rest of her crew stopped moving forward. They spread out, forming a semi-circle that all pointed back at Abby. Aisli and she were at two distinct points from each other, forming a right triangle with the base of the house between them. Her men had their guns out but she, for once, did not. Her hands were at her side and at the ready, as though she were prepared to bring them up at any moment. "I am, I suppose," she said. Her cadence was off, like someone just learning language for the first time and not understanding its nuances. It cleared. "But you are, too. You're trespassing in this world. We have so much of it – so many dark corners – but there are always some who want more and just *do not understand* that none of that is *for you*."

Abby swallowed, and it almost didn't make it down, her throat had become so tight. She steadied her stance, legs apart, ready.

"I take it you're saying no to our generous offer," Aisli said, that false, learned-from-television geography-less accent returning. She tilted her head at Abby and waited for a response, found none, then smirked at Alice. "I know *you* did."

Alice stiffened, enough to make Abby turn to look at her in the corner of her peripheral vision.

"We didn't consider the offer that generous," Abby said, steadying her grip on the gun.

Aisli smiled, nodded, then looked down as she scuffed her boot along their lawn, ripping up a long tear of grass as she did and revealing the moist, carefully maintained lawn underneath. She laughed humourlessly to herself, long enough that it made Crenshaw and the rest of her men unsteady on their feet. She turned back up the women on the balcony. "You expend energy when you are in the presence of death," she said, addressing Abby. "I'll be honest, that's interesting. We don't have a word for that and that's... that's interesting." She turned to Alice. "And you, you can't die. You're that part of the equation. Death twins." She held both her hands out in front of her, palms up, fingers curled into talons. They started to glow the deep orange of smoldering embers in the pit of a flame, casting her face in light from below and making the shadows of the daylight fight for purpose. She smiled and motioned to her men on either side of her. "They carry guns. I don't need one." When she spoke, the words slid out of her like a hiss. She motioned up towards the balcony. "You need guns, don't you? What you do, it's defensive. Reactive." She smirked, raising her hands high, all her fingers pointed out towards them. "Want to see what I can do?"

A blast of hot air and flame arose from somewhere in her middle, a glow travelling up from her stomach and splitter at her bust. It went down both arms and shot – with incredible force – out and up, blowing the corner off the east wing where it met the roof and lighting the parts that remained aflame.

Abby and Alice stepped back from the wall of heat that came at them, and Abby lowered the barrel of her rifle towards Aisli.

Aisli smiled, and the six of them stood in stasis like that for a long moment. Then finally, low and under her breath, she said: "Havoc."

Her men pressed forward into the house in a charge while she remained still.

Abby cursed, even as Alice fell back into the home. She kept her sights trained on Aisli's smirking visage for a moment, then retreated as well.

Aisli's men entered the house through the west entrance, and the alarms that had been rigged to them began to blare. Sparks flew from the corner of the east wing that was now missing – the wires that had been within it now exposed and spilling their static innards with seizure and circumstance.

"Christ!" Alice said, making her way to the eastern corner and finding it aflame and exposed to the open air of the late evening all around. She stepped to the closet and withdrew a fire extinguisher and was about to bring it into the room and douse the flames.

"Hey," came a gruff, deep voice from up the hall, behind her. She turned slowly and found Davies, his gun lowered at her. "You leave that alone and come with me."

Alice swallowed. She turned towards Davies, slowly facing him until they were two gunslingers, standing across an open expanse.

"I want to take you alive."

"You actually don't have a choice in that."

He scoffed, and she realized that despite everything he must have seen, this man was still skeptical of any power that could not be demonstrated to him. He lowered his weapon towards her, as if seeking proof.

A shot rang out, and Davies screamed in pain, a mist of blood spraying out from the meat of his leg. He clasped as it and fell backwards, back down the stairs and into the main hall, as Abby appeared in view. "You are staying. Down. There." She spoke with clipped words as she approached the balcony and looked down at them, shotgun with birdshot in hand and leveled at them. She quickly ducked back out of their line of fire.

"Took you long enough," Alice cuffed, then turned on

the extinguisher and pushed out the flames that were consuming their home.

Aisli smiled, from pointed ear to pointed ear. She honestly could not remember the last time she had smiled so truthfully – the last time she had allowed herself to fully cut loose, and feel the heat and power of the world flow through her and out of her. It was ecstatic and intoxicating, feeling the pressure of each blast as it built in her centre and then *released* out into the world at her command.

Each blast bred fire and that fire called back to her, swirling around her and becoming the next blast. If there was no fire in reach as she made her way in a slow circle around the home, she took from her own energy or from the ground beneath her. She did not do this consciously and had never thought of it before, but now that she was cutting loose and free she could feel it – feel what her body did when there was no flame and no more left of her to give. Feel the pressure build from her toes as it took from the grass and the earth beneath it and travelled up through her legs and into her middle, revving up there like a fire in a pressurized oven.

She extended her hand with abandon, rather than precision, an artist making careless strokes as her mood took her. She stepped around the house, ignoring several feet before finding an errant corner or a window or a collection of discolored brick that offended her and she moved her hand at it, and in a flash of light it ceased to be what it was: now shouldering stone or broken glass or simply nothing at all. She stepped around it like a child, gleefully knocking over a building of blocks they'd created while pretending they were large and powerful.

Except she wasn't pretending.

"Come on," she said to herself, the crimson burning in the whites of her eyes like a drug.

She brought both hands up, tucked them close to her chest, then pushed them out towards the sky. The blast came from her like wave, tearing through the air and blasting the roof off of one of the house's peaks, sending tiles fluttering in all directions. She laughed and shot them out of the air as they fell, like a hunter practicing by shooting skeet. Much of it turned to ash on its way to the earth, and was caught in the swirl of the updraft as she made more heat, until the entire property was a snow globe of swirling, turning ashes.

The house had chunks out of it like a Jenga tower, revealing the world inside. Like the doll houses she imagined some children got to play with – the ones where you could open the walls and see the rooms inside, with all their little eccentricities. Here's Ken's room, he likes sports. See the plastic hockey stick glued to the wall? Ken likes sports. Here's Abby, she likes to paint. See the easel there? She likes to paint.

She pushed out, slamming a second blast into a hole she'd already made, attacking the interior wall beyond it now. The paint chipped and peeled and buckled for a split second before the second wave came, knocking the wall in and collapsing it into the hall.

The Dreamhouse had to go, and everything that came with it.

She would rip it down, brick by brick if she had to.

Crenshaw wrestled the gun from Alice as Forrest tried to restrain her. There were bruises growing beneath their Kevlar from where she had tried to warm them off, but they'd kept coming. Now Forrest had her pinned by the shoulders with one strong arm and she was biting at him, trying to tear a sinewy chunk out of that mass to make him stop.

"Got it!" Crenshaw said finally, as he unwound enough of her fingers in order to pull the weapon free.

"Finally," Forrest stressed, with sarcasm and annoyance. In that moment, Alice's teeth found his flesh. He screamed and reeled and pulled back, and the moment he was out of range that they could both be hit, Abby emptied both barrels of birdshot into his chest.

He screamed again and fell back as Crenshaw did the same, retreating.

Crenshaw moved to go to the back room where she was herding him, but when he touched the knob it sent a blazing shock through his system. He stayed there a moment, transfixed and unable to withdraw his hand from it, until Alice descended upon him and swiped at his legs, forcing him to the floor and breaking his contact with the conductor.

Forrest began to struggle to his feet, his breath labored.

Alice looked for her weapon but saw that Forrest was between her and it, and turned to make her way up the stairs towards their cache.

Crenshaw turned to Abby. "Booby traps? Really? The

fuck you think this is, Home Alone?"

"Because swarming a home with a militia feels like a fair fight to you?" she asked, squinting. She cocked the newly reloaded rifle again and aimed it at him. "Honestly, just the fact that you knew you had to team up to beat us shows that you know how *nothing* you really are."

His jaw clenched, and he stared up the barrel of the gun at her. "What's you waiting for?"

Abby winced, realized he was looking past her, then turned in time to see the butt of Davies' rifle coming towards her face.

CHAPTER 30

The front doors to the house blew back off of their hinges, scattering to the floor and skidding across the hardwood, making deep gouges in it. Aisli stepped into the smoke of where they had been before the dust had settled, fire licking up from her fingers and caressing the fibres of her jacket, fusing them in place. Her too-red hair was pushed back from the updraft she was creating, moving to either side of her and revealing those pointed, white ears. The whites of her eyes caught the gleam of the fire they made, turning them a deep orange. Red themselves, in places.

Crenshaw turned to her, his mouth agape. "My God," he said, his voice haggard and dry from her sucking the moisture out of the air. Being inside with her was like being in a pit with a fire: even if it wasn't touching you, you could feel the burn.

Abby was kneeling on the floor next to him, and Davies behind her, fastening his handcuffs. There was a thick stream of blood cutting a red line across the lower half of her face from her nose. Her sneer cut through the red sash like a knife, teeth stained orange showing. "You know if my powers activate, these won't help."

"Your powers won't activate, though," Aisli said, moving towards the stairs. She turned to Crenshaw, only slightly. "Get her outside. Prep her for the car."

He nodded, and watched as she made her way up the stairs. She almost floating on the air currents she was building with her heat, her feet barely seeming to touch the floor. He swallowed, and found it hard, then brought Abby to her feet by hauling her up by the cuffs.

Aisli heard the sounds of struggle from the east wing from the top of the stairs, and turned to step down it. There was so much hot air pluming around her that she could barely feel the floor beneath her boots. She had the sudden urge to be barefoot, but resisted it.

There was a muffled cry and a pained gasp, each from a different voice, though it was genuinely difficult to tell which was from which, and she moved towards it.

The first room on her left was clean, with everything folded and tucked. There was a desk was free of clutter, and the room looked like a tomb in all ways save the photos on the wall: one of a very young girl, the rest of adults merely clinging to youth. The bed was made, there was a dent in the top of its sheets, as though someone had wanted to be on the bed but had not wanted to disturb them. The same indent was on the pillow.

Aisli continued, the whimpered sounds of struggle getting louder but she had not found them, yet. The next room down the hall was a cluttered mess of paintings and paint supplies. The bed was covered with them, piled high and packed tight in the space between the bed and the dresser.

There were still no humans, no sources of the sound. There wasn't room for them in that room, amidst all the clutter.

The last door on the left was open and the light was on. Even before she reached it, she could see the shadows playing on the wall from within, the blast of light from a powerful book lamp making dark silhouettes of the actors within. There were two of them, but their shadows were never far enough apart to be two separate images.

"Stop it," she heard Forrest below, in a way he did that made his cheeks shake. "They say you can't be killed but we can test that. And they didn't say nothing about you can't be hurt."

She rounded the corner and found them there, in the last room on her left. There was a weapon – a bat with nails in it – not far from Alice's arm but she could not grasp it. She was on the floor on her stomach and Forrest was on top of her, his large legs weighing hers down.

His hands were wrapped around her neck, plump fingers like sausages pressing with force on her thyroid cartilage. She was gasping for air but didn't seem to be feeling the effects of gasping for air, her abilities keeping her stuck in that middle-ground stasis between the two states when most people would have fallen over to the other side.

Alice stretched, trying to reach the bat that was partially under the bed, her fingers nails scraping against the wood floor and making deep gouges in it as she did.

Aisli smirked. "That's enough, Forrest. Cuff her."

"Fuck no it's not enough," he growled, turning to her only slightly. It was enough that Aisli could see the deep gouges that Alice's nails had also left in his face, streaming blood in a red sash much in the same way Abby had been.

"Forrest. It's enough."

He pressed harder, leaning into it.

"*Forrest.*"

Aisli felt the heat rise from her fingertips again as she stressed his name, and as she did her eye caught the motion of a new assailant hiding in the corner of the room. She turned, hands outstretched and prepared to fire a blast at whomever it was, then stopped short.

It was a mirror.

She saw herself then, lit from below by the heat from her fingers, casting strange, sinister shadows all up and along her face. She saw that smile for the first time and wondered, briefly, why it was there. But more than anything, she saw the unbridled *red* of her own eyes.

The smile faded.

The house at the far end of their vision erupted, its front door bursting clear. What came out was large and black and hulking, a mass of swirling black muscle and sinew and teeth. It was easily seven feet tall and as broad across as Crenshaw was up and down. It leaned back its massive head and bellowed: "Za-Kron!" It had glowing, monstrous red eyes.

Steam shot out from between the creature's fingers where

they touched, filling the cavern with it until the air was as thick as a sauna. It was close enough that she could see that its eyes were not completely frozen, there were just thin sheets over them... and that they were red. Not bloodshot, but the same glowing, bestial red of the monster she'd encountered at Stapleton.

∞

Aisli stared at herself, the last lingering remnants of her smile leaving the corners of her lips, and saw the glowing, bestial red of her own eyes. They caught the fire that came from her, looking as though it were reflecting hell itself. It was so bright she could not even see her own pupils for it: just that same, monstrous glow.

She turned back to Forrest and Alice, the scales now removed. Her mouth was slack, all trace of the grin that had adorned it gone. Alice was on her stomach, prone, still struggling her reach the bat. Forrest was atop her. He was three times her weight, and this was one of the rooms of her own house. He was pressing the air from her lungs with the force of his knee and those plump, callused fingers were preventing her from drawing more. She was too weak to fight from the lack of oxygen, but was incapable of expiring.

And he... was smiling.

The smile disgusted her: not only because it was revolting in and of itself – it was – and not only because he was taking such glee in the pain he was causing... but because she recognized it as the same smile the girl with the glowing red monster-eyes in the mirror had had, only moments ago.

"Lillian, sweetheart," the Colonel said, his voice as easy and

*as soothing as it had ever been. It made her want to throw up.
"I really would hate to have to kill you for the experiment, but if
you can't hand it over, I'm going to have to." He spoke in a way
that made clear he would not have hated that, at all. He smiled,
and it was so like the way he used to smile that she realized it
must have been an act all along.*

Aisli raised her hands and pointed all of her fingers at
Forrest, the flame building behind them already. "That's
enough."

CHAPTER 31

"That's *enough*."

Forrest turned, his head snapping towards Aisli. The smile melted into a sneer. "What the fuck are you doing?"

"Giving an order. Just like always. Nothing's changed, so get off the girl."

Forrest narrowed his eyes at her. "It's funny you think you're in charge," he said, his voice a growl of contempt. "Everything you did was what they would have had to do anyway, but you tell yourself that you're the one barking the orders. But really you're so deep in you can't feel the puppeteer's hand up your ass." He turned back to Alice and applied even more of his weight to her. "We follow your orders until your orders don't make sense. And your orders, *Captain*, don't make sense."

His smile returned as a haggard death-rattle-that-was-not-a-death-rattle sound escaped Alice's lips.

Aisli let loose with a full force blast, the heat coming with such force that it blew Forrest off of her.

The wall blew out of Maximus' room on the east wing

and Forrest fell onto the roof beneath. He scrambled for purchase on the melting tiles, but they pulled free and he continued his decent, tumbling end over end until finally gravity grabbed him and pulled him down to the grass.

Crenshaw and Davies watched this, eyes wide, from the knoll outside the house. Abby was on her knees in front of them, the wet grass soaking into them, and she grinned.

Aisli helped Alice to her feet. "Can you get air?"

Alice nodded, clutching her throat. It was sore, and it was hard to breathe the hot air that occupied to space that surrounded Aisli. "I'm fine," she said, her voice croaked. "Thank you."

Aisli held her jaw firm, nodded once, then stepped to the hole she had made it the wall with Forrest. She looked down and Crenshaw and Davies, much in the way that Abby and Alice had from their perch along the balcony. When she spoke, she did so loud and clear, with gravitas that would have been able to have been heard anywhere on the property: "Let her go. Now."

Davies laughed, shaking his head. After a moment's pause, his smile faded. "You're kidding, right?"

The white of Abby's teeth cut across the ribbon of blood covering her face, but this time it was with a rueful smile.

"Let her go," Aisli repeated. She raised her hands. "I won't say it again."

"The fuck you say," Davies started.

Crenshaw took out his pistol, stepped back, and turned it on Davies. "The keys. Un-cuff her."

Davies squinted. The gun was aimed at his armor, but

the intent behind the action was still clear. He paused for a long moment, then brought his keys out. "What're you even doing?"

"Following orders."

CHAPTER 32

The Quarry seemed less a deep scar in the flesh of Payson in the bright sheen of the Arizona sun, with hundreds of men walking from one task to the next, focused and driven like worker ants tending to their hives. It ran with such efficiency that it was almost beautiful, now, less a gash and more a womb that birthed out its treasures onto those who thought to work to maintain it.

Aisli stood at the far edge of one of the quarry's declines, not alone but far enough from any of the action of the day that she wouldn't be confused by it. She had a coat on despite the heat coming from above and below, and the wind of the day caught it and her hair and billowed them both out over the fall before her like a flag.

"I got your message," Abby said, stopping a few feet behind her. The El Dorado's engine was humming several feet back behind that, though it was empty.

"Thank you for coming," Aisli nodded, not turning to look at her but continuing to stare at the men at work underneath. "I wasn't sure you would."

"You said you had something for me?" Abby was trying to keep her tone neutral, but was finding it hard to keep some of her knife's edge wit out of it. The struggle between the two was apparent in her voice.

Aisli nodded and reached into her coat, turning around to face her.

Abby flinched, on some level, expecting an attack.

Aisli withdrew an envelope packed tight with papers, held shut by thick elastic bands that wrapped around it both lengthwise and widthwise. She stepped forward with it extended and Abby stepped back a pace, so she stopped. She tossed the package down at Abby's feet. "That's what they had on you."

Abby raised an eyebrow, but squat to pick it up all the same. She riffled through its edges, seeing the first lines of many paragraphs and the edges of her own ID photos. "I mean... thanks. But I was there for my life, so I'd think I'd have all this, already."

"Don't be so sure," Aisli stressed, turning back and looking over the maw that was the quarry. "Years of research and following, documenting, analyzing... they keep track of you. You've fallen off the grid in the last year or so, but not totally. Facial recognition has picked you up in a few places. None of them Payson... yet. No digital traffic cams. But that's not how I found you anyway."

Abby nodded, thumbed through the document edges one final time, then tucked them under her arm.

"Aren't you going to ask *how* I found you?" Aisli smirked.

"No. Not really."

"Well... it's in there, too. The last few pages. I hand-wrote some notes, just in case. Some stuff in the margins all the way along too, to give some context." She paused.

Abby stared at the back of her head, at the way her hair moved in the wind, whipping and catching the air and travelling in all directions.

The workers below went about their tasks, sweating and moving from one set of earth to the other, molding and shaping small fragments of something as large as a planet.

"I wasn't wrong about you, you know," Aisli said, her voice as low as it could be while still reaching Abby.

Abby stiffened, tightening for an attack that she knew she couldn't have prepared for.

"Back at the University, when we spoke. I don't want you thinking that I was wrong, and that you can just go back to your life like it was. You are a tool in this system. The other one gets that, I think. She'd change it, if you would, but she doesn't want to leave you." She grinned. "I hated you both so much for being a *part* of that. For being a part of these things that have oppressed me and oppressed us for... generations. Going back now to the start of modernity. I hated you both." Her lips curled a little, it was visible from the side of her pale cheek. "You wanting to use the system that they left behind for you, and just keep perpetuating the same problems. The other one, wanting to start fresh but making the same mistakes, so it just winds up the same system but with a different skin on it." She tisked. "And she can't really make it different anyway, not while she's bolted at the hip to you. To everything that came before. Smart men in suits, poking and prodding."

Abby's lip was a thin line, her lips pursed tight. She

understood. She did not like that she understood. "Why'd you stop then? If we're so bad?"

Aisli smiled. "I was so angry at everything you were doing. I wanted to stop you so badly... I didn't realize I was doing their work for them." She paused. "I'd always assumed I was on the right side of things just because I knew the people I was fighting were wrong. Then I saw myself, with those red eyes, and the way I was acting and the way my people were acting... and now I don't know if I'm better." She forced a humourless smile and turned back over her shoulder to Abby. "Simply opposing an evil system isn't enough to make you good."

Abby nodded, slowly. "What will you do now?"

"They're teetering. The systems. They're right on the edge, that's why they're scrambling. When they're gone, people like you and I... we'll be able to stop fighting about what the world *is* and start fighting over what to do *next*."

"Does there always have to be fighting?"

Aisli smirked, and let out the first honest laugh Abby had ever heard from her. They were both silent for a long, empty moment. "I guess the question is: what will you do now?"

CHAPTER 33

Alice brought a box filled to the brim with knick-knacks and folders out to the back of her car. She laid it on the open floor of her hatchback, paused, then pushed it in as far as it would go. She stood back, staring at her whole life packed into the back of a car and at the totality of her work, then shut the trunk with a hard slam.

She made her way to the passenger side door and got in. Abby was waiting in the driver's seat, the engine on and the radio playing smooth jazz. Her hands gripped the wheel at ten and two as though she might float away if she lost her grip.

"Did you get everything?" Alice asked, pushing back her purple hair.

Abby turned and looked into the backseat. There were paints both new and old in a box behind Alice's seat, and laying across the back were five brand new mounted canvases, pure white and still wrapped in cellophane. "I did," she said, then pushed the car into gear.

As they made their way down the driveway, Alice rolled down her window and let her arm fall out of it, travelling along the hot currents of air like a feather on the breeze. She looked forward – forward through the part in the trees that surrounded Victor's home, forward to the road that would take them to the highway, forward to the wide world that lay beyond it.

Abby held her grip on the wheel, so tight that her knuckles were white. She kept her gaze focused and steady on the road ahead, but every so often she found it flitting up into the rearview mirror to Victor's house.

She looked in the rearview as they pulled out of the driveway, and as they passed out of the tree line. She looked into the rearview long after the house could be said to still be there.

Victor's cab pulled up to the Infinity House and he got out, slowly. The driver asked him if he was sure he wanted to be dropped off and he did not respond, merely stood with his bag slung over his shoulder until the driver pulled away.

The lawn was filled with debris that made no sense to his analytical mind, parts blown this way and that and coming from no consistent direction. There were large chunks gone from his home, opening up its innards as though it were prepared for surgery.

He stepped up to it, and up through the archway where his front doors had been. He walked through each room silently, surveying the damage with stern detachment.

He made his way to Alice's room, stripped bare of the posters and pegboards she'd adorned it with. It was just bare walls now, even the holes where they had been filled with spackling paste. In a home where the walls had been blown off, Alice Loveless had still chosen to fill in the holes left behind by an inspirational poster.

He moved on to Abby's room. It had also been stripped bare – the dresser drawers were open and emptied. The bed had been stripped of its sheets and they were folded, neatly, at the foot of what had been her bed. Her photo albums were gone.

Victor stared at that room for a long, silent moment, then let his head fall. He pushed off from her doorframe gently and continued up towards his study.

It had been untouched by the chaos: the same desk, the same pegboard on the walls with names, the same bookcase. On that case his gun box was there, opened, and the weapon cleaned and displayed out of its grooves. The cot was there, the blankets on it tucked into military corners. It was as he'd left it.

Frozen in time.

Victor sighed, placed his bag down onto the corner of the cot, and unzipped it. He withdrew a single sheet of paper that read 'Today is Going to be Fucking Awesome' on it and posted it onto the wall over his desk.

He sat back onto the cot with his back against the wall, staring at it.

ENGEN TIMELINE

With over twenty-five novels spread over multiple series by many different authors, the Engen Universe of titles is growing every day and into genres we couldn't have imagined! From the original ten book *Coral Beach Casefiles* thriller series, its crime novel sequel series *Xander Drew*, our flagship science-fiction thiller title *Infinity*, or single-novels like *Jacobi Street* and *Exposure*, there's something in the Engen Universe for everyone with more books by more authors on the way soon!

...But how do the events relate to one another, chronologically? While some astute readers have guessed at the potential timeline (some accurately, some not), we're going to finally set the question of the Engen Timeline to rest.

Turn the page for an up-to-date guide of the ever-widening world of Engen, featuring the works of Ali House, Ellen Curtis, Erin Vance, Matthew Daniels, Andrea Hackett, Sarah Thompson, Jay Paulin, and Matthew LeDrew!

In the 10 Years Prior Black September

"Reptilia" by Matthew LeDrew
published in *light | dark* & *Collected Short Fiction*
"Reptilian" by Paul Carberry
published in *Undead Rebirth*.
Danger descends on a small secluded town in the form of a deadly virus with fantastic and terrible side-effects. Can a small group of doctors escape alive?

Compendium by Ellen Curtis
Three short stories forming the basis for the Engen Universe's ties to suspense, genetic engeneering, and the supernatural. Features the stories "The Tourniquet Revival," "Falling into Fire" and "At Midnight, the Dawn."

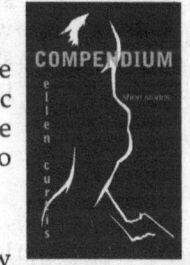

"The Theogony" by Matt LeDrew
published in *light | dark*.
A tale of young Theo Flaherty of the *Infinity* series and his time admitted against his will to the Black Springs hospital, where he learns to paint, and seeks out his father.

Black September

"Revving Engen" by Matthew LeDrew
published in *light | dark*.
A direct lead-in to both *Infinity* and *Black Womb*, Tasha travels to Coral Beach, Maine on a hot tip about a recently discovered young man with incredible abilities.

Infinity by Ellen Curtis & Matthew LeDrew
Faced with a destiny he's uncertain of, the enigmatic Victor must bring together four unique people with very special abilities... or face the tasks ahead alone. Guaranteed to excite!

Black Womb by Matthew LeDrew

Fifteen years ago, something happened in Coral Beach, Maine that resulted in the present death of a seventeen-year-old boy. Now four high-school students must try to solve the mystery… before the killer picks them off.

Jacobi Street by Matthew LeDrew

When a mysterious painting shows up at an art gallery he works at, Bob must work with Eddie and Sloan to track down its sinister origins and convince the people living on Jacobi Street of them, before its too late!

Transformations in Pain by Matthew LeDrew

When two girls are assaulted, the residents of Coral Beach must put their shared tragedies behind them and stop the man responsible, as well as unlock the secrets behind the true nature of the Womb…

Variety Show by Ali House

Local performer Wendy is introduced to the drama and mystique of The Quaint Little Theatre of Jacobi Street. But backstabbing aren't the only dangers at play in this venue...

Smoke and Mirrors by Matthew LeDrew

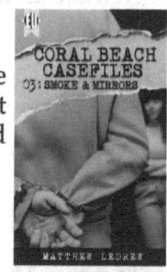

The approaching trial of Genblade brings closure to the people of Coral Beach, until people start showing up dead in the same manner they did when he was at large.

"The Inevitable" by Ali House
published in *The Lightbulb Forest*
A young woman must contend with the emergence of a frightening new power alongside the emotional high of a first date.

The Tourniquet Reprisal by Curtis & LeDrew
A man lives in Atlanta, Georgia that people don't talk about, but everyone knows he's there. He arrived a year ago and turned a gaggle of uneducated youth into something new, something to fear.

Roulette by Matthew LeDrew
As the teen suicide rate in Coral Beach starts to climb astronomically fast, Xander travels to Los Angeles to fight his most terrifying adversary yet... and learns that the only thing worse than looking for release... is finding it.

Year One: November

Exodus of Angels by Curtis & LeDrew
Victor's enigmatic past is illuminated when Jaycee accompanies him to visit a new friend in the paliative care ward of the Black Springs hospital, where Theo also happens to be searching for a cure for Leigh.

The Irony of Glass by Matthew Daniels
published in *Undead Rebirth* and *Interstitches*.
Abby and Chad track down a man with the ability to project his emotional state to a remote town, and struggle to escape.

Ghosts of the Past by Matthew LeDrew
Coral Beach faces its most awesome threat when one of Engen's past mistakes is unleashed upon the unsuspecting populous. Friends and enemies unite to fight a common enemy… but will even that be enough?

Touch Your Nose by Matt LeDrew
Simon Monk must infiltrate the San Fransico branch of Shane Industries, a massive company with deep ties to the Engen Universe. Where do his true loyalties lie? And can he get out without causing harm?

Ignorance is Bliss by Matthew LeDrew
After being set through the ringer one too many times, Xander decides that his life with Julie needs a little more attention… which is bad news because a new villain has come to town with his sights set on Adam Genblade.

"Gristle While You Work" by Jay Paulin & "Scarlett" by Andrea Hackett published in *light|dark*.

"A Night to Forget" by Kelly Rose & "New Employment" by Sam Bauer published in *Undead Rebirth*.

Becoming by Matthew LeDrew
For months Xander Drew has been doing his level best to keep the streets of Coral Beach clean, which means it's time for the forces of darkness to strike back… all at once.

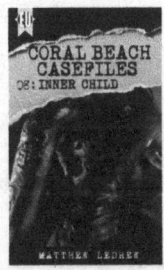

Inner Child by Matthew LeDrew
Julie is hospitalized with life-threatening wounds to both body and soul. But the real threat comes from the hospital walls themselves, as a demonic presence makes itself known to Xander and his friends.

"Comfortably Numb" by Ellen Curtis
published in *Undead Rebirth*.
Xander and Cathy spend an evening hunting the remnants of Coral Beach's gangs when Xander begins to lose control of the Black Womb, threatening their secret.

End of Year One

Gang War by Matthew LeDrew
The Tees, a homicidal gang of evil men, has finally been taken down by Xander Drew. But his victory is short lived, as retired Tees are mysteriously killed. With a town of suspects, anyone can be the culprit... including one of their own.

Chains by Matthew LeDrew
Sociopath Derek Smith has been freed from prison and is praying on the weak; and none are weaker than August Styles: a pregnant girl with Down Syndrome who has run away from home.

"Omega" by Ellen Curtis
published in *light | dark*.
A sinister division of Engen begins a series of experiments on pregnant women in a fashion eerily similar to those that created the original Black Womb project.

The Long Road by Matthew LeDrew
Xander meets the American people — and realizes that the world is harsh and wicked, but can also be soft and gentle, even loving. Xander Drew comes of age on the road, and sets his new direction.

Year Two

Cinders by Matthew LeDrew
Detective Horton enters a violent and dangerous world he didn't know existed beneath the veneer of order and structure that he has based his entire deductive method around.

Sinister Intent by Matthew LeDrew
One of the killers Detective Horton could not catch has resurfaced: a serial killer who flaunts his sinister intent in front of the Los Angeles Police Department, making it so that no one is safe.

Faith by Matthew LeDrew
Xander's mysterious and troublesome past returns to haunt him on the streets of Los Angeles; a place where even more people can get caught in the crossfire of the games of death and deceit that makes up his life.

Flickers in the Night by Matthew LeDrew
Lisa Rowdan is hunted by her haunting -- and powerful -- ex-boyfriend Ryan through a lonely city street. Can she escape him?

One of over twenty great sprine-tingling short stories!

Garden of the 8th Circle by Curtis & LeDrew
Victor brings Chad, Abby, and Alice into a dangerous conflict a decade in the making, fighting an out of control cult for the fate of a young soul. Meanwhile, Theo investigates a mysterious event in Los Angeles.

Family Values by Matthew LeDrew
Xander and his new friends Crowley, Lisa, and Tim investigate a series of kidnappings and murders that stretch back decades, all of which have the same similar twist: victims being found after years of being missing.

The Rats of Refraction by Curtis & LeDrew
When Abby and Alice's secret lives are discovered, they must defend their home and way of life with everything they have against the forces of Circe, a shadow agency that will stop at nothing to abduct people with supernatural abilities.

Fate's Shadow by Matthew LeDrew
When one of Xander's old cases comes up for trial, Megan Greene returns with it. The former friends are led into conflict regarding her client's innocence. However, they put their difference aside when they both become targets of the vigilante known as Shiro Gilbert.

First Aid by Matthew LeDrew
Xander takes his feud with mob boss Stephen Fields to the streets, and his attracts the attention of the *Infinity* team. Before the arrive, he'll have pushed the mob boss into an all out gang war, the likes of which the city will never recover from.

As Loved Our Fathers by Matthew LeDrew

Jona's plans come into view as he travels to the island of Newfoundland in search of a mystical item: the Holy Grail.

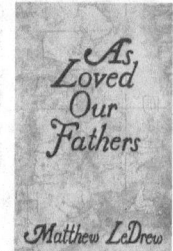

Gone by Curtis & LeDrew
Chad's sister has gone missing, resulting in him upending heaven and hell to get her back. His quest embroils him back into the dangerous world he'd hoped to escape, and unlocks the terrible secrets Jona has been investigating.

Moments by Matthew LeDrew
The Shane murders have been happening for months, dogging Xander at every turn. They've been happening for longer than even he knows, stretching back to the Black September. He's taken down Fields. He's taken down Murdock. Now the stage is set for this part of the story to also end.

Exposure by Erin Vance
Joshua Deering just wanted was to pass his final photography project. But that's not what happened. But hindsight is 20/20, and now creepy cemetery guy Adrian, Josh, and Josh's two friends are being stalked by nameless, violent strangers.

"The Port 13 Motel" by Erin Vance &
"Living Light" by Sam Bauer
published in *Undead Rebirth*.

The unlikely return of both Kemp and a cannibalistic serial killer to the Engen Universe.

The Future

"Remers" by Sarah Thompson
published in *light | dark*.
In the not-too-distant future of the Engen
Universe, young athletes are the targets of a
scouting program to create the next stage of
super soldier with cybernetic enhancements.

Timeline I - V by Matthew LeDrew
published in *Undead Rebirth & Collected Shorts*
Faced with the death of his wife, Mikhail
breaks the laws of time and space to find a
way to save her, only to discover that her fate
was sealed in the distant past...

DARK STORIES FROM ENGEN BOOKS

THE HOWL BECONS

Werewolves and a dark family secret in Northern Labrador! Growing up without his father, Tyler had no way of knowing the horrible secret that has plagued his family for generations. To free himself and find the cure, he will have to look beyond himself and into his dark history.

"The perfect mix of suspense and literary storytelling, Werewolves as metaphor for the original sins of Newfoundland & Labrador make this book the best in its class ,"
— Matthew LeDrew, author of *Infinity* and *Xander Drew*.

WESTON'S WAR

Something evil grows in the heart of Colorado. Bill Weston was a man of the West. He knew it – its land, its people, its stories. It was where he plied his trade, hunting men for money. His life wasn't easy, but it was predictable. That all changed when he captured Faraway Sue and he was led on a trip through the Colorado forests

"Take a little Zane Grey. Add a little Penny Dreadful. Read with Sam Elliot's voice. Discover Jon Dobbin's masterful The Starving." — Darrell Power, Great Big Sea

The early years of **Xander Drew** as he struggles with the evils of his small rural hometown of Coral Beach, Maine. Cursed with the heart of the Womb and the gift of seeing the world around him for what it really is, Xander must learn the hard lessons about the nature of humanity to traverse the minefield of criminals, gangs, and abusers that stand between him and ultimate happiness -- but most of all that **sometimes it takes a monster, to catch a monster.**

"THE WRITING OF ITS GENERATION- - VISUAL, TO-THE-POINT AND IN-THE-MOMENT."
-- *The Northeast Avalon Times*

The Coral Beach Casefiles series by Matthew LeDrew:

For more information, please visit

www.engenbooks.com

ENGEN
BOOKS

about the authors

Ellen Curtis is a writer born and raised in St. Johns, Newfoundland; whose aptitude for the written word began at a young age, when she began writing short stories, poetry, lyrics and novellas.

Her first collection of stories, *Compendium*, was published in October 2009. She has gone on the be the co-editor of the bestselling *From the Rock* series.

She has written four novels for the Infinity series.

In her spare time she enjoys reading, art, music and spending time near the ocean.

Matthew LeDrew holds an Honours Degree in English from the Memorial University of Newfoundland with a minor in Anthropology, and studied Journalism at College of the North Atlantic in Stephenville, Newfoundland. He was honoured to be a jury member of the 2018 NLBA awards.

He has written twenty-four other novels for Engen Books: the ten book Coral Beach Casefiles series, *The Long Road, Cinders, Sinister Intent, Faith, Family Values, Fate's Shadow, First Aid, Jacobi Street, Touch Your Nose, Slipstreamers, Infinity, The Tourniquet Reprisal, Exodus of Angels,* and, *Garden of the 8th Circle,* the latter four of which with co-author Ellen Curtis.

He lives in Newfoundland.